How To Escape
An Arranged Marriage
in High Heels

Tanima Kazi

To: Safa & Farzana, the loves of my life.
Remember that the world is infinite in its possibilities

CHAPTER 1

I'M GETTING MARRIED TODAY...to a guy I barely know. And I'm not quite sure how I got here. "Here" being in my bedroom, dressed up in my incredibly uncomfortable red silk sari. The matching silk veil (although fastened by 200 tiny bobby pins painfully pricking my scalp) insists on slithering off my freakin' head, so I don't even look like the demure Indian bride I'm supposed to.

Well, hell, I don't exactly *feel* like a demure Indian bride . I've been plucked, prodded, and poked by so many perverted aunts in the past two days, dodging awkward questions like, "So tonight's the big night, huh?" *wink, wink, nudge, nudge.*

I've had various thoughts of nausea, hunger, and blind hysteria, ranging from *What have I done?* to *I can't, I can't, I can't.* But the biggest problem of all (and I think the one most damaging to my health) is the fact that I've had to pee since 9 am, and it is now noon. I have to pee and I don't know how.

Well, I know *how* to pee, obviously, I just don't know how to pee with a sari on. I can't navigate the folds and creases. I'm terrified that if I go to the bathroom and mess it up, everyone will try to help me fix it, which would result in me having to talk to them. Something I definitely *don't* want to do. So I sit on the edge of my bed, my hennaed decorated hands clenched into the folds of the most beautifully suffocating sequined sari I've ever worn, wanting to pee and not wanting to get married.

"Maya," my mother taps on the door tentatively. "We're going now." She walks into the room beaming with pride, joy and a feverish glint of victory in her eyes (or maybe that's my own imagination).

I take a deep breath and exhale. "Ma, I don't want to do this. I don't think this is a good idea. I don't want to get married."

"Nonsense," my mother says, "you're twenty-seven years old—"

"Twenty-six," I interrupt.

She blithely continues, "If you don't get married now Maya, you never will. After you turn twenty-seven, no one will want you. You're not exactly an Aishwarya Rai or a Rekha, my dear. You should be grateful that Hamza is giving you a chance. He's tall, handsome, and —"

"Needs a green card so he doesn't get deported," I supply.

"Mastering in finance and business. He is the best man for you. You'll see he'll make you happy beyond your wildest dreams. And in a year, you'll give me beautiful grandbabies," my mother waves away my concerns with a toss of her hand and strides across the room to open the curtains. The bright sunlight makes me wince.

"Grandbabies?" I echo.

"Of course, you should have all your children before you turn thirty, it's easier on your body."

"Why? Will my ovaries wither, blacken and fall out after I'm thirty?" I ask sarcastically.

My mother gives me a look that says she is only holding her massive anger in check because she is dressed in her best sari wearing her best makeup and doesn't want to wrinkle the outfit or the face.

"Okay, Maya, so you want me to call off the wedding, after everyone has flown here from New York City, Atlanta, and Miami? You want me to break Hamza's heart? Tell all the guests, please take your presents and go? I asked you when we started this, if there was someone else and you said no."

That gives me pause because there *had* been someone else (a girl doesn't get to be twenty-six without feeling out some of her hormones), but that someone else definitely *could not* get married. "Why does there have to be someone else? I'm happy being alone."

"It's not normal to be alone. Look at me and your father, we've been married for almost thirty-two years—"

"But you guys *hate* each other," I protest.

"That's not the point, the point is we're not alone." She says, with a perfectly arched eyebrow. I have no doubt that, somewhere in her mind, that argument made perfect sense. Her face softens slightly, "I know what's best for you. All your aunties and uncles are so proud of you for doing the right thing and being a good girl. I know tonight will be a little scary for you, but it's your wifely duty, and you won't have to do it often."

Ah, yes, if arguing didn't work, my mother could easily call up and play the guilt card, and even though I could see it coming, it still worked. Because the truth is I'm not that "good" of a girl, and as for my wifely duty, I was still contemplating on how to fake my virginity tonight.

"We'll be waiting in the car for you," she says as she leaves the room.

This is it, the turning point in my sad, boring, and useless life. I could get married, have kids, and be everything that everyone else wanted me to be. Or I could go to the bathroom and relieve myself.

Washing my hands, I stare into the mirror. Who was this girl? Terrified brown eyes stare back at me underneath layers of eye shadow, kajol, and mascara. The ornate gold headpiece feels like a tomb on top of my head. I am being buried alive and doing nothing to save myself. The veil slithers and falls off my head once again, but this time I let it fall to the ground. I then slowly unwind the sari from my body and feel the sweet air kiss my skin.

I can't do this, I won't do this. I have to leave. I run around my bedroom in my undergarments—a red crop top and skirt— until I find my trusty duffel bag. I frantically pack anything and everything that will fit.

How to escape?

My parents are in the front of the house, waiting in the car. My bedroom faces the backyard. Thinking quickly, I wind the heavy sari around my four poster bed and secure it into the best knot my inadequate hands can muster. Sweating profusely, I pray to any and every God that might be listening before swinging the duffel bag around my neck. I hold the sari tight as I crawl out the window and scale down the house, biting my lip as my hands slip. Never mix sweat and silk; you might break your neck.

I hit the soft grass and then run for my life.

The cruddy thing about the north side of Chicago around Devon Ave is that it is crawling with other Indians—Indians who are related to me, Indians who are friends with my mom, Indians who are jealous of my dad, Indians that have dated my elder brother. So walking along the regular sidewalks is not an option.

I cut across the back alleys, my ankle bracelets echoing off the metal frames of the fire escapes. I am conscious of the sounds of traffic in the distance. I keep waiting for my family to yell, "There she is, grab her!" Scenarios of being gagged, bound and thrown into the back trunk of their car keep playing in my mind. Is my family capable of that? Remembering my mother's vow of shipping me off to India if I didn't cooperate, I concluded that they most definitely were.

I swipe my cell phone open and dial the only person who won't judge: "Nefertiti's hair salon, how can I help you today?"

"Angie," I whisper, "I need your help."

"Who is this?" she asks, snapping her gum.

"It's Maya. I'm on my way to the intersection of Devon and Western, you have to come and get me." I try to walk soundlessly, which is difficult, given that my ankle bracelets jingle with every step.

"Maya, aren't you supposed to be getting married this morning? I already dyed my shoes for the reception tonight. Girl, let me tell you, they are fab-u-lous."

"There's not going to be a reception. Or there might be, but I won't be there."

"Why not?" she asks.

"Because I'm running away," I grit my teeth in frustration, "please come get me and I will explain it all to you when you get here."

"Sherry is going to kill me; I already came to work thirty minutes late because my nails needed to dry this morning. The nails that matched the dress and the dyed shoes that I guess I won't be wearing tonight." She harrumphs into the phone, obviously put out. I swallow against my dry throat, "Oh, well, in that case I can wait."

"I'll be there as soon as I can."

CHAPTER 2

TEN MINUTES LATER, I see Angie's trusty Saturn pull into the busy intersection. I scramble inside, grateful that I have not been found by my wedding-compulsive family.

"Damn, look at you! You look beautiful. I love your outfit," she exclaims.

"Thanks, these are the undergarments," I say wryly as she peals away from the curb. My red "blouse" or top ends right under my lower boob area and is held together tightly by metal clasps in the front to give the illusion of a cleavage. My "petti-coat" is a long red skirt from waist to ankle held together by a drawstring.

She gives me a second as I jostle around trying to find the seatbelt and then asks, "What is this about?"

"I freaked, I couldn't do it, I just stood there and I couldn't make myself go to the ceremony. I felt like I would morph into my mom or my cousins, and not that there's anything wrong with them, they're just not..."

"You," she supplies, "or the you that you want to be."

"Exactly," I rest my head against the back of her car seat.

"This has nothing to do with Damascus?" she inquires.

My heart still clenches and breaks a little at the sound of his name. "No, it has nothing to do with Damascus."

"You didn't think he would rush in, save you and whisk you away from it all?"

"No," I scoff unsuccessfully, "not at all. I am over him. I mean, I am sooo over him that I'm practically around the bend and... under a bushel," I laugh haltingly, "or however that saying goes." I close my eyes and picture ebony skin, tangled limbs entwined in sweat, whispers of love, togetherness, and forever—

She snorts, breaking my sensual daydream, "I didn't realize that was a saying. So what are you going to do now? You can't go home. Your parents will kill you."

Oh God. The enormity of what I have done hits me like a tidal wave. My parents faces will be filled with rage and disappointment, my mother will throw in a few slaps for being insubordinate, while my father would walk away, giving me the silent treatment. That always hurt more. My stomach rumbles reminding me that I haven't eaten since last night. My eyes water as I realize I would have no biryani waiting for me, no samosas and tandoori chicken with yoghurt salad. I already missed them, my crazy family.

But I couldn't go back, because if I got married I would miss who I was even more.

I clear my throat. "I guess I have to find a place to stay."

"You could stay with me for a few nights. You could stay longer, but Tyrone is back in town and my place is so small that we wouldn't have room to breathe."

"No, I completely understand. Thanks Angie, I'll just stay a few days and be on my way."

To where? I had no idea.

***

We walk into Angie's apartment, my big duffle bag hitting the door on the way in. Angie gestures around vaguely with her hands, pointing out the rooms. "You know the digs—kitchen, bathroom, bedroom, living room, sofa. For the next couple of nights it will be your sofa. Tyrone is out right now kickin' it with his boys. He'll be back around five, at which point he'll watch court TV, yell at the television and doze off around midnight. You have my permission to kick his behind to the bedroom whenever you're tired."

Given that Tyrone scared me (just a little bit); I probably will fake insomnia before daring to speak up to him. In the bathroom, I shrug out of the wedding gear and clean off my face so I didn't look a kabuki made-up bride.

Feeling more refreshed and relaxed, I leave the bathroom and slump down on her couch, a.k.a. my temporary oasis. My mind goes blank.

Then all at once, my thoughts start colliding into each other. *What do I do now? Oh my God! I have no money, no family, nowhere to go outside of Angie's living room. I forgot to pack my deodorant.*

My eyes start to water again. "Oh my Gosh, I'm homeless," I blubber. "What have I done?"

Angie hands me a dish towel to dry my eyes.

"Maybe I can still fix it. Maybe they haven't detected I'm gone and I can just sneak back into my own wedding. Do you think they'll notice?" I wail, blowing my nose loudly into the dish towel.

Angie sits in front of me and shakes my shoulders. "Maya, there's a reason you did what you did. It didn't feel right to you and there is nothing wrong with that. It took a lot of guts. Now you gotta take stock of what you want and don't want. And do you know who gets to decide that?"

I nod slowly; of course I know that. "Oprah." *Duh!*

Angie rolls her eyes up to the heavens, "No, Maya, the answer is you. You get a clean slate. You can be anything you want to be. No one can tell you when to come home at night, what to wear, who to hang out with. Maya, you've been in limbo for twenty-six years. You had to choose at some point."

"I can't go back to my old job," I worked as a receptionist at my dad's clinic.

"You get a new job," Angie says with enthusiasm.

I try to crack a smile. It makes my face hurt

She continues to beam, and it's beginning to blind me, "Ultimate, complete freedom. You can be anything you want to be."

A bolt of lightning (filled with genius power) strikes my brain. I know what my calling should be, what I am meant for. My heart races with adrenaline, conviction, and (dare I say?) strength. "I'm going to the tryouts for America's Next Top model. I'll be the first Indian supermodel in the world." Ooh, I can see it now, runways, and catwalks, designer clothing worth a small fortune.

Angie grimaces, "O-kay… um, I think there are other Indian supermodels in the world and what about the fact that you're only 5 feet 4 inches and not a size zero?"

"Oh, I'll wear really tall heels. No one will notice," I say distractedly, "Heels are slimming, so I could pass for a size 4."

"From really, really far away," I hear her mutter.

I can see it now. I will run into Ryan Gosling at the Victoria Secret Fashion show, who will (inevitably) fall madly in love with me. We would re-create the Notebook love scene very Wednesday before dinner.

A newspaper hits me on the side of my head. "What's this?" I ask.

"The classifieds, Tyra. I'm headed out. Be back in a few," Angie says as she sashays out of her apartment.

Spying a bag of chips on her countertop, I pounce and devour them as I peruse the classifieds. My eyes start to droop, and I conk out. It has been a long day.

***

I wake up to the sound of muffled arguing, "Where have you been all night?" That sort of sounds like Angie.

"I was out. My boys are saying that, since I've been with you, I've started acting like a punk." A very defensive male voice answers.

I pinpoint the direction of the smothered yelling as Angie's bedroom.

"Does being out til 5 in the morning prove that you're a man? Because being a man means getting a job, helping me with the bills, doing your share around here." Ooh! Angie is getting really mad.

"I can't talk to you when you're like this," he retorts.

"Like what? Like tired of paying the bills and not getting a dime out of you? Like fed up with your lazy ass for spending all day at home and not cleaning up after yourself?"

"Whatever. I'm outta here." As he comes out of Angie's bedroom, I dive underneath the blankets. After the door slams shut behind Tyrone, I cautiously poke my head out and hear Angie sniffling softly in her bedroom. I wonder if I should go in and offer support. Except I shouldn't have heard the argument in the first place. I shift deeper into my blanket and pretend not to hear my friend's heart break from less than fifty feet away. Lying here and feeling crummy is not going to help anyone. I throw back the covers and decide to make her breakfast. After reviewing my culinary skills (non-existent), I pour her a bowl of Lucky Charms and a spash of milk.

"Knock, Knock," I say tapping on her door, "I made you breakfast."

She raises a brow at the bowl.

"It's a lot harder than it looks," I say in defense.

"Maya—thank you. But I have to get ready for work, and I—I need to be alone right now." Angie struggles to keep her face neutral.

"Yeah, I get it. No problem, I'll be out there if you need me." I shut the bedroom door behind me, feeling awful. In public, Angie is flippant, loud, and sometimes too close to the mark for comfort. But once you get to know her, you realize she has a huge heart, loves deeply and is just as vulnerable as the next girl. Seeing her dejected and lost, well, it makes me feel a little hopeless as well. If she can't make it, what chance do I have?

CHAPTER 3

IT'S BEEN TWO DAYS. Tyrone hasn't come home and I haven't found a job. I struggle to keep my hopes up. I'm not totally broke. I found a place that buys gold for cash, so I parted with my bridal jewelry for a cool $2K. Not bad for a day's work, huh? The problem is, it's hard to keep money when you don't have a steady income. I never realized how much I ate until I started paying for it. The more anxious I became about finding a job, the hungrier I became. I could feel my thighs expanding beneath my skin—disgusting!

I also wanted to repay Angie back, but she wouldn't take a dime until I found a job.

This makes me feel like mooch number two, (I don't want to mention mooch number one because that's a sensitive topic around here and none of my business).

"Find anything?" Angie asks as she flips through the channels.

"Well, there's waitressing, retail, and dog-walking."

"Nix the retail and waitressing, you might run into your family." She finally settles on the six o'clock news.

"What can they do? I'm not a fugitive or anything," I couldn't do anything when I lived with them, I'll be damned if they run my life when I'm living without them.

I snap out of my pity party to hear the TV report, "In local news, we have the case of the missing bride.

Twenty-six-year-old Maya Khan was last seen on the way to her own wedding when she mysteriously disappeared. Police have yet to say if there is a suspect or foul play involved."

My mouth drops in disbelief. I stare at my high school picture from freshman year. There I am, big wire-rimmed glasses, face full of cystic acne, mouth open wide with shiny, metal braces glinting in the camera flash. I gasp in horror.

"That's not pretty," Angie commiserates.

The anchorman's voice continues to blast from the TV, "If you or anyone you know has seen this woman please contact the number below or call your local authorities."

"So...?" Angie says thoughtfully.

"I—I— gaa," were the only sounds emitting out of my mouth. Why that picture? What had I done to deserve this? Was I Hitler in a past life?

"Now might be a good time to call your folks," Angie says casually. As if seeing her best friend on TV as a missing person is an everyday occurrence.

"Yeah, I was hoping I wouldn't have to do that—ever," Confrontations aren't my strong point. I look over at my cell phone. There it sits in the corner of the room, plugged in but turned off. I had turned it off the minute Angie had picked me up on my wedding day. I gingerly turn it on, and it vibrates back to life, flashing colors. Twenty voicemails glare back at me. Taking a deep breath, I sit down to listen.

"Maya! Maya! Where are you? What happened—" my mother's frantic wailing follows.

"Maya, this is Hamza. I am very sad. I hope you are okay. Please call me so we can talk. I hope you are safe." Aww my sweet, dull ex-fiancé.

"This is your father, I will not tolerate this behavior from you, Maya. Come home right now!"

And on and on it went. My family and friends in tears, either berating or consoling me.

I glance at Angie, she shrugs her shoulders in return. I didn't blame her, dealing with an over protective family is not her area of expertise.

I take my cell phone to the tiny bathroom filled with way too many of Angie's hair products and shut the door. Sitting on the toilet lid, I smooth my hands over my pants to wipe away some of the sweat.

I dial home and pray that they will understand.

"Hello," my mother answers.

I inhale, exhale, and speak. "Hi, Ma," I say softly.

"Maya, Maya is that you? Where are you? What happened?"

"Ma, I couldn't do it. I couldn't go through with the wedding. I had to leave." My hand grips the phone so tightly my fingers hurt. "I'm safe, but I need to be on my own right now."

"Come home, please, *beti*," she sobs into the phone. "We are so worried, Hamza is so worried. Please. We need you to come home—"

There is a jostling sound. A few grunts later, my father gets on the line. "Maya, what is the meaning of this?"

"*Abu*, I couldn't get married. I'm sorry, but I couldn't." Tears stream down my face making it hard to get my words out.

"Come home and we will settle this. You don't have to get married if you don't want to. Just come home and we can talk." My father's voice sounds old and heavy and I regret hurting him.

My heart leaps at the idea. I *could* go home. It was still an option. Everything could go back to normal. Home cooked meals, freshly laundered clothes, Fabreeze-smelling carpets. My parents never being satisfied with who I am, never encouraging me to have or follow my dreams, just pushing and prodding me towards marriage. In my heart, I knew there was no going back. I had already taken the hardest step. If I went back now, I might not get this chance again.

"I'm sorry, Abu, but I'm not ready to come home now. I have to be on my own." The lump in my throat makes it hard for the words to squeak out

"What about money, Maya? At least meet me so I can give you some money." His voice takes on a frantic edge and my heart breaks.

"I have to go now. I'm sorry. I'll come home soon to visit. But I'm not ready right now."

"Maya, no—" I hang up quickly. Before I change my mind. Before I place their needs above my own and forget myself completely. Besides, there was nothing left to say. I'd made a clean break. After twenty-six years I could finally live like an adult. So why did it feel like I just divorced my family?

CHAPTER 4

"I COULD ALWAYS SELL my eggs," I say to Angie.

We stroll down Lake Street in the Oak Park area. The hot summer sun beats down on our backs. I have a hazelnut gelato in my hands that is oh-so good, and Angie has a low-fat smoothie in hers.

"You could, but you might miss your eggs," she says as we pass the African Arts store.

"Oh, discount on Bob Marley CDs," I say, looking at the display, "Miss my eggs? Puh-lease. They go down the toilet every month, and I don't exactly cry a river over them."

"Okay, well, what if you sell your eggs and they get used and there's a person out there with half your DNA and then you decide to have a happy family and have a real kid, and then one day, what if your first non-kid meets your real kid and they fall for each other and then they start having kids? What happens then?"

I stare at her in disgust. "Ewww!! Where do you come up with this stuff?"

"Well, that's what happens when you start letting your eggs loose—all willy-nilly like that," she slurps up the lasts of her smoothie. "Oh would you look at that sign? It looks like a room for rent. And right by the Green Line. How convenient for a person who may not have a car…"

"Uh-huh, real convenient." I dive back into the cup. There has to be more gelato in there. I paid $3.21 for the stupid thing.

"Well, since we're not doing anything this fine Saturday morning, why don't we take a look?" she suggests with an arch of her brow.

"Yeah, sure, right after the movie. It got four stars." I head toward the movie theatre.

Angie grabs my elbow and yanks me in the opposite direction, "No, I think we should do this first. I mean, there's an afternoon showing for the same movie."

"I guess..." I say uncertainly.

So, we walk up to the little brick bungalow house that has a pink neon sign screaming the word "Psychic," in broad daylight on a Saturday. Ooooh-kay, just a little creepy. Not wanting Angie to think I'm intimidated, I continue onwards. Next to that sign is a little cardboard cutout with the words, "Room for Rent" scribbled on it in black marker.

We attempt to knock on the door, but the door swings inward of its own volition. What's next? Eerie music and flying bats?

"Enter ladies, back room on the left," we hear a melodious voice call out to us.

I grab Angie's arm and mutter, "Okay, Hansel, if she tries to bake you in the oven, I'm running for my life."

"It's just psychic talk, to set the mood. Chillax," but I notice she hesitates a little bit herself before walking to the back.

We enter a dining room lit with candles. The hot humid weather we experienced outdoors ratchets up quite significantly in here, causing sweat to stream down my sides. I surreptitiously pat my t-shirt down around my torso to absorb the excess moisture.

At the head of the dining table sits a petite woman, her face overshadowed by a tangle of blond curls, which spring forth in every direction. She is encansed in a—hey, is that a salwar kameez? It sure is, an Indian jersey top with ballooney cotton pants. She raises her face from her tarot cards and greets me with a warm smile and mischievous eyes.

"What can I do for you today? Palm reading? Tarot reading? Looking for love? Guidance—"

"All of the above," I snort.

Angie elbows me in the ribs, cutting off the rest of my words. She sure is abusive lately. Is this a pattern? As I contemplate if we should seek counseling, Angie says, "Actually, we were curious about the room for rent."

"Oh, of course. I'm Penny. Shall we take a tour? The entire house is available for use. There's one and a half baths, the kitchen is in the front," she stands up and starts walking; we follow suit. As she names the rooms and gestures towards them, her bracelets tinkle, drowning out most of her words. "And this is your living area," Penny beams at us. We had followed her all the way up to an attic. Seeing my disgruntled face, she quickly says, "I'll let you think it over," while she gingerly climbs down the ladder. *A ladder for God's sake!* What is this? *Little House on the Prairie?*

"It's cozy," Angie says.

"It's an attic. I am not Anne Frank or the incestuous kids from "Flowers in the Attic." I don't *do* attics. As evidenced by my two examples, nothing good happens in attics.

Angie sighed. I don't blame her. Tyrone is back, and my back is ready to give out from her sofa. We both need me gone. But to banish me to an attic, isn't that a bit extreme?

"I guess it is cozy." I mean, "Little House on the Prairie" isn't that bad. Shannon Doherty guessed starred in it, and she turned out okay—sort of.

We stand there, rocking back on our heels, neither one of us able to come up with any other word except "cozy."

The house was rented out to three or four other people? I'm not quite sure how many people I need to share a toilet with.

"I'll take it," I mutter.

Angie clamps down quickly on her smile and says, "Are you sure? Only if you really want to."

I shoot her a look of hope. "Really, because if you don't mind me staying—"

"Look at you spreading your wings, leaving the nest, you're going to soar, Maya." She gives me a tight hug that squeezes any other words I may have wanted to say right out.

***

The house belongs to Penny, and the attic belongs to me and my meager belongings. Angie makes me purchase a mattress and a chair. She also gives me some "odds and ends" that she no longer needs, along with a miniature TV. The rent is $400 plus the security deposit of $400. If I continue to eat Raman noodles on a daily basis, I could go roughly 2 and half months without a job. I laugh, looking around. Growing up, I had a playhouse that was bigger than this and filled with way more things. I was one step ahead of being homeless and a million steps behind the rest of the human race.

***

I wake up confused, groggy, and hot. The freakin' wooden attic suctions heat in like a greenhouse. I open my tiny hatch window to let some air in. I can barely sleep; every sound and shadow scares the bejeezus out of me. Twice I think for sure I am being robbed, until I realize I have nothing worth stealing.

I lie back down on my hot mattress, and my mind wanders to other hot summer nights where I lay in bed, except I wasn't alone—I was with the man I thought I loved. I scowl up at the darkness. Damascus McCarthur. *That bastard!*

***

Damascus had walked into my dad's clinic with a pulled hamstring and the nerve to smile at me, flashing twin dimples. It wasn't a normal, friendly, "Hi, how ya doin'?" smile. It was a "Me man, you in my bed soon," smile, and my idiotic twenty-four-year-old heart had tripped over itself at the attention it was receiving. And then that cocky son of a gun left me his card, as if I would be interested enough to call. So what if I called 27 hours 34 minutes and 15 seconds later? I was bored and curious. I wasn't exactly the kind of girl who turned heads, and the fact that I could (maybe) turn his head had me feeling mighty good.

But I wasn't going to sit around and be manipulated. I had my own plans for this guy. He could help relieve me of my whole virginity thing.

I had gotten to the ripe old age of twenty-four with a few pecks and awkward gropes from various encounters, but I hadn't really experienced anything major with a man. I was tired of having the sex life of a nun. All of my friends and female cousins had either gotten married or laid (not in that order) and would go on for hours about how they loved it when their husbands touched them *there* and how amazing their sex lives were. Usually when these conversations occurred, my paltry contribution consisted of a knowing smile and a nod. Though, I seriously doubted I was fooling anyone.

He took me out to dinner at a French restaurant where I couldn't pronounce the names of any of the entrees. Feeling gauche and about as sophisticated as an Amish girl in a burlap sack, I blundered my way through the conversation. By the time dessert came around, I knew I had botched the whole evening by talking about the various stool softeners my grandmother was using to help with her hemorrhoids.

Later, when he drove me back to "my house" (decoy house that was two streets over and 4 blocks north of my actual house), I was pretty sure I would never see him again. So, feeling brave, I tentatively asked if he would have sex with me. My request was met by laughter.

Mortified, I started to cry.

He held me and asked why in the world I would pose a question like that.

Between hiccups and a snotty nose, I confessed that I was a virgin.

He asked if I was sure. I nodded eagerly.

He booked us a hotel room for the night and I became lost in the headiness of him. He was a former athlete who had a gorgeous body. I traced his biceps with my hands, watched his stomach muscles jump underneath my finger nails. And then it happened—he took my virginity. It was agonizing and horrible, but in between the shock and the pain, he whispered in my ear that the first time was always the most painful and it would get much, much better.

And it *definitely* did.

We met whenever I could sneak away. He didn't question my schedule or ridiculously short curfew—a fact I was immensely grateful about. I actually thought it was funny that he had the same schedule I did; he also had to be home by 6pm to help his elderly mother prepare dinner.

I didn't question it, because I was just happy to have a man's attention. It was also curious that whenever he received phone calls, he had to go in the washroom and shut the door. And if I was never invited to his home or met his friends, I couldn't complain, because I couldn't extend the same invitation myself. So I shrugged everything off and just lived in the moment. I ignored reality completely until it jumped up and bit me in the ass.

***

It was a Saturday afternoon and Damascus was in the shower, (I swear I wasn't snooping, I was just looking around for the remote to the TV), when his phone rang next to me. Trying to be helpful (because that's the type of swell girl that I am) I grabbed his phone intending to hand it to him in the washroom when I noticed the ID as "wifey" came up. Hmm… Well, that was curious. And then the text came through: *Baby, come home now. I miss U so much.*

Shocked, I realized I was having sex with a man who was with someone else, even possibly married to someone else. Bile began to rise in the back of my throat.

"What are you doing?" He had come out of the washroom and was staring at me, staring at his phone.

"I—uh, your phone rang and here ya' go." I handed it over like a hot potato.

Now what? Big confrontation? Mini confrontation? No confrontation at all? Well, since I'm not one to initiate arguments, I would have preferred to remain silent. However, just because I was a dysfunctional Indian girl who had sex in remote motel rooms with potentially married men didn't mean I was a coward. Not a big coward anyway. Playing out a hunch, I said, "You're wife called." If only I could keep my voice from quaking.

"What do you know about my wife?" he snapped, dark eyes flashing. Twin dimples long gone.

"Well, I—uh, I know you have one," I said lamely.

"Did you talk to her?" he asked, towering over me.

"No, no she called you and sent a text—which I did not read." Why was *I* lying? Why was *I* the one answering questions? Why did *I* feel like I had done something wrong? "Wait a second—why are *you* married?" I asked, trying to act indignant.

His shoulders relaxed when he realized his two worlds hadn't collided. "Oh Maya, you just don't know. I met her when I was in college and I was playing basketball…" They had sex a couple of times and she ended up pregnant. Trying to do the right thing, he had married her, but he didn't love her. He loved me. He was going to divorce her; he just needed time to get his finances in order.

I wanted to believe him. I so desperately wanted to be wanted. When I heard the words, "I love you" fall from his lips, I sighed, "I love you too!" while flinging my arms around his neck.

I continued to see him because I believed I loved him. Plus, it was sooo convenient having multiple orgasms and being home in time to help with dinner and catch the latest episode of *Scandal*.

We continued to lie to our families happily with no remorse (wince), until last year when my mother cornered me at the breakfast table.

***

"Maya, you're going to worry your father and I into an early grave," my mother had moaned. This is how my mother started most conversations.

"What did I do now, Ma?" I grabbed a bagel and was about to head off to work.

"You are the only girl on both sides of the family that is not married. Your cousin, Fatima, got married in April. Even Meena and Neena, who are three years younger than you, are married with kids. I can barely hold up my head when I go to their houses."

"Your *only son* Amir is married. Why do I have to get married?" I should have ignored her. Stupid me!

"You know your father had open heart surgery last year; you not getting married might kill him."

I rolled my eyes. How can a person not doing something cause someone else to keel over? I mean I was a good kid. I didn't do drugs. I helped around the house. I wasn't promiscuous. I mean, I was only sleeping with *one* married man. Alright, so my moral compass had laxed a bit and wasn't on the complete straight and narrow, but overall, I was pretty wholesome. At least my lies were.

"Your father and I were talking…"

She was probably the one talking, he just happened to be in the room.

"…And we spoke to Hamza's uncle and he thinks you're very nice. *Verrry nice.*"

I tried to picture Hamza and came up with a brown-skinned, gangly guy who hid his face behind a scraggly goatee. "He's agreed to marry you."

Wait—what? Hold the phone!

"Agreed to marry me? I never asked!" I sat down. Being the boss's daughter was sometimes very convenient. Dad would understand if I had to kill Mom before coming into work late.

"No, but we've been looking for you for ages. Given your attitude and age, and not to mention the fact, that," she lowered her voice to a whisper, "you're a bit dark."

Yes, apparently Indians found it shocking to be with other Indian people who had brown skin. Thank God Angie introduced me to Ebony and Essence magazine in high school. She also took the time to explain to me about the 'Black is Beautiful' campaign from the 1960's. I adopted those mantras as my own. Anytime I would hear my mother comment about how fair skinned and lovely my cousins were, I would quickly reminded her that "Brown is beautiful too."

My mother was blathering on about an August wedding.

I interrupted her, "I don't want to get married. Not now—not ever!" *Whoa, where did that vehemence come from?*

She blinked at me and her mouth curved into a hard smile. "Maya, if you don't get married here, I will take you to India and find you a husband. And you won't return from India until you are married. And, if you don't get married by the end of this year, you can no longer live here. Is that understood? I have put up with your directionless life for twenty-five years. I have indulged your little hobbies. But unless there is someone else, I don't understand why you can't get married. Is there someone else?"

And what could I say to that? So I shook my head no. "I need time. I—can we just not announce it right now?"

"Of course. First our families have to meet, and then there's the…" And she was off. I was no longer needed in the conversation.

***

"I might be getting married," I told Damascus as we lay in bed watching an old re-run of *Seinfeld*.

He let out a chuckle as Kramer entered Jerry's apartment blustering, "What now?" he said, waving me away. I sighed in exasperation and turned off the TV.

"Hey!" he protested.

"Damascus, my parents are pushing me to get married to a nice Indian man. They say I'm too old to be single, that it's unnatural." I stood up and folded my arms across my chest, waiting for his outrage.

"Really… Wow, that's…great," he said smiling.

Did I miss something?

"I'm sorry—*what did you say?* 'The-love-of-your-life' might be getting married in six months and you think that's great?"

"You getting married doesn't change anything, Maya. We'd still be here like this every week, completely in love." He rubbed his palms down over my shoulders and tried to coax me back into bed.

"Wait—that's sick." I pushed his hands away.

"How is it sick? I don't love my wife and you won't love your husband. We'll still be together, and nobody would have to know a thing," he tried to kiss the side of my neck, but I jerked away.

"I love you. Your son is nine. Why can't you leave her and be with me? Don't I matter to you?" *Please, please tell me that you don't want me to belong to anyone but you. Please declare that you'll marry me and take me away from this horrible predicament. Please tell me that I haven't wasted two years of my life to be with you.*

"Of course you matter. I just don't see a problem here. I think you're making a big deal out of nothing." He sighed and gave up trying to coax me back into bed.

He flicked the TV back on. "You'll see everything will be the same."

Just like that, I was dismissed. Apparently Jerry Seinfeld was more important than I was. I might as well have been a used tampon. Disposable and slightly bloodied from the carnage of this love affair.

I was getting married, so, no, everything would not be the same! I would not be the same.

***

And here I am, my skin itching from the heat in an attic far away from everything, feeling so depressed that I just want to climb into a dark hole and never come out. I haven't seen him since, but I still think of him more often than I care to admit. I wonder if he's okay. If he's found someone to replace my time slot. If he ever loved me. Or if I was just a fun distraction. I wish I could take it all back. Maybe if I hadn't wasted my time with him, I could have found a real guy, a good guy, someone who may have thought I was worth spending the rest of his life with. Ah well, so much for regrets, they don't get you anywhere except a hot, stuffy attic at 4 in the morning..

CHAPTER 5

I AGONIZINGLY WATCH THE CLOCK on my cell phone turn to 7:00am before getting out of bed. I contemptuously look at my meager bundle of clothes and pick out a pair of black pants and white dress shirt. That looks professional-ish, doesn't it? One coat of mascara and a touch of lip gloss later, I feel like a new woman.

I creep downstairs, unsure of the house etiquette. The kitchen is blissfully quiet, except for Penny, who sits at the kitchen tables staring at her cards. Her curly blond hair is still in a wild tangle around her face, and she is wrapped in a silk kimono. The woman is beautiful.

"Hello, Maya," her voice is soothing, melodious, and kind, making it hard for me to hate her.

"Hi Penny, I was just on my way out," I was planning on heating up my cup of Ramen noodles, but I feel uncomfortable eating it in front of her. She might assume I'm poor, and the last thing I need her to think is that I can't afford the rent.

"Sit down, have some breakfast." She pushes a plate of blueberry muffins towards me.

I sit down and take a bite and almost moan out loud at the joy my taste buds are experiencing.

"Have you ever had your cards read?" she asks, shuffling the deck.

"My what read?" I have no idea what she's talking about.

"Tarot and psychic readings, my dear. They originated in India." She looks at me with a meaningful expression on her face.

I nod, agreeing with her. Of course they originated in India, that's probably what Columbus was looking for on his search to India. Screw the spices; psychics are the real "it" thing. It's a shame that the big goofy continent of North America got in his way. She keeps staring at me, I feel like I should say something. "Yes, yes they did," more nodding ensues.

"Do you mind if I practice on you?" she asks me, expectantly.

"Um… do I have to pay you?" No way am I shelling out any dough on this nonsense.

"Consider it on the house." She cuts the deck neatly into three piles.

"Okay, but I really should get going. I don't want to be late for… work," Well, what can I say? *I don't want to be late for looking for a job, looking for a life!* I'm already twenty-six years late, I'm sure 10 more minutes won't kill me.

"Hmmm… interesting," she hums, flipping the first card.

Call me a sucker, but I wanted to learn more. "What? What's interesting?" I mean, the woman did want to talk about *me* for free. I'm pretty sure I'm absolutely fascinating.

"You're on a journey, a deep and meaningful journey."

Really lady? Aren't we all on a journey?

"You've been deeply hurt and betrayed by everyone around you," Penny says flipping the next card. "It will take you a long time to recover."

"How long are we talking about here? Around the time I start getting subscriptions for AARP?" I laugh nervously.

"Don't interrupt," she says sharply.

"Oh—okay, sorry." Shoot, I had interrupted her again.

"You will find your calling in letters that are wet." I try to absorb her words like a sponge, but that's not working out too well. "Love will take time to find you. But when it does, it will be like a burning flame full of fire and sparks. Eventually it will dim into contentment and deep happiness. There will be much trial and tribulations for you right now. There is a reunion in the future, either with yourself or with others. You will feel like you are hitting many dead ends. But have faith and keep walking. Wear comfortable shoes."

She lifts her head away from the cards and smiles at me.

Seriously? That's it? Wear comfortable shoes. That is my destiny. Well, the love part wasn't too bad. Burning, huh? Knowing my luck, it probably means Chlamydia. Note to self: invest in latex.

I thank Penny and get up from the table. The entire time I was getting my cards read, clouds had gathered outside in dark ominous shades of grey. As soon as I shut the door behind me, the skies open up and begin to pour rain down in sheets. I manage to scramble towards the subway and purchase the Sun-Times for a buck fifty. Cripes! $1.50! My cash would be gone soon at this rate.

Scanning the classified section, I circle the most promising ads and head off with a somewhat optimistic—meaning apprehensive and slightly terrified—attitude. Twelve hours later, my feet hurts, my throat is dry, and my back aches. I felt like an 80-year old woman stuck in a 26-year-old body. I have filled out 10 job applications ranging from shoe salesperson to data entry agent. All I can do now is pray my phone rings… soon.

Walking back to my attic, I contemplate the meaning of life—more importantly the meaning of *my* life. Is there a plan? Will I make it? What if there is no plan and I suffer heat stroke in the middle of the night and am devoured by gnats? Would anyone notice? And now that I've told my parents to piss off, would they even know?

High-pitched laughter interrupts my morose thoughts of sexy Shemar Moore on Criminal Minds shaking his head over my decayed and half-devoured body.

I frown in the general direction of the laughter and am blinded by the pulsating red and gold neon lights screaming, Hookah Lounge. My ears register the rhythmic Arabic music. I walk on past the laughter, the music, the blatant display of fun and good times. I'm not in the mood.

Curled up back in my attic, I check my phone for non-existent messages and chew thoughtfully on a piece of burnt toast. I turn on Angie's small black and white TV and am pleasantly surprised I can watch the local WGN channel. Oh goody, the news is on. What's happening now?

"On the North side of Chicago," the anchorwoman reports, "a rapist is on the loose. There have been three attacks since Sunday—"

I snap the TV off. I'm pretty good at scaring myself; I don't need any assistance from the local news team.

The rest of the week passes by in the same blur of job hunting and morose thoughts intercepted by phone calls from Angie checking up on me.

***

Friday night, dejected and bored, I decide to check out the pulsating rhythm of the Hookah Lounge. I am ready to get "Hookah-ed out." I feel like the whole world is conspiring against me. I mean, how hard is it to get a job in this city? I have good hygiene, I speak English. I am a nice person, so why can't I get a job? I am willing to do lavatory inspections, for Christ's sake!

I walk into the dimly lit room and am hit with the smell of incense. The patrons are mostly men—actually they are all men—and they look at me like I have a third eye. For a moment I consider walking out ass backwards, but I straighten my shoulders. I deserve a hit of Hookah too.

The room is covered in red: red tablecloths, red lamp shades, red carpet. On top of the tables are the communal Hookahs, which look like Aladdin's golden lamps. The men smoke on the hookahs, leisurely, imbibing and exhaling colorful smoke rings. Women walk by in glittery bras and chiffony, transparent black skirts, carrying drinks.

I make my way to the bar and am about to place my order when the bartender snaps at me. "You're late." Her green eyes flash. "And you used the wrong entrance."

"I— What…?" Words escape me.

"You're the new girl, aren't you?" Her eyes rake over me.

"I—well, I just moved to the neighborhood a week ago," I stammer.

She nods and mutters something under her breath that I don't quite catch, but it seems to rhyme with *numbass*. "Wait here—I'll get Oliver to see if he still wants you."

Good God, what horrible service. All I wanted to do was try the apple-flavored hookah and this crazy witch is talking in riddles. I turn to leave. But stop in my tracks when the bartender returns with the most beautiful man I have ever laid eyes on in my life. He looks like a dark-haired Orlando Bloom but prettier.

He smiles and I hear birds chirping and bells ringing. "You must be the new girl."

I smile back dreamily. "I must be." *Darling, I can be whatever you want me to be.*

"Well, let's get you in the back so I can see what your measurements are. You're tinier in the front than I expected, but at least you have a big rear. That's the popular look this year."

Tiny in the front? Big rear? I try to ignore the tiny thrill his half-baked compliment gives me.

"I'm sorry," I say, blinking slowly. I instantly regret losing eye contact with him. "Fitted for what?"

"You're here to apply for the hostess/escort position, correct?" He lifts one sexy eyebrow in question.

Oooh, I could swallow him whole.

Did he just say *apply*? As in job interview? As in, what I've been praying for all week?

"Yes," I say, smiling, flashing all my teeth (even the back molars). "I am your perfect hostess/escort."

"I like your enthusiasm," he says winking at me. "The customers will like it, too."

I follow him to the back dressing room where glittery bras, thongs and skirts are haphazardly strewn about. My mind is racing, so I chatter nervously, "What exactly are my specific duties. I mean, I know you described them in the um…ad, but I just want to re-confirm so I can nail it perfectly." I titter self-consciously. "I'm a bit of a perfectionist." *Or an idiot. Or a perfectionist trying to be the perfect idiot.*

"Oh, I'm sure you will nail it just fine," he says, chuckling. "Your duties are to make sure the customers are comfortable and that they have enough drinks, food, and entertainment to keep them satisfied for as long as they're here."

Okay—so waitress/lackey for rich, fat men. I can do that. Piece of cake!

He turns me over to a woman who roughly resembles Attila the Hun. "Yakisha, get her dressed. She goes on in twenty."

I curve my lips in a smile at Yakisha, trying to make friends with my eyes—I had learned this trick from Oprah. In one of her episodes, a therapist suggested that when faced with an opponent, use soothing body language.

She glares back in return as Oliver walks away.

"What girl like you doing here?" she says gruffly as she hands me a black push-up bra stuffed to resemble Double Ds and a sheer piece of chiffon clothe.

"Oh, well, I need a job, and I can't believe how lucky I got that you guys had an opening." Palming the chiffon I looked at her quizzically, "what do I do with this?"

"That's your skirt," she replies.

"Oh—and underneath the skirt goes what exactly?" I say slowly. There is only so much the world needs to see of Maya Khan.

She squints at me, "I like you talking girl, I give you this, no extra charge." She reverently gives me a pair of leotards for which I am eternally grateful. *See? If*

I hadn't made friends with my eyes, I'd be feeling some major drafts tonight!

I walk into the dressing room so excited my fingers shake as I shove my 'tiny in the front' boobs into the bra and slip the chiffon skirt on below. I stare at the mirror in the dressing room and can't believe it's really me.

As I walk out and Attila barks, "Wait—you need face done." She shoves me into a chair and proceeds to spackle brown mud onto my face and apply ridiculously long false lashes, the kind that keep going into my eyes, making them water. Add ruby red lipstick and a smearing of blue eye shadow a la 1987, and I am ready to hit the floor. From the neck up I look like a brown, weepy, Bozo the Clown, and from the neck down I looked like Princess Jasmine. Correction: Princess Jasmine in drag.

"You ready now," Attila says, smacking her lips in satisfaction.

Before I leave the room, I hear her say hesitantly, "Give the man drinks, make 'em forget their problems, and then maybe they go home with no special requests."

I nod appreciatively, albeit a bit confused at her advice.

I shuffle over to the bartender in my new harem slippers. She proceeds to roll her eyes at me.

"Stacy, this is the new girl. She'll be shadowing on tables 1 and 2, the last hour she gets table 3. No special requests for her tonight, that'll start tomorrow."

I smile brightly at Stacy, a blond-haired, blue-eyed girl with freckles. She looks like she should be in a cheerleading squad instead of this locale. She doesn't even bother glancing my way.

"Follow me," are the last words she says before I plunge into the world of harem waitressing. The men are insatiable, arrogant, thirsty beats. They want their drinks, now! They want their hookahs filled, now! They want their appetizers 15 minutes ago! My feet throb; they have stopped being feet, they are just pulsating nerve endings held together by the miserable harem slippers.

I get my own table at 2 in the morning and go home at 4 in the morning $150 richer. I have to be back Saturday night at 7pm. I crawl into bed smiling. I finally have a job as a sexy harem girl.

Mother would be so proud.

CHAPTER 6

"I GOT A JOB!" I shriek excitedly into Angie's ear.

"That's awesome," she says, mustering up enthusiasm.

I pretend not to notice. "I'm a hostess/escort at the Hookah Lounge, it's a block away. I don't even have to pay for transportation," I whisk eggs in Penny's kitchen so giddy to be making a breakfast that didn't consist of dehydrated vegetables. I had woken up this morning (well, noonish) and purchased eggs, chili peppers, tomatoes, cilantro, and a loaf of bread. I am making myself a spicy omelet to celebrate my accomplishment.

"Escort?" Angie questions, "what kind of escort?"

"Oh—you know," I say airily. "The kind that escorts drinks out, escorts the customers in, ya know. How have you been?" I politely ask, figuring my boasting time is about to come to an end.

"Not good, Tyrone left." Her voice indicates that this is not a good thing.

So I hold in my shout of joy and instead respond with, "Oh no! What happened?" *Hopefully he got run over by a car on his way out and will never disappoint or hurt her again.*

"I got pregnant."

I almost drop my mixing bowl. "Angie...*what?* Are you sure?"

I hear her sigh, "I'm four months along."

"What? Why didn't you tell me sooner?"

"You were so busy with the engagement parties and then the wedding preparations. Plus I knew how miserable you were and I didn't want to burden you with another problem,"

"You are never a problem Ms. Angie Wesley. You are my best friend and you can always come to me, I wish I hadn't been so self-involved. I wish there was something I could do."

"Maya- you couldn't have done anything. I actually want to keep it, Maya. I know it isn't reasonable. I'm just so tired of being alone. I've been on my own since I was 18, and I want to take care of someone who will love me back."

"Oh Angie…" I pause and try to speak with a little compassion "I'm no expert, but I don't think mother-hood should be entered into out of loneliness."

"I know, but I'm perceiving this as a gift. I don't want Tyrone. I don't care about him. But I do want the baby."

I lean against the kitchen counter and shut my eyes. Does she have any idea what she is getting into? "Well, then I'm here for you. For whatever you need."

"Thanks, Maya, I appreciate that."

"I am glad he's gone, Angie. That man was garbage. When your house is full of garbage, you have no room to let anything beautiful and new in. Now that he's left, you have this big opening and something new and wonderful is coming in."

"Are you quoting Oprah again?" she asks, irritated.

I actually had to rack my brain to see if I had committed inadvertent plagiarism, "Nope, that was all me. Original Maya Khan, words of wisdom learned on the streets of Oak Park. Word to your mother, yo."

I get her to emit a slight chuckle on that one. "Thanks Vanilla Ice. I'll keep it in mind."

"Oh, don't get me started." In my best Vanilla Ice impersonation, I start to rap, "Yo VIP, lets kick it! All right stop! Collaborate and listen. Ice is back with my brand new invention."

"I'm hanging up now, Maya!" Angie says, laughing. I hear a click on the phone as I do my Vanilla Ice shuffle. What can I say? Baby got back, and she knows it!

***

I work two straight weeks in a row, dodging grimy paws and lecherous looks. I smile so hard, my jaws clamp shut and I fear that all my teeth will fall out. I put up with catty remarks like, "Do you pad your ass? Or is it really that big?" and "Why does it smell like curry in here?" I usually get the worst tables in the house. I have never gotten the "special requests" that the experienced waitresses got. I assume these requests consist of bachelor parties, since they are usually handled in the private suites upstairs.

I work so hard I almost forget the mind-numbing loneliness and the always swirling question , *What am I doing with my life?*

As I wipe down the counters and fill the Hookahs with strawberry-flavored tobacco, the doors bust in. "Police—nobody move, hands up!"

I lift my hands up and promptly drop the heavy silver tray on my big toe. Squelching a yelp, I hobble around in pain as the rest of the girls try to run out the side doors and windows. They quickly stop when they realize the building is surrounded.

The cops march through the bar with their big, stomping feet and shiny guns. Attila comes out of the dressing room. "What is the meaning of this?" she asks, her face red, arms akimbo.

"Yakisha Waheeda?" one officer asks.

"Yes-I," she nervously jumps when an officer comes up behind her and proceeds to cuff her.

"You are under arrest for trafficking and the solicitation of prostitution. Do you know an Oliver Waheeda?"

"He is out of town—business," she says angrily.

"We have a warrant for his arrest. He is also charged with trafficking sex workers. If you tell us where he is, we can be more lenient with your charges."

"I don't know. You are incorrect, we no do that." She looks like she is about to spit in his face when he jerks her forward.

I am frozen, rooted to the spot like a gnarled oak tree.

"Ma'am," an officer looks at me and nods in the direction of the main door. "You're going to have to follow the other women to the squad cars."

"I—I," I say haltingly, "I don't exactly understand what's happening here."

He nods and speaks slowly to me. "You're under arrest for prostitution which is the act of exchanging money for sexual activity."

I almost faint from the sheer mortification. I have been working in a freakin' brothel and didn't even know it!

"But I never—"

He abruptly cuts me off, "We'll take your statement down at the station."

***

I have never been to a police station—never needed to go. They are loud, busy, and filled with possible criminals. I am now in the "possible criminal" category. The girls that I work with all sit next to me, snapping their gum and looking bored, they seem all too familiar with the process.

"Stacy, they're wrong, right? I mean, none of us do that—those thing," my words break off into the stale air.

She adjusts her bra strap and says in her nasally tone, "We all do it, sweety, but you were never requested."

"Never requested?" I repeat, puzzled, "Wait, that was the 'special requests.' Oh my Gosh!" I whisper in awed horror.

"For $800 a pop, I was saying OMG every night myself," she pulls out a compact and smoothes out her non-existent eyebrows.

I sit there in disbelief, a plethora of conflicting emotions washing over me. I am getting arrested on charges of prostitution, working in a brothel, where not one man thought I was worth paying for?

Okay, that's coarse and twisted, but come on! It's not like I had diphtheria. Did Attila the Hun get propositioned? My deflated ego hides behind the comforting emotions of rage and bitterness.

"Khan, Maya Khan, you're up next." I follow Sgt. Rodriguez to his desk, noticing his fine derriere along the way. *God, what have I turned into? A depraved fake prostitute. The kind that got arrested but never put out.*

"As per earlier statements from Yakisha Waheeda—she states you never engaged in inappropriate acts with the patrons—is that true?" he asks.

"That's correct. Apparently, I was never requested," I say with a touch of indignation.

Officer Rodriguez looks up from his paperwork, his grey-green eyes slightly amused. "Did ya' wanna be requested?"

"No, I was unaware that was even going on. I was hired as a hostess/escort." When he lifts an eyebrow at the word escort, I hastily add, "Escorting drinks and patrons around."

He smiles. "You seem like a nice young girl, Maya, whachya doin' at a joint like the Hookah Lounge?" Before I can open my mouth to speak, he continues, "Look, I see your type around here all the time. Indian girls that go out

on their own and bite off more than they can chew. You should go home and make nicey-nice with your family."

I flinch at the word, "your type." There were two types of Indian girls. There are the ones who completely forget their own culture and embrace being the "all-American" girl. This includes the clothes, the boys, the goals, the ambitions, and the mannerisms. Oh sure, they'll put on a glittery Indian costume every once in a while to show off their exoticness and get frothy compliments from their American friends. But they are usually swigging Vente Lattes in their brand new Porsches at the time, their noses turned up at the Indian girl who wears baggy sweaters and jeans to hide her confusing curves.

Then there is the other type of Indian girl. She never ventures out of her Indian comfort zone. She is helpful at home, maintains good grades, and does what she is told until her parents marry her off like a sacrificial cow to a lucky fella who happens to be walking by.

I am the latter, and I have always been miserably jealous of the former. Oh, to be so carefree, so unburdened by everyone's expectations.

And now I am just confused. To my utter horror, my eyes start brimming with tears, right in front of the delicious Officer Rodriguez, and I can't get them to stop.

"I tried," I blubber, "but my parents wouldn't listen and they told me I had to get married but then I—I—I just couldn't do it and so I ran and I couldn't find a job and I looked and I looked and this was the only thing available but I had no idea it was a brothel until today and then I found out that I hadn't even been re-QUESTED!" I wail, grabbing at the tissues on his desk and blowing my nose loud enough to be mistaken for a lawn mower. I am just grateful that I hadn't sprayed snot in his general direction.

I look up to see a decidedly uncomfortable Officer Rodriguez.

"Look, kid, the charges against you have been dropped. My advice: go to school. Become a pharmacist or a medical assistant. People keep getting older but aren't really dying. Ya got a second chance here. Don't blow it on a dead end, and that," he says, gesturing towards my sequined bra, "is definitely a dead end."

Oh, he was so wise and so cute. I could see it now: our wedding dinner would be a combination of Indian and Mexican cuisine. Maybe I'd wear a white dress this time, red really isn't my color. The D.J. would have to do a mix of Bollywood dance music with salsa and meringue. I was so caught up in our dance number that I almost missed the tail end of our conversation, "because I got two little girls at home and it would break my heart if they ended up at a joint like that." His head is bent down as he signs his paperwork and crushes my multi-cultural wedding dreams all at once.

***

I scramble out of the police station. Angry, relieved, sad and hungry, I hail a cab to the nearest Walmart, purchase a sweat suit, one with an elastic waist band and then head off to the nearest Indian restaurant to drown my sorrows in lamb kabobs and jasmine rice.

Officer Rodriguez may have been cute and married, but he was also right. I am so busy running away from everything, I have no idea what I am running towards. What do I want? Stable employment is definitely at the top of that list. But it can't just be any job, it has to be something that I like. What do I like? I have no idea. I know for sure what I don't like: arranged marriages and prostitution are at the top of that list. But what am I passionate about? What makes me happy, what do I love?

I frown, how have I gotten to the ripe old age of 26 not knowing what makes me happy? Am I so distracted by my family, my married boyfriend, my girlfriend's problems, TV, music, and TMZ that I have never thought about me? Have I always settled for "not completely miserable" instead of happy?

Sitting alone in the booth, I write a list on my napkin stating all the things I love. I love to eat. The stretched-to-the-max elastic waistband surrounding my ample middle could attest to that. I love sex—when I am getting it. Back in the day, way back. It was freakin' awesome. Now it is just another ache I ignore frequently. I stare at my list: sex and food. I have somehow gone backwards in the evolutionary food chain and have the same desires as a horny hyena.

Okay, this is too hard. I start another list titled: **Things I Need ASAP**. A job, another place to live. That attic is killing me. Sharing a bathroom with invisible strangers is absolutely disgusting. I have never seen so many shades of pubic hair floating around in a tub, sink, or floor. Ick! The fridge needs to have been cleaned months ago. The fragrant moldy smell permeates through the walls, making the whole house smell like rotten cheese. I feel quite satisfied with my list. I should start applying for other jobs. I should call Angie to give her an update on my miserable life. I should at least buy a newspaper. I, instead, buy a romance novel, a box of chocolates, and some ice cream and take my leftovers home. I alternately read, watch TV, and eat for the next 3 days. I also think some more, which by now is becoming a dangerous hobby.

I don't know how to navigate in this new world. My whole life has been run for me—meals were always prepared, laundry always done. Sure, I did a few chores, but I was cocooned from a lot of life's harsher realities.

I enjoyed American culture through the delightful prism of TV and books. It was something to be looked at for entertainment value, but never explored or tried through personal experience.

I am floating in a kind of cultural prison. I can mimic the jokes and conversational banter, even the layered haircuts, but I don't know if I can actually live in it. Sticking a spoonful of Rocky Road ice cream in my mouth, I let the chocolaty marshmallow goodness trickle down my throat and try to empty my head of all unhappy thoughts. The last thought that goes through my head before I conk out is, *Does this ice cream make me look fat?* To which my inner-voice replies, *Yes! Lard-ass.*

CHAPTER 7

DAY 4 OF HIDING FROM life is interrupted by Penny poking her head through my floor. "Oh, hello, Maya, I haven't seen you around the last couple of days. I just wanted to make sure you were doing okay."

I quickly grab all the empty foil wrappers from the chocolate bars and throw them in the wastebasket. "Fine, fine and you?" I run my tongue over my lips and chin, hoping I don't have any food stains on my face. Oh yeah, Maya Khan is one classy broad.

"Good, I haven't seen you go to work lately. Is everything okay?"

"Oh well, the place got shut down," I avert my eyes from her gaze and instead stare at the wooden floor. *Please leave*, I scream to her psychic brain, *can't you tell I'm embarrassed and ashamed and my breath smells like something died in my intestines?*

"Perhaps that's for the best. Maya, I don't know how to say this, but well, I'm afraid the house is going into foreclosure."

My head snaps up in attention, "What? Why?"

"I was behind on a few payments, and, well, my business isn't making the revenue I had hoped it would make, that's why I rented out this storage space—uh, I mean extra room," she quickly corrects herself. "But it still hasn't helped, and I can't keep this up."

"What do we do? What are you going to do?" I look at her, willing her to say that everything will be okay. How could she have not seen this in her tarot cards?

"We have another month, and then I'm going to Houston to work at my brother's diner." She wrinkles her nose, "blek!"

"But what about your psychic business? Who will tell people their inner truths and stuff?" I protest. Psychics are already such an endangered species.

She holds my gaze and smiles, "We can't always do what we want to do, Maya. Sometimes there are sacrifices that we can't foresee. We'll keep in touch. In the meantime," her gaze skims over my disarrayed clothing on the floor and the overflowing wastebasket, "let's clean this up a bit for prospective buyers."

***

"I'm going to be homeless!" I wail to Angie. I have taken a train over to Lincoln Square with the sole purpose of unburdening all of the bad things that continue to happen to me—in short, whining like a 3-year-old until I got a commiserating, "mm-hmmm."

Unfortunately, Angie is working at the hair salon, which means I have an audience. So, deep in my depression, I can't even expend the energy to be embarrassed.

"You're not going to be homeless," Angie says as she fluffs her client's hair out, "You know Tyrone's ass moved out, and I need someone to help massage my feet at night."

I give her a quizzical stare, "By *someone*, I hope you mean your pedicurist Latisha right around the corner. Because I don't do feet."

"Oh, beggars are turning into choosers now? Well, this is interesting." She pulls a bobby pin out of her teeth and sticks it underneath the side part of her client's hair.

"Great, so now I live with you and I have to find a new job too. I'm right back where I started. Why do bad things always happen to me? It's so unfair. I mean, I'm such a nice person, why don't people just give me a job and an apartment that's affordable?"

"While they're at it, they should give you a brand new car and your own personal chef," Angie quips with sarcasm.

I shrug. "I mean, it couldn't hurt. If I just had one thing going for me, everything else would fall into place, right?" *Why do thoughts always sound better in my head than when I say them out loud? I'm so smart to me, when I'm all by myself. Hmm... that didn't sound right either.*

"Well child, what did you major in?" A gravelly voice emits from Angie's chair.

Silence meets her query.

"What did you go to school for? Get your resume out there and see if you can get a few interviews," the sentence ends in a fit of coughing.

"Maya didn't finish college, Mrs. E. She majored in the school of life." Angie smoothly responds. I cringe. Why *hadn't* I finished college? Oh yeah, two years into it, my brilliant 20-year-old self had decided it was too much work, and instead I settled like a comfortable parasite at my Dad's medical clinic working as a receptionist.

Ah, the path of least resistance was coming back to bite me.

"Well, then, get your ass back to school; that's the answer to your problems. No place in the world for another uneducated, illiterate bumble-head," Mrs. E gingerly lifts herself off the chair and pats her hair into place, "Great job, Angie, you always know how to keep me in style."

"You're welcome, Mrs. E. Have fun at tonight's Steppers Set," Angie says with a wink.

"Oh, you know I will. Arthur was eyeing me last week. I'm going to show him some moves this week. Uh-hugh-hugh," she gurgles out a laugh and slowly shuffles out of the salon.

"I'm not illiterate," I blurt out behind her in my clever, sharp manner (if clever and sharp were ever interpreted as awkward and dim-witted). All I hear in response is laughter.

"Alright, Miss Maya, you know what will make you feel better?" Angie asks me.

I raise my eyebrows in response, "A deep-tissue massage by Colin Farrell while he's whispering sweet Irish nothings in my ear?"

"Even better: a haircut," Angie says. She catches my look of disbelief. "It'll be fun. Trust me."

I look in the mirror and immediately wish I hadn't. In my haste to share with Angie all of the perils that had befallen me, I had not taken the time to shower or change out of my sweats. Funny, I don't want to end up homeless, but I have no problem looking the part.

"C'mon, M, there ya go." Angie coaxes me into the chair. Before I can protest, she quickly whisks a cape around my neck and gets to work. I watch in shock as the long black tendrils slither this way and that before finally falling off my cape and onto the floor. It is oddly liberating. I feel the weight falling off my head. In its place is a great sense of freedom. The old Maya wouldn't dare cut her hair off. Her mother would purse her lips in disapproval, shake her head, and say things like, "Is this why we brought you over to this country, so you can wear short skirts and have Americanized hair?" Her tone always implied that anything American-ized was negative. The old Maya would have stared at her mother in mute fear and toed the line because she didn't know any better. But the new Maya would stand up and say, "Yes! Dear mother, that is why we're in America, to wear what we want, have whatever hair we want, and pierce our nether regions if we feel up to it." Of course, I wouldn't be talking about *my* nether regions, as I'm averse to both pain and strange people looking at my girly parts. But if my mother were here, I would give her a piece of my mind or maybe a lock of hair to remember her baby girl by.

My hair, my long, tangled mess of ebony tresses, was gone. In its place was a short, sassy, edgy cut. It shaped my head and ended at my chin. The cut brought out my eyes and made me look... a little bad-ass. Hey now! Check me out!

"Oh my gosh, Angie, it's awesome!" I grin and then instantly stop. Smiles don't match the haircut; instead, I practice a steely-eyed gaze of sexiness.

"Oh, Maya," Angie bursts out laughing. "What are you doing now?"

"This is the new me, edgy, funky Maya. Maya the rebel. Raawr!" I make exaggerated facial expressions of toughness.

"Maya the rebel, huh? Well Maya the rebel, don't forget to get your stuff out of that attic before that witchy looking creature hawks it on eBay."

I grimace. Great! More moving ahead.

***

I wander down Lake Street, taking in the evening. I have said goodbye to Penny and the invisible residents of the Psychic House. All of my belongings are back in my trusty duffel bag.

The sun is setting, and families are sitting down to dinner. I can see them through their bay windows, the lamplight creating halos over their heads. Watching them makes me feel hollow inside. I miss my family all the time. I am usually able to sidestep the feeling by focusing on the essentials, like shelter and food. But there are moments like this one when I can't escape the extreme ache for home.

My family had laid out my life long before I was born. There were expectations from the cradle regarding who I should become. I had no say in the matter. Now that I have escaped their gridlocked outline, I feel like I am freefalling through thin air and there is no safety net that will keep me from smashing my face against the pavement. The worst part is that there is no one to talk to about this feeling. Angie tries to understand but can't really get where I am coming from. Her mom kicked her out when she was 18. They speak once in a while but live completely separate lives.

My parents, on the other hand, live for my brother and me. We were adored and coddled—as long as we stayed within that gridlocked outline. I stop looking into the windows at other people's lives and focus on the sidewalk. *Don't look up, Maya, don't look to the side, just put one foot in front of the other, just keep moving, the sadness will pass, and so will the hurt, the fear, and the resentment. Just keep moving.*

"Free books," a booming voice interrupts my introspection.

I glance up, startled.

"All books free—sales over, we gotta offload the merchandise," the same gruff voice says through a megaphone.

Oh no, Anderson's Bookstore is going out of business? Is nothing sacred??

"You wanna book, kid?" The voice belongs to an elderly man in a tweed jacket and baseball hat.

"Sure," I answer—anything free at this point is a bonus.

"Here, you'll like this one," he shoves a book in my hand and I glance at the title, "Letters to a Young Journalist," by Samuel G. Freedman.

I smile in thanks and continue towards the park, peering at the first couple of pages, "In Egyptian Mythology, there existed a God named Thoth…"

Oooh—have I mentioned that I love Egypt?

***

"I think I want to be an archaeologist," I say brightly the next morning, plopping down on the barstool by Angie's counter.

I wrinkle my nose at the stench permeating through the air. "What is that smell?"

Angie is hunched behind the refrigerator door. I can hear a crisp snap and then chewing.

"What are you eating?" I ask her.

"Nothing, just a snack," she jerks up and closes the door. I see the pickle in one hand and the jar of peanut butter in the other.

"Do I want to know?"

"I'm pregnant—I'm allowed to eat whatever I want without judgment."

"Judgment is form of love too," I remind her, "If I don't judge you first and correct the bad choices, I wouldn't be a very good friend. Because then you would go out into the world and be judged by others who wouldn't be as sensitive as I am. So when I say that's the most disgusting thing I have ever seen, I am saying it with love."

Angie proceeds to bite into her pickle defiantly.

I delve back into my book. The title catches Angie's eye and she snorts. "Only you would read a book titled, 'Letters to a Young Journalist' and want to be an archaeologist."

"There are subliminal messages in here," I snap, irritated by her lack of support once again. I stare at her dubious expression, "What makes you think I can't be an archaeologist?"

She starts counting her fingers:

Index— "You don't like dirt."

Middle— "You don't like bones or skeletal remains."

Ring— "You don't like dark, confined spaces."

Pinkie— "You hate sweating."

"Okay," I wave off her reasons, "I could be in the elite jewelry-finding tomb section.

"Well, whatever—archaeologist, journalist, neurologist, geologist—anything with an *ist* at the end of it means a degree. Something you don't have."

I inhale, frown, and decide to change the subject, "So how's the baby?"

"Baby's fine," she drops the dish towel and starts fiddling with the tea bag in her cup, refusing to meet my eyes, "Baby's daddy skipped town. He sent me a text saying he was going to New York to find a job or something."

I feel an intense sense of relief. Thank God! New York is ten hours of driving distance away. I would have preferred he'd been shot out to the moon with a giant rubber band, but I feign concern for Angie's sake, as I don't want to appear smug or superior. A tap dance (although appropriate) didn't seem fitting.

"Oh," I say with empathy, "And we're still…?"

"Keeping the baby," she finishes my sentence.

"Angie, I'm not trying to talk you out of this, I swear. You are woman and I hear you roar, but how are you going to juggle baby, work, and all the bills that come with it?" I tactfully left off, *and my unemployed ass.*

"Well, I've been talking to my mom and Nefertiti. I think if I rotate my shift around my mom's, I can take care of him during the day and pick up the evenings and weekend shifts. On Sunday I can bring him to work, so she has that one day to herself. The girls are okay with watching him on Sunday when I'm with clients."

"I can help too," I impetuously offer, doing God knows what. But I had to say something, right?

"If I get that desperate, I'll let you know," she glances down at my book, "Seriously, honey, you need a degree, otherwise it's a bunch of dead-end nothing out there. Especially now that mommy and daddy aren't giving you an allowance,"

"It wasn't an allowance," I say defensively, "It was a weekly stipend."

"Tom-ay-to, tom-ah-to."

I hang my head, "I miss them, Angie. I'm so lost and everything is so damn expensive and I don't think I'm cut out to be on my own. I thought I could do this, but I don't know how to navigate out here."

"In a world where Kim Kardashian has somehow transformed from pathetic wanna-be porn star to reality TV queen, not only can you make it, you can destroy those petty little goals your parents had for you. There's more to life than being somebody's wife or girlfriend." Angie's hand flutters over her stomach, and I wonder which one of us she is talking to. "It's August, Maya; you can still make late registration for fall."

Okay, so it wasn't like I had no education, I had two years of Gen Ed's tucked away from UIC, it was only when I hit the advanced Biology and Chemistry courses geared towards getting me into med school that my anxiety overrode my reasoning and I dropped out. Which brings me to the Maya Motto in life: "When things get hard—QUIT!" Like it? I coined it myself. The As started slipping to Bs, B-'s, and then eventually C-'s and D+'s. I was surrounded by super-smart Indian people who could do quantum physics in their sleep and dissect a hamster's appendix in three seconds flat, while I was struggling to keep up. I couldn't keep up with their conversations; I couldn't keep up with the lectures. Everything that came out of their mouths sounded Latin, and I just couldn't decipher it no matter how hard I tried. I was never invited to their gatherings after class where they all made fun of how dumb the professors were. I secretly wondered if they made fun of me too. I was like the defect Indian in a sea of uniform genius.

I came home for Spring break and didn't go back. My dad gave me the pity job at his clinic, where I stayed until well... you know the rest of the story.

"But I hate school!" I grumble feebly.

"You hated pre-med and the idea of being a doctor. You could go back and get a degree in something you actually want. If I didn't have my cosmetology certificate, I would be flipping burgers at Burger King, and you know my hair does not go well with excess grease.

"Mmmmm," my eyes flicker over to the TV, where naked Game of Thrones characters grope each other. "College kids get laid a lot, right?

Her eyes follow mine to the TV screen, "Yup, they hump like fuckin' rabbits," After a particularly vigorous thrust on TV, Angie sighs and fans herself, "I think I need a little education myself.

It's settled—I am going to school to get laid. And, oh yeah, to get an education.

CHAPTER 8

"WELL, MAYA, your high school transcripts are quite impressive and so is your first year at UIC; unfortunately, your second year tapers off a bit at the end," my admittance counselor's enthusiasm falters slightly. "But that's okay, we'll take only the good and just omit the bad, how does that sound?" he adjusts his glasses and shoots me a buck-toothed smile.

I am shocked that anyone even has buckteeth anymore. I thought by the age of twelve, kids got attached to braces like pre-pubescent magnets to a fridge. I myself had the good fortune of going through high school with coke-bottle glasses, braces, and full-blown cystic acne. You can imagine the booming social life that invited.

"So I can transfer my Gen-Ed courses over?" I ask hopefully.

"Well... eh... some of them, yes. Based on my calculation you fall in as a second-semester sophomore. This might be a good thing. Gives you a chance to declare a major. You better choose wisely, a major in art history only gets you so far," he laughs nervously. "...as far as the nearest bottle of Jack Daniels," I hear him mutter as he opens a drawer and pulls out more files.

"I um... also need a job," I venture nervously.

"Yes, well, that's where we hit a bit of a snag. You're going to have to go over to the Financial Administration office. There seems to be a hiccup in your credit history. You have some outstanding loans." He notices my perplexed expression, "It might all be a mistake, but you should drop by there and clarify the matter. From the academic side, we are full steam ahead, but we can't fully admit you until you clear those loans up."

I nod stiffly and make my way over to the Finance Office. What is it? The late Victoria Secret Card payment? The one time I over-exceeded my debit card? It turned out to be far, far worse...

"YOU BOUGHT DAMASCUS A CAR?!" Angie screeches at me.

I wince and open my mouth to explain, but she beats me to it. "How in the hell could you purchase him a car? Why would they give you a $40,000 vehicle when you made $10 bucks an hour and lived at home?"

"*Refinanced*. We refinanced the loan, and it ended up being in my name. It was prior to the recession and the housing market crash," I offer feebly.

"Well, no wonder the bubble burst, they were offering anybody and everybody a freaking Navigator." She turns back to me, her hair whipping around her face in a dramatic frenzy, "How could you put your name on the refinance paperwork?"

"I loved him," I say in a very small voice.

Angie's face turns red and her knuckles turn white. "Ooooh! Somebody should take that man and just hang him by his balls and cut out his—"

"Anyways," I quickly interrupt her, before her unborn child overhears her cussing like a sailor. "According to the bank, he's about 2 months late, but the upside is the car should be fully paid off by October."

"Unless he's late," she says accusingly.

"Well yeah—unless he's late."

"And it's all in your name, title, registration, everything?" She asks.

"I'm not sure."

"Maya, I am not going to sit by and let that man take another day away from you. You are going to school. You are going to get laid by someone else in this lifetime, even if it kills me. Come on," she throws my purse at me and walks to the door.

"Where are we going?" I ask, tottering behind her in my new platforms (I needed a treat, they were on sale—don't judge me).

"The police station."

"Maya," Officer Rodriguez sighs, looks down at his paperwork and then looks up at me, "don't take this the wrong way, but I had hoped I would never see you again."

"Officer Rodriguez, I took your advice: I registered to go back to school."

"That's good," he sits back in his chair and smiles. "I'm happy to hear that, so what can I do for you?"

"I'll tell you what you can do," Angie interrupts both of us and leans so far forward, her booty is elevated a good two inches above the chair she's supposed to be sitting in. Her chin, practically resting on Officer Rodriguez's lap, "She used to date a low-down, lying scum bag who took advantage of her naiveté and had her purchase him a car."

Officer Rodriguez's eyes widen in surprise.

"Yes, my poor baby." Oh God, she is laying it on a little too thick. I *think* she is trying to work the sympathy angle. "That's not the worst of it. Now that she's finally getting her life back together, mending the broken pieces," I am starting to sound like a sad country song, "fate rears its ugly head. Guess who is denied her student loans because of her terrible credit score, thanks to you-know-who?"

"The naïve girl—I mean Maya Khan?" Officer Rodriguez guesses.

"Exactly!" Angie says triumphantly, "All we need, Officer," her voice drops and catches a little, as if she's about to cry. I'm touched that she cares so much, "is to see if the vehicle belongs to her and if she's within her rights to reclaim it," end scene with the heroine batting fake eyelashes at a man in uniform. Ladies and gentlemen, we gotta give the woman an academy award here, or at least a glue gun to keep the lashes in place, because one side is starting to droop a bit.

Officer Rodriguez clears his throat, obviously touched by her plea. I mean, who wouldn't be? "Well Maya, your…" he hesitates, *partner* here is very convincing. I'll see what I can dig up. Give me a moment, I have to go into the other room and look up the information. May I have the VIN number and license plates? Also, do you have any paperwork stating that the vehicle is yours?"

I write down the information and hand him my paperwork. Luckily, the lady at the Financial Administration office sympathized with my plight. When I had complete selective amnesia and was adamant that this was a case of identity theft, she had me call the bank. I made the call right in front of her, convinced that the bank was wrong. I boldly asked them for proof that I had purchased the vehicle. My voice was loud, clear, and direct. My conviction was strong. Stupid banks. Everyone hates banks. I am the 99%. Boo, banks! Well, the bank happily faxed over the paperwork, with my signature, date, and photo ID saying that I willingly refinanced the loan on a 2005 Silver Navigator. That I had plopped down $3500 on it (Damascus had promised to pay me back… but stuff happened, so he never did). I then sat in stupefied mortification.

I mean, I didn't even know where this guy lived and I had refinanced a car in my name for him! The worst of it was that I knew I had Angie to face when I got home. Good ol' Angie, who would make me go to the police station and relive the horror of what I had done, over and over again.

"He called me your partner," Angie hisses at me, her dark eyes flashing.

"What?" I glance at her, startled. "What are you talking about?"

"He paused and then said 'partner', like I was your bitch." Angie is clearly in a huff.

"Oh Angie, if we were in a relationship, everyone knows I would be your bitch," I say, trying to console her.

"Really? Wait, what are you saying? That I'm masculine? That I'm too aggressive? That I don't let a man breathe? And that I cut off his balls? Is that what you're saying, Maya?"

Me thinks I have touched a nerve. "No, not at all. But you know if we were ever in a *girl fight*, with other *straight* girls, you would be kicking ass. And I would be in a fetal position on the floor. Hence, I would definitely be your bitch."

She straightens in her chair, slightly pleased with my comment.

Thankfully, Officer Rodriguez returns before Angie gets riled up again. "Maya, I'm happy to say that the vehicle is yours. Registration, plates, and the VIN number all point to the fact that you're within your rights to request the vehicle back. I mean, if he can prove he's been making payments, he could take you to civil court and dispute your claim. But given his negligence on the account, the judge could rule in your favor."

My heart does a deep dive and sinks to the bottom of my stomach. I sooooo do not want to drag this to court.

Angie chimes in, "So we're within our legal rights to take the car?"

Officer Rodriguez nods.

"Thank you, that's all we needed to hear," Angie inclines her head gracefully to Officer Rodriguez and sweeps me out of the office.

I have just enough time to swerve my head and stammer, "Thank you very much," before being yanked away by a very strong pregnant woman who is out for blood.

As soon as we get into her vehicle, she turns to me, "You have the extra set of keys, right?"

I sink down in the passenger seat uncomfortably, "Well, I did kind of run away from home a few weeks ago, I didn't exactly think to take my ex-boyfriend's car keys.

"Check your key chain, maybe you put it on there and forgot. And he thinks you're too much of a pushover to do anything about it two years later. But we are going to show him," the latter part of the sentence is delivered in a growl.

I rummage around in my purse, pull out my keys, and go through the assortment of metal. And there it was, a pointy silver tip enclosed in a black rubber base with the Navigator symbol on it. I had found our beacon of hope.

"Yes!" Angie yelps as soon as I hold up the key in timid victory, she bangs her hand on the dashboard, "We are going to get that son of a bitch!"

"Yay," I say weakly. I think I am beginning to understand Angie's master plan and that it will involve me having to confront my biggest fear: Damascus McCarthur.

"We're doing it tonight, Maya."

"But I don't want to do it tonight. Besides, I have no idea where he lives."

"Thank God for Google. Look it up on your phone, we'll do a drive by of it right now."

"What? No, it's too soon, I have to mentally adjust to this new development."

"How is it too soon when your education depends on it, Maya? You don't owe him anything. He used you, he took advantage of you, and now it's affecting your future. You have to put a stop to this shit. You finally confronted your parents after all these years, and it's time you confronted this asshole and put it behind you. You think he's sitting around his house with his wife and kids worrying about you? I highly doubt it."

I will myself not to cry, but Angie's words just remind me of what a colossal fool I had been to trust this man, and before I can help it, hot tears run down my face, "I feel sooooo stupid!"

"Aw, hell," Angie pulls the car over and awkwardly pats me on the shoulder.

"I need a tissue," I sniff. Actually what I *really* need are extra-absorbent 3-ply paper towels.

Angie rummages around in her glove compartment and hands me some wrinkled napkins. It will do. I blow my nose loudly.

I am hurt and upset and embarrassed, so naturally I lash out, blurting, "You know, you're not a total genius when it comes to men, either. Tyrone was an asshole too. He used you. You couldn't see that he used you when he didn't pay his rent and ran around the city?

Doing God knows what and with who?" Angie's eyes narrow into dangerous slits, but I am past the point of caring, "I mean, you're carrying a baby from a man who isn't concerned about you or his baby. He ran all the way to New York to get away from the responsibility. He didn't have the money to cover his phone bill, but somehow he was able to gather enough pennies to get to New York. How does it feel? Huh? When people sit around and judge you and think that they're so much smarter than you? It feels crappy, doesn't it?"

After a brief pause, Angie says, "I don't think I'm smarter than you."

"Well, you always act like it," I say sullenly.

"Do you feel better?" she asks.

"Not really."

"You know what would make you feel better?"

"Ice cream?"

"Stealing that asshole's car!"

The betrayal, the sadness, the hurt, and the confusion of the last four years churn inside of me, giving away to a pulsating, red, hot anger directed towards Damascus McCarthur. "You're right! Let's go get that lying, no good, needle-dick fucktard!"

We hide across the street in the cover of night, looking at the house with mini-binoculars, "We can't just steal it!" I hiss. "Maybe we should have the police talk to him."

"Just focus on the car, is it your car?"

I looked at the back of the silver Navigator, "I guess," I say tentatively.

"Look at the license plate, does it match the license plate you have?"

"Yes, it does."

"All right, here's the plan. We wait until all the lights go off in the house and wait another thirty minutes to make sure they've all turned in. You sneak out to the car, put the key in the ignition and slightly turn the key. You don't want to start the car, just unlock the steering column. We push the car down the driveway and maybe another block over. You then gun the engine and we're out of here."

"We're going to push a 5000-pound vehicle down the block?" I say incredulously. "I can barely lift a 2lb dumbbell."

"It's fine, the driveway inclines down. Once it's in neutral, the car will be easy to maneuver. Just harness that anger. Mothers have been known to lift buildings off their children through pure adrenaline alone, just think of this Navigator as your child, and you are freeing it from the shackles of late payment."

"That's like the worst comparison I've ever heard."

"Well, it's all I've got, now shut up and let's get back to the stake-out," Angie slurps loudly on her Coke.

"Aww, man!" I groan.

"What? Did he see us? What happened?"

I lift the top of my sesame burger bun and show it to her. "I clearly said, I wanted the spicy grilled chicken sandwich, they got me the classic grilled sandwich. I mean, my God, how hard is it to get an order right?"

"Probably as hard as it is to order a stake-out buddy who keeps her mouth shut. Have you never seen the movies? They don't talk about their pickles during a stake-out."

I glare at Angie; however, the darkness prevents her from feeling the full effect.

***

We sit in her car three hours later listening to Marvin Gaye crooning about love. The rustle of cellophane from our burger wrappers mixes with the sounds of crickets in the sticky summer air. It is almost a perfect evening, filled with the contentment that only summer can bring, and if not for the upcoming heist, I might have enjoyed it. As it is, my stomach is tied up in knots. *What if I get caught? Will he recognize me? How will I explain myself? Will he be able to go to work? What if he loses his job? Will I ruin his life with this plan?*

As I mull over the questions in my head, another set of questions arise. *What about me? Don't I deserve to go to school? Does he think about me every time he makes a late payment? Does he laugh because my credit score is being dinged and not his? Does he take his other girlfriends on trips to Lake Geneva in the truck that I had refinanced for him?*

"Maya," hisses Angie, "All the lights are turned off. Start your timer—we're going in after 30 minutes."

I program the timer on my phone, my heart beating erratically, the back of my neck covered in sweat. I am really going to do this. I try to take a deep breath.

Angie rubs her hands and cackles with glee. "Oooh, he isn't going to see this coming. Can you imagine the look on his face tomorrow morning when he comes out to his driveway and his truck his gone? Is he going to report it stolen to the police? I hope so, I can't wait!"

"How can you enjoy this so much? I'm having trouble remembering to breathe."

"Because you're not seeing how fun this is."

An eternity later, my timer goes off. My heart races. I creep out of Angie's Saturn. Trying to act nonchalant, I cut across the street. I have donned my best car heisting outfit for the occasion, which consists of a black t-shirt, leggings, and flip flops. I hope his neighbors don't call the police. Yes, I am in the right. But I want to do this without seeing or hearing him. I especially don't want to stammer out an explanation in front of the cops *and* his wife. I imagine it would go something like this: "Hi, Mrs. McCarthur, yeah I um… was sleeping with your husband for two years and decided to refinance the car as a present to both of you, and now I want to take it back. I know I totally sound like an Indian Giver—but I *am* Indian. So I think it's okay if I call myself that." Yep, I'm sure that explanation would go over real well.

My hands are slippery with sweat; I nearly drop the keys when I get to the driver side door. Swearing and praying, I put the key in the lock and turn it. It unlocks soundlessly. I slide onto the leather seat and frown, the seat is inclined way too far back, and my butt keeps sliding down the leather slope making it impossible for my feet to touch the brake or gas pedals. I feel like a four-year-old trying to ride around in her daddy's car. My nostrils flare in agitation. *What if I can't drive this thing?* I turn the key anyway. I hear the soft click and put the car into neutral. True to Angie's word, the car automatically slides down the driveway. I try my best to steer it out and around. I am now on the street. A light rap on my window makes me jump out of my skin. I manage just in time to stifle a scream so that it comes out as a wheeze.

"Get out here, we both have to push," Angie is oblivious to the mini heart attack she has just caused me.

"I thought I could handle the steering," I protest. "I mean, that takes a lot of work too."

She gives me her "look," the one that means she's two seconds away from using her fists to "persuade" me to change my mind. Grumbling about my lack of upper body strength, I slide off the seat and walk sluggishly to the back of the truck. Trying to shove a 5000-

pound truck is not fun. Grunting, moaning, and heaving, we push for a good ten minutes. The truck does not move.

"Angie," I gasp panting, "I can't do this. I think I dislocated a kidney."

"Yeah, well, I think I pulled my groin muscle," she says in between grunts.

I turn around and try pushing the truck with my butt—easily the strongest muscle in my body. "But don't you see that this is helping your uterus stretch out. In 7 months, your baby is going to do the electric slide on its way out."

"Maya, shut up before I slap you."

I hear commotion in Damascus's house before the lights flicker on. I turn to tell Angie to run, but realize I'm opening my mouth to thin air. She is already waddling away to her own car.

I run around to the driver's side seat and crawl inside. Trying to start the truck quietly was useless because, as soon as I turn the ignition, the massive engine roars to life. Lowering the windows down, I breathe from my mouth, taking shallow gasps of air, because the entire truck smells like sweaty gym soaks and moldy take-out food.

I push on the gas pedal just as I hear, "What the hell?" I see Damascus running out into the street in his boxers in my rearview mirror. As he tumbles over the sidewalk, I abruptly slam on the brakes, stick my head out the window and look at his stunned face, "I'm taking MY truck back, you turd-suckah!" I flip him the bird with both hands. Before he can recuperate, I quickly slide back into the truck and roar away. Flipping on the radio, I turned up M.I.A.'s song, "Bad Girls."

I shout the lyrics out the window, "Live Fast, Die Young! Bad girls do it well! My chain hits my chest when I'm banging on the dashboard! My chain hits my chest when I'm banging on the radio!" My eyes flick over to the rearview mirror one last time and I watch his dazed face get smaller and smaller behind me. I smile. Sometimes life can be so sweet!

Three blocks later, I notice the lights flashing on the dashboard. Chewing on my lower lip, I'm not sure what to focus on. The smell, the check engine light, the tire pressure light or the gas light. I need both hands to steer the massive thing. My previous experience with cars consists of the much smaller variety. Inside the Navigator, I feel like I am charting the deep seas in a submarine. I stop at a light and quickly call Angie.

"I'm right behind you. Can you go any slower?" I do not need her sarcasm right now. Why can't my best friend be more cuddly and huggable?

"He has no gas, his check engine light is on, the tire pressure light is on. I think a small animal died in here. It smells like throw-up and gym socks. My feet can barely touch the pedals. Can I please get a little sympathy?"

"There's a gas station a few blocks down, let's try to get it down there."

"We have no choice, you and I both know we can't push this thing anywhere."

I turn down the radio and concentrate on breathing out of my mouth for the rest of the trip. God, what has he done to this thing? Two years ago, it was brand new and sparkling. Now there is garbage strewn everywhere. The gear shift is sticky, I don't even want to know what I am sitting on, and there are peanut shells all over the floor.

"What side is the gas nozzle at?" Angie says to me on speaker phone.

"I don't know, I just bought the thing, I never drove it."

"Well I guess we'll find out."

I gingerly pull into the parking lot of the gas station a few minutes later, my heart beating wildly. I keep picturing Damascus chasing me down and demanding that I hand over the truck.

I walk out of the driver's side door and breathe a side of relief; the gas nozzle is located in the back of the truck. Thank God I don't have to reposition it. Sliding back onto the car seat, I stare at the dashboard dazzled by the array of buttons and lights. Gas nozzle opener, gas nozzle opener… where are you?

"Any luck?" Angie's voice pipes up beside me and I jump, knocking my head against the roof of the truck.

"Geez, a little warning next time," I snap at her.

"What are you doing?"

"I can't find the gas nozzle opener thingy," I say to her.

"Hmm…" I hear Angie walk to the back of the vehicle and then a large thump, "it's open," she calls out to me.

"Aw, did you break it? I need the vehicle to get as much value as possible," I say as I walk back around.

"Really? I can see used condom wrappers from back here; you really think a loose fuel door is going to bring the value down? You have to clean this truck out before taking it into CarMax."

"Me? Oh, now it's me? Back when we were stealing the truck, it was for the sisterhood and for womankind everywhere."

"I don't do hard labor," Angie swizzles her head at me and looks at her nails. I open the fuel door open and put in $20 worth of gas, which gets me maybe a good three gallons.

"Okay, we need to take this back to your place. He doesn't know I'm staying with you. Well, obviously, we haven't talked in six months. I'll um… clean it up in the morning and take it to CarMax."

"Fine by me," I follow Angie into the night, hoping that tomorrow turns out better than today.

***

I chew nervously on my thumbnail. The sales representative smiles at me. All blond hair and blue-eyed, he wears a carefree expression on his serenely all-American face. I bet he's never refinanced a vehicle for his girlfriend as a bartering tool for love. I bet he's never worried about his credit score or wondered what he should do with his life. Nope, the man in front of me looks perfectly content in his pleated khakis and brown loafers. He seems like he is exactly where he wants to be, living the life he is destined for. Unlike me—I always imagine myself in other, more interesting lives than my current one.

I would give anything to trade my reality with someone else's today. I had gotten up at seven o'clock this morning and spent quality time with the following items: gardening gloves, a surgical mask (you know the kind that people wear during a SARS epidemic), five garbage bags, one can of Lysol, one bottle of Clorox wipes, and a half bottle of Febreeze. The first sweep of the area involved removing the trash. So I put away the empty potato chip bags, chocolate and gum wrappers, the paper bags from McDonald's, Arby's, and Wendy's, and my all-time favorite: pistachio shells conveniently scattered all over the floor. The second round of cleaning consisted of scraping items off the seats and doors that had gotten dried over time and stuck to the interior. This included moldy lasagna (ick), lollipops, hair gel, toothpaste, Kool-aid, and gum. The icing on the cake was when I opened the glove compartment and found a family of slugs living there (this may have been met with a few screams). There was also some interesting reading material—2010 tax returns anyone? There was a family photo of the whole gang at Disneyland, and then there was a photo of me, which caught me off guard. We had driven to Lake Geneva one rare weekend, and he had taken a picture of me on a boat with my face tilted towards the sun, my eyes closed with a dreamy smile on my face. I ripped the photo into tiny little pieces. *Stupid girl*, I scowled at the tattered pieces, *what were you thinking?*

At the end of the scrubbing and wiping, the car still smelled like death, but death covered in a lavender scent with lemony undertones.

"So, bet you're glad you won't have to fill that gas tank anymore, huh?"

I nod my head and smile, because I've been told that's what normal people do.

"Well, our auditor will be able to get you an assessment in a jiffy; in the meantime, can I get you anything?"

"No, I'm fine." *I have $1800 saved, and I currently owe $2300 on the car. If they can just give me $500 for the stupid thing, I can cover the rest. Please let the computer say $500 or higher, God. Please, please. I'll start praying again. I'll start to believe that even some of what was written in the Holy Books is true. Even though all the prophets are male and always skew everything so that every disaster is a woman's fault, I'll make peace with that. I forgive you, God. You didn't know that, when you were passing down the rules, the men you entrusted them with would be a bunch of dumbasses.*

The computer starts flashing, numbers whirl on the screen, and I almost collapse in my chair. The monitor reads $3000. Holy cow! I am going to get $3000 for that piece-of-shit smelling car? I thought the smell alone would make them vomit and I would be pushing that thing back to Angie's.

"So does that work for you?" The sales guy, Aaron (I think), asks me.

With tears of joy in my eyes, I nod. "Yes, that'll do just fine, Aaron. That'll do just fine."

CHAPTER 9

I STRUT INTO THE FINANCIAL Aid office a week later. My credit may be a little frayed around the edges, but my pride is intact, and I am beaming ear to ear. All financial matters from my past had officially been resolved.

I sit in front of the same Financial Aid Administrative Assistant, challenging her to say no to me. "I see that the account is closed. It takes a few months for your credit to recuperate; however, given how quickly you've been able to resolve the matter, Columbia College is happy to offer you a private loan, alongside your regular FAFSA loans. Whatever FAFSA can't cover, the private loans will. Please fill out these forms and we'll get this started for you."

I sit and fill out the endless stream of pages, I whip through them, inputting my name, social security number, and birth date over and over again until the letters start to blur in front of me. I don't care if I am signing my life away; the truth is that, without this opportunity, I won't have much of a life. Instead of viewing college as the enemy, I now view it as my sanctuary. This is the institution that will help me become financially independent. Hopefully, with this degree and the job that will come along shortly after, I will no longer be dependent on a husband or a set of parents to take care of me. I will finally be taking care of myself. The office is silent except for the slight hum of a desk fan and the sound of my application pages being turned over. After reviewing my responses for the third time, I hand the packet over to the woman behind the desk.

She flashes me a smile. "Welcome to Columbia College, Maya. I know you've already had the campus tour, but is there anything else I can help you with?"

I shake my head and stand up. I just want to have the acceptance part over with—I want to leave before the other shoe drops. As my hand turns the doorknob, she starts to speak once again, and I wince, "Maya, unfortunately the semester starts this week. Given your situation, I thought it best you start this semester and not delay things any further. By the time your application and the financial aid paperwork go through, you'll be two weeks behind in the semester. Sorry about that!"

I turn around and shoot her a relieved grin. Is that all? This girl has no idea, I mean, I could steal trucks for a living now if I wanted to. Two weeks behind. Pshhhh! Ain't no thang, chicken wang! "No worries, I enjoy a challenge."

"Oh, and you'll be working at the student bookstore. You need to check in with Andy this Monday. Pay will be $12.75 per hour. Roughly 20-25 hours per week.

"I can't wait. Thank you so much for all your help. I'm really glad it all got resolved," I am filled with the greatest sense of optimism. I can make this work. I know I can.

I return to Angie's, jubilant in my victory. I have a job, I am going to school. The energy in the apartment, however, did not reflect my jubilance. There is no music on, no TV. Nothing blaring in any of the speakers. I walk into the living room to find Angie staring at the calendar, circling various dates.

"Hey, I'm a student at Columbia and I have a job. Pizza on me tonight! I got $20 in my pocket and this is freakin' awesome!" I sing the last part off key.

All I get in return is a sigh.

"Angie, what's up?"

She sighs again, "Nothing," she looks over at me and shoots me a tired half-smile. "Yay! You got a job and it isn't at a brothel. You are moving up in the world."

"Shaddup!" I wave my hand at her. "Seriously? What's with you?

"My first ultrasound is tomorrow, and I don't know if I should take my mom, call Tyrone, I just... I just don't know." She runs her hands through her hair and laughs haltingly, "Look at me, I'm starting to sound like you. All confused and unsure. This isn't like me. I'm, I'm..."

"Acting human?" I supply the words. I grab her hand impulsively, "Luckily I'm free tomorrow, and I can't wait to see my future niece or nephew." I squeeze her hand gently, "Don't beat yourself up about being unsure. You're in a situation you've never been in before. All the guidebooks in the world won't ease the nerves. But I'm going to be here Ang, no matter what."

She squeezes my hand in return and looks away, when she stares at me again, she arches her eyebrows, "So what's this about money in your pocket? Because I could sure go for some egg foo young."

"They better deliver, because I'm about to slip into some sweat pants and not crawl out of them for another 10-12 hours."

"Your fat ass complains about all the weight it's gained but can't be bothered to walk 4 blocks to get a pregnant lady, your *best* friend, some Chinese food. The best friend that you said you would be there for. No matter what."

"Um... I meant that more in a cerebral context—you know, mentally, not so much physically."

She throws a couch cushion at me, "Order the damn food, Maya."

I chuckle as I dial the number to Happiness Chinese Restaurant. How appropriately named.

***

"Ma'am, the doctor should be with you any minute. If there's anything I can do for you, my name's Antoine."

"Antoine, please don't call me ma'am," Angie sits demurely on the examination table, clad in an ice-blue paper gown. Her face is filled with haughty irritation.

"Yes ma—well, is there something else I can call you?"

He is met by silence. "Her name is Angie," I offer helpfully. Mostly to kill that awkward silence that happens when Angie ignores someone. I feel the heat of Angie's death stare, so I pretend to admire the blood pressure valve.

Antoine continues to talk, "Well um... Angie, did you want any water or anything? If you feel your blood sugar dropping I can get you a lollipop. I have some pull on the pediatric floor." Antoine flashes Angie a sheepish grin.

She shoots him a look that could curdle milk. "I'm fine."

I clear my throat, "Actually I'm feeling a bit parched," I offer.

"Sorry, we only offer refreshments for the patients." He doesn't even bother sparing me a glance, his eyes are glued to the girl in the paper gown. He continues to press, "Are you cold, Angie? Because I could get you another blanket or another gown."

"I would love for you to be quiet," Angie snaps back.

Looking at Antoine's woebegotten face, my heart contracts in empathy. I, too, know what it's like to love someone who treats you badly. I mean, you met my mother at the beginning of this thing, right?

"Ahhh, don't mind her Antoine, it's her first baby and she's a bit nervous. What with her boyfriend bailing on her and leaving town," Angie grabs my hand and gives it a warning squeeze. I keep talking, "Angie's had to work out all the details on her own. Not that she can't handle it. She's, she's fierce—" I gasp as her nails dig into the top of my knuckles. I continue on. I am doing this for her own good! The path to true love is never easy. "She's fiercely single and very capable of handling it all on her own. But she's also a very loving sou—ow! Ow! Ow!" I stop, as I think she may be quite capable of amputating my finger off with her acrylic nails. Antoine is on his own now.

"Hello all!" A fine-boned elderly man walks into the room, his shiny dome covered in wisps of black and grey hair, "I'm Dr. Chang, pleased to meet you all." I shake his hand gingerly, as all of the feeling in my fingers has disappeared.

"Well, I see you are about 18 weeks along. How are you feeling, my dear?" He asks Angie. Thankfully, she has managed to turn her mutinous expression into one of cordial hospitality.

"Fine, just a little hungry, other than that nothing else feels odd."

"Looking at your chart, you seem to be progressing nicely. Did you want a look to see at what's in there?

We may be able to see the sex of the child at this stage. Did you want to know?"

"Yes!" I shout excitedly.

Just as Angie interjects with a hard, "No!"

"Oh, oh my. Your partner seems to be very excited. Should I only tell her?"

"She isn't my partner, just a good friend," Angie says through clenched teeth.

"Her best friend," I supply and nod to the doctor with a knowing smile.

He winks back at me, "Oh, I see!"

"Can we please get on with the examination," Angie says, sighing.

"Sure, let me have Antoine put a little gel on the tummy. It's a bit cold, don't be alarmed."

Antoine doesn't look at any of us. He seems extremely focused on putting the gel on Angie's flat tummy. After applying the gel, he quickly backs away from us. Oh no, I can't gauge his mood. Has she scared him off?

Dr. Chang moves the probe over Angie's tummy and a faint, fuzzy image comes on the screen. The room is filled with the sound of a quick, steady heartbeat. It reverberates through me, and I am shocked to find my eyes watering. Oh my goodness, this is actually happening, we are going to have a baby!

"Angie," I whisper, "Oh my gosh. This is amazing."

She turns her head towards me and I see her eyes are filled with equal parts awe and fear, "It's really real, isn't it?"

"It doesn't get any realer," I say in return.

"I'm going to be a mom," she whispers to herself, our heads turn toward the grainy image on the ultrasound.

"As you all heard, the heartbeat is steady. Vitals look good for both mommy and baby. If you can make a follow-up appointment in 4 weeks, I think we'll have a better chance of getting a glimpse at this fella or filly," Dr. Chang smiles. "I'm going to write you a prescription for some prenatal pills you need to start taking daily...

The rest of what he says fades away. My eyes are still glued to that screen. A baby is coming into our lives. A baby filled with possibilities. A being not corrupted by pain or hurt or disappointment. I am going to love that baby. I vow to shield it from all the ugliness in the world. I am going to wrap it in a cotton candy bubble where it would only know love, peace, and laughter.

I tune out so completely I don't completely catch what Antoine is saying to Angie when the doctor leaves the room. "My aunt is a lawyer who does pro-bono work. If you'd like to hold your baby's father responsible as far as child support payments are concerned, my aunt could help you... if you'd like," Antoine's eyes skitter over his shiny, white running shoes.

"I'd like that," Angie says softly, "I could um... use the help."

Antoine's face breaks into a tentative smile, "Well, uh, we're actually having a birthday party for my grandma next Saturday, you're welcome to come. My aunt will be there. She's usually kind of booked at work, so it's hard to get a hold of her. This might be the best way for you all to meet."

Angie looks up at Antoine's face. Her expression is unreadable. I hold my breath—*please don't screw this up, Angie. This guy seems genuinely nice.* "If your aunt is busy at work, don't you think she'd mind me interrupting her at a family function?"

"Not if I tell her that you're my friend. She's got a sweet soft for me." Antoine's face twists in horror, "not that we're friends, obviously. But you know, I hope we can be someday," Antoine stops speaking abruptly.

"If you're sure she won't mind, then yeah, I'd love to come over next Saturday. Do you mind giving Maya the details out in the hallway while I change in here?"

I try to keep the big goofy grin off my face. *Shake it off, Maya! We gotta play it cool.*

"Are you going to be free that Saturday?"

"Absolutely," I gush, "wouldn't miss it for the world."

"Cool," he hesitates and then said, "you're a good friend to her. She's lucky to have you."

"Well, I think Angie is open to having more friends. New friends," I say meaningfully whilst arching a brow. Subtlety isn't something I excel at.

"I hope so," Antoine says blushing, "I sure hope so."

We exchange addresses and phone numbers. Angie comes out of the exam room and walks towards us.

"So, I'll be seeing ya," Antoine says, walking away slowly as another patient enters the hallway and heads towards us.

"I guess so," Angie then lowers her head, looks out from underneath her lashes and throws him a look that makes him stumble as he walks away.

My oh my… what have we here?

CHAPTER 10

I'M LATE, I'M LATE, I'm late. This morning has been an absolute scramble. I haven't gone to school in so long that I completely forget to get a book bag or any of the normal school supplies. I did manage to scrounge up an extra-large tote bag with a legal pad and some pens I had hawked from the Navigator's seat cushions (waste not, want not, right?). The stupid train halted twice. The morning has brought a downpour, so the subway has a wonderful mildewy scent to it.

Mercifully, the train finally arrives at my stop, and I push along with the rest of the crowd to exit. Checking my cell phone, I swear under my breath. I am already ten minutes late. I debate whether or not I should wait for the bus or just run the other eight blocks to class. I look at the streets congested with cars and construction signs. I decide to make a run for it. I mean, I am always saying I need to work out, right?

Part jogging, trotting, and speed walking, I finally arrive at my classroom. I am officially two weeks and twenty-two minutes late. I pray that the professor is benevolent.

I open the door and the hinges screech wildly, begging for the entire class's attention. I try to hide my face in my hair.

"Well, it appears our star pupil has finally arrived, I presume you are Maya Khan," the Professor raises her face from her podium and looks at me.

When my eyes lock on hers, I freeze in disbelief. "Matisha?" I ask, my voice squeaking in surprise.

She visibly stiffens and says, "Professor Zeniya, thank you very much, Maya. Please take a seat, you're extremely late and have a lot of catching up to do."

Isn't that the truth? I couldn't believe it—Matisha Zeniya is going to be my professor. She *hated* me in high school. Remember the cool Indian girls that have the BMWs and vente lattes? Well, she was one of them. She always tripped me in gym class and would walk down the hallway sneering at everyone around her.

It is so odd seeing Matisha like this. Hair in a chignon, a cream-colored blazer over a knee-length skirt and sensible pumps. She looks… old. She looks forty-six instead of twenty-six. I guess the vente lattes have taken their toll. I wonder if it's spiteful to get joy out of the fact that she has not aged well.

I quickly trot over and scramble into a seat. She begins to speak about alliteration, and I try my best to follow along. I chose the Women's Literature class because I am a woman, and I want to know what being a woman means in this day and age. I also want to redefine who I am. I figure the best way to redefine myself is to read about great women and impersonate them until I get the hang of it.

"Earth to Maya, hello Maya," I hear a derisive tone and automatically look to Matisha. Wow, there are a lot of creases on that forehead!

"Did you want the syllabus? Or did you think showing up was enough?"

I *was* thinking that I would love to strangle her with her hideous caramel-colored scarf.

I force a smile on my face and bare my canines, "Sorry about that, I thought I would ask you after class what I needed to catch up on."

"No need to wait, I can outline it for you right now. By next week I'd like a 1000-word essay on your response to Virginia Wolf's 'A Room of One's Own.' I'd like you to have read the first three chapters of "The Awakening" by Kate Chopin with a brief summary, also the first chapter of Maya Angelou's 'I Know Why the Caged Bird Sings' with the Q&As mentioned in the packet I enclosed," she flashes me a tight smile. "I think that should keep you a bit busy."

My head is swimming. I haven't even purchased these books. Hopefully I can check some out of the library. The rest of the class passes by in a blur. I watch Matisha's lips move as she points to pictures on the projector of female authors (all could do with a bit of a makeover if you ask me). Matisha is a Professor at Columbia College, and I am a sophomore and a half. Just when I thought I could pull myself out of this black hole called my life, I look up and realize I'm very, very behind.

At my age, women are getting married, having babies, or conducting themselves in professional environments. They are NOT stuck in a classroom with 18-year-olds who smell like Red Bull and Skittles—most of whom are half asleep or texting under their desks.

The class finally (thankfully) ends. I try to skedaddle out but am halted at the door, "Maya, can I see you for a moment?"

I square my shoulders and brace myself for the next round with Matisha. She has already won Round 1. Hopefully I can hold my own in Round 2.

She looks up at me and her face rearranges itself into a plastic smile, "Oh my God, how crazy is this? You being in my classroom?"

"Yeah, weird," I mutter back.

"I mean, your name didn't even register to me, be-cause there's like a million Maya Khan's out there—"

"Not a million," I quickly correct her with a fake smile of my own. I mean, I've never met anyone with my name. I think it is pretty unique, and cool.

"Well, you know what I mean. So what are you do-ing here? I mean, you got a 4.0 and were in a bunch of different clubs in high school. You were so driven back then." *If by driven she means propelled forward by parents with high expectations, then, yeah, I guess I was 'driven.'*

"Oh, well, I got... ill at UIC and they suggested that I take it easy. So I took a break, and now I'm back trying to finish up my Bachelor's Degree," I fib. I mean, what else could I say?

Her eyes widen, "Oh, how awkward... for you," she says in a syrupy tone that means completely the op-posite, "Well, it's been a whirlwind for me since high school. Let's see, well, I got into Northwestern, where I just excelled. There's no other word for it. I rocked that campus. I was in the Delta Gamma Sorority. That helped me get connected to the CARE organization. You know about CARE, right? The charity organization that helps impoverished women around the world? I was lucky enough to go to Afghanistan where I taught women's literature to young girls. I was also working on my Masters Degree online at the same time. So imagine getting internet in Afghanistan and completing a the-sis?" She emits a tittering laugh that makes my left eye-lid twitch, "Luckily the profs at Northwestern were so understanding. They were absolute dolls about it. It was such an exhausting but exhilarating time for me," she then sighs and looks wistfully over my shoulder, as if she's posing for the cover of *Time Magazine*. I can just imagine the title: 'When Narcissistic Girls Travel the World, They Still Make it All About Themselves.'

I tune back in, to hear, "I'm actually working on a novel based on that profound experience," she ends her soliloquy with a smug smile, "So after UIC what did you do?"

My brain freezes, the woman has been around the world and back and I have been sulking in my bedroom for most of my adult life. "Oh, you know…stuff." I say lamely.

She nods as if she knows exactly how dull my life has been, "Well, just because we used to know each other doesn't mean I'm going to cut you a break. I expect all of the assignments to be turned in on time. I hold myself and everyone around me to high standards," she feigns looking at her watch, "Oh, I have to go. Well this has been fun. Ciao!" she turns on her heel and clicks out of the classroom.

Who the hell says 'Ciao'? I mean, besides Italians?

***

"Hey now, I'm Andy, this is Van. We're the guys. And you are the only gal in this little hell hole we call the bookstore," Andy says to me with a nervous chuckle, "So you'll be doing a lot of shelving and re-shelving. The shelves are labeled, so I think that's self-explanatory, unless of course you can't read. In that case, you have bigger problems than not knowing how to shelve the books if you catch my drift, ugh-huh-huh-ugh," more nervous laughter.

"I can do that, no problem," I say with what I hope is a reassuring smile.

"Great. Books are in the back, Van is minding the register. I gotta make a phone call," he half-walks, half hobbles out the door in a hurry.

Van and I stare at each other. He shrugs and goes back to watching Netflix on his phone.

***

"Matisha? No way!" Angie throws a grape at me, "I loved her. She was hilarious!" It is late in the evening, and I am attempting to put together spaghetti and meatballs while Angie is arranging a fruit salad.

"What? How could you like her? She was mean, and she thought she was better than everyone else," I say, tasting the sauce.

"I mean, I know she wasn't cool with you. But her and I had some good times. Aww, maybe I'll drop by and say hi," she bites into another grape.

"So how's Antoine?" I ask, deliberately changing the subject, not to sound like a third-grader, but *I* am Angie's friend. Not Matisha. "And stop eating all the fruit."

That wipes the smile off her face. "He called the other day."

"I know, I took the message," I raise my eyebrows at her, "and...?"

"I called him back and we had a nice chat. So, you're not busy Saturday are you? Can you go with me to the party?"

"Angie, I don't know. I have a ton of homework."

"Please, I don't want to go alone. Our first date is going to be me meeting his whole family."

"Oh it's a date, now is it?"

"No... I don't know. Is it? What do you think? Is it weird that he wants to go out with me when I'm pregnant?"

"No. You're beautiful, funny, and smart. And he is smart because he's able to recognize and appreciate those qualities. Based on my *one* conversation with him, I liked him. And I definitely think you should get to know him better."

"So how many classes are you signed up for?"

"Just two. Figured I'd get my feet wet first."

"So you're going to bail on me for two classes."

"Two classes which I'm two weeks behind on."

"Maya, make it happen. Bring a friend. I don't think Antoine would mind."

I sigh. She isn't going to let me out of this one. "Fine, I'll be there."

Angie throws her arms around me in a hug, "Thank you!"

At least I'd get free food.

***

"Class, welcome Maya Khan. She is two weeks behind, so let's all catch her up shall we? Morrison, why is being a journalist the coolest job in the world?"

A rail-thin white kid with black eyeliner answers in a monotone voice, "It is the only profession listed in the U.S. Constitution. It is the only profession that can take down presidents, help enact laws, and shed light on injustices around the world."

Professor Wiseman interjects, "Hathfield, how did people communicate back in the day?"

A voluptuous red-headed girl answers in the breathiest voice I'd ever heard, "The newspaper was Twitter, Facebook, and YouTube, before those things were invented. It was the forum in which everyone communicated with everybody." Oh my Gosh, she could be a sex-phone operator. I am getting turned on listening to her.

Professor Wiseman takes a deep breath and says, "That being said, in this new day and age, people are saying that journalism is dead. Why do you think that is, Hudson?"

A young black man with piercings in both eyebrows answers, "Because there's no need for an elite group of snobs to dictate and decide which news is important and which news remains on the cutting room floors. You have blogs, you have citizen journalists, to hell with newspapers and news shows who tell us what to think!" he ends on a snarl and a curled lip.

Professor Wiseman smoothly interrupts as he walks to the front of the classroom, "So, now we have newspapers filing for bankruptcy, serious evening newscasts featuring American Idol and Lindsay Lohan to lure viewers in," the prof turns around and rests his hands on the podium, "I'm going to be honest with you kids; I have no idea what the future holds. I can tell you that journalism is never going to be dead because people read now more than ever on their smart phones, tablets, and e-books. People are sucking in information like the blood-sucking maggots they are. It could be crap information, but nonetheless, they are reading about it. So I can't guarantee you a job out there or predict how this is all going to pan out. Who knows— in three years, you might have salon.com etched into your brain matter and all you have to do is blink twice to retrieve the movie reviews. But what I can guarantee is that, when you get out of this class, you are all going to know how to write like journalists. You all are going to be brief, concise, articulate young men and women. And if I see an "LOL" or "TTYL" on any of your articles, I will personally hang you by your ankles over the side of this building and let you go. Your parents will probably thank me. All right, Maya, you are officially caught up. Let's open up chapter three, people." The professor turns back around and draws an inverted pyramid on the blackboard.

I take a deep breath and exhale slowly, overwhelmed by the amount of information that had been thrown at me. I look down at the notes I have managed to scrawl. The words "journalism" and "dead" stare back at me.

"Ay, for this I blow $40,000? I could 'av gotten a manicure and a new outfit instead of being yelled at by an old, white guy. Ay mija," I hear a girl with a husky Spanish accent mutter next to me.

"At the end of it, you do get a Bachelors degree," I timidly remind her.

She looks at me as if I've lost my mind, "Honey, I don't need a degree, I don't plan on working after this. I have a rich husband in my future, none of this working my fingernails to the bone."

"So what are you doing here?" I ask, puzzled.

"To keep my parents' mouth shut. They don't want me to be a bimba. So they can brag to their friends in Ecuador how educated their little Isabella has become—"

"Ahem—am I interrupting you ladies?" The professor asks us pointedly.

We shake our heads no in reply.

Isabella emits another sigh, "Dios mio, my youth is fading as he speaks."

I stifle a laugh. I couldn't believe it, I so desperately did not want to get married in a cold, calculated manner, and here I am, sitting next to a girl who wants the exact opposite. Muy loco!

CHAPTER 11

"CRAP, CRAP, crap," I mumble under my breath. This isn't happening. I had worked on this paper for three days straight. I had arrived on campus an hour prior to class to print out my essay, wanting to submit it to little Miss Snotty pants without hearing any condescending remarks.

"No!" I moan out loud when the monitor flickers and dies in front of me. I am in the computer lab surrounded by computers, and the one that I am working on suddenly decides to glitch out. I shake the monitor with trembling fingers.

"I don't think it responds well to assault," I look up to see a clean-shaven jaw. Large glasses frame a narrow face that is wearing an amused smile.

"I am trying to retrieve my essay, it's wiped out. Gone. And of course it's due in 20 minutes," I say, irritated and not feeling very cordial.

"Mind if I check it out?" He asks, sitting next to me, "Do you have it on the USB drive?"

"Yup, and it's jammed in there. I can't get it out. I can't bring it up. I can't do anything!"

"Hmmm, let me try to unjam it," I watch him yank it out forcefully. I am impressed—he doesn't look that strong. "All right, let's reboot this puppy."

As he watches the monitor, I watch him. He has hazel eyes that are currently narrowed in concentration and long fingers that tap softly on the keyboard. Everything about him looks lean and long, like human taffy that someone has stretched out.

"There we have it," he says, smiling and turning towards me, "you wanted it printed out, right?"

My eyes widen in surprise, "You did it? Really?" I hear the hum of the printer as my essay shoots out, "Thank you so much. I owe you big."

"You can buy me a drink sometime," he says easily. "I might even let you assault me."

"Sure," I say, distractedly in return, my eyes skimming over the essay. My heart rate returns to normal, and I register his comment and think of something. "Actually, my friend is going to this party Saturday night and she wanted me to bring someone along. No pressure, but there's going to be free drinks and food."

"Who can say no to that?" he responds.

"So that's a…?" I trail off.

"That's a yes, I'm Eddie by the way."

"Maya, Maya Khan," I reply, smiling at him. Cool, I've never had a guy friend before. I should start practicing. "Oh, bring your girlfriend too, if you want." Why not? I'm feeling generous. I'm the kind of girl that has guy friends.

"Girlfriend? Oh well that won't be possible, but I will be there and maybe you and I can tear up the dance floor. I got moves," he says, trying awkwardly to jiggle a hip.

"Mmmm," my glance fell on the wall clock above his head, "Oh crud, I gotta go. Um… here's my number, and here's the address for the party. I'll see you there Saturday around eightish, okay?" I scribble the information down and turn tail to run, not bothering to wait for his reply.

***

"Since when do you ask guys out?" It is Saturday afternoon. Angie and I are both critically eyeing ourselves in the mirror.

"I didn't ask him out. I invited him to a party. That way, when you get all moony over Anthony, I'll have someone to talk to. I think he has a girlfriend."

"So? Why does that matter? All that matters is if he's happy with his girlfriend. If he is happy, that's a tough situation to break, but it can be done. And if he's unhappy, that's like taking candy from a baby," Angie holds up a red dress.

I shake my head no. Too many sequins. It looks like a throwback from the '80s. "Stop it! I am done playing the mistress. He seems nice. He helped me out. I'm paying him back by bringing him somewhere other people will feed him, thereby repaying my debt."

"You are a cheap little thing, you know that?" she says as she rummages through her tiny closet, sighing loudly she cries out, "Help me find something to wear. I have to be sexy but not slutty. I want his family to like me."

"I can't figure out what you're going to wear until I do your hair and makeup."

"Hell no! Why would I trust you with either one of those two things? I have to face the man. I can't arrive to that party looking like a jacked up clown because I let someone who never fixes her own hair mess with mine."

"Okay fine, you do your own hair. But I get to YouTube the style." I log onto her laptop.

She hesitates and then gives in by shrugging her shoulders.

"It should be an updo, something that shows off your long neck. Classy but sexy. You'll look like a grown woman. I showed her a photo of a very beautiful, classic chignon, "But first you're letting me do your makeup. I'm feeling inspired. And if you don't like it, you can wash it off."

"I—"

"You asked for my help, and now you have to take it." I forcefully sit her in a chair and brandish some makeup brushes in front of her. She winces as if in pain. I do know a thing or two about makeup. I worked as a receptionist in a hair salon when I was 16, so I picked up a few tricks. I give her a sultry smoky eye, with black, grey, and light blue eye shadows blended together on the top of her lids. I then edge out the bottom of her lid with an electric-blue eyeliner. I give her a cat-eye using the grey eye-shadow again but dipped in water for a clean line. A few coats of mascara, touch of concealer under the eyes, a little pressed powder, a smattering of light blush along her high cheek bones, and a nude lip gloss completes my masterpiece.

I step back to admire my handiwork. She could give Tyra a run for her money. My girl looks fierce!

She looks in the mirror and smiles, pleased. I rummage around in her closet and find a flirty, silver dress that shimmers, "This is the one. Has a nice retro vibe. Classy and sexy."

"All right, and what about you, missy? How are you going to make your little nerd-boy drool?"

I eye both my side of the closet and hers critically. My closet consists of basic jeans and t-shirts. I have no choice but to borrow a dress from Angie. Unfortunately, our bodies are complete opposites; where she has a bust, I have the Great Wall of China. Where I have a booty—I mean a shelf you can practically set your drink on—she has nothing. Her backside is as flat as a pancake.

"Since you picked the dress for me, I'll pick for you. You should definitely wear this one," she pulls out a short leopard dress that looks like it was made out of velvet.

"No way, I'll look like a 40-year-old divorcee who's willing to bang anyone that looks at her," I protest.

Angie arches her eyebrow at me, "Well, aren't you?"

"No, I have standards now. Standards like he should have a job and not be married. There is no way I am wearing that dress," I vehemently shake my head in denial.

***

Five hours later, I stand on the outside edges of someone's living room itching in my hot, velvety leop-ard-print dress. My hair is in a big ol' bouffant, and I am trying to blink away the false eyelashes that keep poking me in my corneas. My bra is filled with tissue paper so the top half of Angie's dress wouldn't sag around my knees. And my butt is straining against the material in the back. Unfortunately, nothing else in An-gie's closet fits me except this sweat suit of a dress. I have to tough it out.

"Isn't this great?" Angie shouts in my ear as she el-bows my left boob, deflating it slightly.

"Hey watch it," I yell back, trying to fluff my itty-bitty titty back up to a C-cup.

"Oh, sorry. I think I see Antoine, gotta go," I watch her sail across the room and land in front of him. I catch the look of sweet surprise on his face before my view is obstructed by a button-down royal-blue check-ered shirt.

I try to strain my neck around the blockage when the voice above the chest speaks, "Wow you're tinier up close. I didn't think that was possible."

I crane my head up to stare at I.T. guy (I had forgotten his name—I know, I'm terrible. But it has been a long week). I muster up a smile and try to play off that fact, "Hey, you!" I say enthusiastically, "You're here."

"Yeah, a big fault of mine. I always show up on time. It kind of removes me from the cool kid club pretty quickly," he has a nice smile. I like how I feel around him. Calmer somehow, grounded.

"I brought you something," he says, holding up a little plastic square, "You left your USB drive at the lab. I got you an extra one that has a key chain attached. If you don't like the key chain, I also get you a lanyard in case you want to hang it around your neck. I mean I know wearing it around your neck isn't the coolest fashion statement, but I thought it could be a helpful reminder. You'd look down and be like 'whoa, there's my USB!'"

I am shocked. The man bought me a little present. Granted, it is probably the nerdiest present one can get another human being, but it is still thoughtful. "Thank you so much. That's very sweet. I'm sorry I didn't bring you anything."

"That's okay, I was in the bookstore and it caught my eye—" he pauses mid-sentence and gives me a very thorough once-over, "you look different. Hmm... what's changed?" he muses to himself.

I blush self-conscious, "It's a friends dress. It— um, fits differently. I don't usually wear this type of cut. It makes my body look a bit different." That and five pounds of Kleenex stuffed down my bra.

The crooning of R. Kelly fills the air and I hear someone shout, "Oh Watch out now, I'm about to get my swerve on. Clear the floor people," I see a woman in her mid-fifties start swinging her ample hips and stepping to the sound of the music. A few more people join her until the entire room is shaking as people form rows, stepping, swerving, and twirling to the music.

"You wanna dance?" asks the man with the hazel eyes. I still can't remember his name and I feel *terrible* about it.

"Sure," I shrug my shoulders in a deliberately casual manner. I hope he is being drawn into my aura of mystique that I am carefully cultivating.

I do not anticipate how utterly uncoordinated we both are. He moves left, I move right, we knock into each other a few times, both apologizing profusely. I accidently elbow his temple and skew his glasses in the process. Laughing, we decide to call it quits until the beat of Sean Paul's monster jam, 'Get Busy,' blares from the speakers.

"I love this song, we HAVE to dance!" I shout and shove him back onto the living room floor. We both proceed to jiggle our booties. I see Angie across the room, her silver dress swaying to the beat. I wave her over, and we proceed to sink to the floor and swerve our hips at the same time. I feel good, I feel sexy, I feel the cool air on my backside—and hear the unmistakable sound of fabric ripping.

I gasp. Angie shouts, "Oh my God!"

"It's okay, I got you. Just lean into me," a low voice intones in my ear.

I nod, unable to think. I slowly stand up and he grabs my hips and positions my behind so that it is directly between his hips. I hope and pray that no one can see my granny purple panties. Sexy girls wear thongs, I know, but there's nothing like all-over cotton coverage to make you feel comfy and coddled.

I am conscious of his fingers on my hips and his breath on the back of my neck as we slowly shuffle and scoot into the kitchen area.

Antoine and Angie are close behind us.

"Maya! —I am so sorry, I never should have made you wear that dress," Angie starts speaking just as Antoine does.

"I'll check if anyone has a coat or anything they can lend you. In the meantime, you can use this," Antoine hands me a red and white checkered kitchen towel.

"It's okay, did anyone see my um… undergarments out there?" I ask them all.

Everyone choruses, "no, no" and "definitely not." But none of them can meet my eyes.

"Okay, stop lying!" I snap, annoyed by the whole bunch. I stretch out the kitchen towel and use it to cover my butt. It manages to cover one cheek. Just dandy!

"I told you to wear the leopard thong," Angie immediately chimes in.

"That neon purple is a bright color," Antoine admits.

"Hey guys, my car is right outside, I may have a hoody or something she can borrow," my courteous date generously offers.

I don't have a chance to reply because Angie opens her mouth first, "Oh, you're the IT guy. I'm Angie, by the way, Maya's best friend."

"Eddie," he says, shaking her hand slightly. *Whew!* What a relief. Now I know his name. Angie beams at him and gives me a not-so-subtle look of approval.

"Aww, man, I'm so sorry you have to go Maya, we were all going to go to Navy Pier afterwards to catch the fireworks display," Antoine says. I notice he casually drapes his arm around Angie's waist. I notice that she lets him.

"Well, maybe I can meet you there. I can go home and change or something," I say to him. Angie proceeds to do a very slow, very exaggerated stretch that involves her head moving side to side in a deliberate no signal to me. I wink back at her.

I stand in front of Eddie once again, as he arranges my bottom so that it is directly in front of his... well you know where. We proceed to do our slow shuffle out to his car as Antoine and Angie snicker in the background.

"Angie, I'm going to get you back for this," I turn my head and say over my shoulder.

"Sure, I'm shaking in my... undergarments." That involves another peal of laughter out of her and a husky chuckle from Antoine.

"I hate people. I'm going to turn into a hermit," I mutter to myself.

"Aww... we're not all bad," Eddie says against my ear. The vibrations from his voice have some very interesting parts of my body tingling. He needs to stop that. I need to take back control here.

"Eddie, I'm sorry the night didn't work out. I'll just borrow your hoody and head home. Sorry about everything," we arrive at his car. He reaches into the back seat and pulls out a large t-shirt. I try to snatch it from his hands, but it isn't budging. He's holding on tight.

"Uh-uh," he places his face in front of my face, so that we were eye to gorgeous- hazel-eye, "you don't get off that easy. You only get the t-shirt if you have dinner with me tonight."

"You're really going to let me walk the streets like this?" I ask, incredulous. "Oooh, if Angie knew, she would never have let me come out here with you."

"Angie's got other things on her mind. Your cute bottom has fallen completely off her radar," Eddie says to me, amused.

"I don't eat dinner. So I guess you can just save your money," I retort. Did he just say cute bottom?

"Actually, you owe me dinner. I've saved your behind twice now. You're lucky I'm a cheap date... I might also be easy." He winks at me as he edges my body into the passenger side of the car, "but we have to get to the end of the date first."

My mouth drops open, I am at a loss for words, "First of all, it's not very gentleman-like to keep score of who helps who. Secondly, this isn't a date. This is just a meeting of two people who may or may not get along," I protest, as he tucks my legs into the car and plops the t-shirt on my lap.

He gets into the driver side of the car and guns the engine. I suddenly realize I am sitting on leather seats in a BMW. Oooh, these seats are comfy.

"All right, you can change once we hit the highway. That way no one will be able to get a long glimpse of you. I got some shorts back there, too. But that's on the condition that we hang out a little longer after dinner," he drops a pair of gray shorts that are super soft and cottony on my lap as well. Mmm... just like my granny panties, but bigger (if that were possible).

"Do you have to bribe people to hang out with you? That's very sad. I am not changing in a car next to you. I don't want you to see me like that," I say holding on to both items in a death grip that turns my knuckles white.

"Fine, then do you propose we go to a gas station, where even more people will catch a glimpse of the grape-flavored fruit-of-the-loom?"

He had a good point. "No peeking," I warn him.

"Eyes will be straight on the road," he promises.

We hit the highway, the windows are down, and the sunroof is wide open. The wind rushes over my skin and through my hair, lifting up the strands. For the first time that evening, my skin starts to cool down from the oppressive heat. I shimmy into his shorts with surprising ease. They are about double my size, so I have to wrap the cords around my waist twice before double-knotting them.

Now comes the hard part. I am having a hard time reaching the zipper on my own. "Eddie?" I ask tentatively. "You mind unzipping the back?"

"I thought you'd never ask," I hear a smile in his voice.

"This is strictly for changing purposes," I sternly say as I shift in my seat and present him my back.

"Absolutely," his warm fingers trail up my spine until he reaches the zipper. I hear the soft slide of the zipper and feel the fabric loosen around my shoulders.

"Thanks," I mumble. I keep my back to him. I figure that is the best angle to keep him from seeing my not-so-ample bosom. I don't expect the Kleenex to escape the confines of my bra, but now that I don't have the elastic of the dress holding them in, the little buggers start flying out.

"What the hell?" I hear Eddie shout. I turn around and see one of the tissues stuck to the front of his glasses.

"I'm so sorry," I reach over, stumble over his lap and accidently elbow him in the groin, he yelps in pain, "Oh my gosh, so sorry, so sorry," I finally get the darn thing off his glasses and scoot back in my seat. I cringe and wait for his wrath.

He grimaces and shifts in his seat. After what seems like an eternity, he finally looks over at me and down at my bra overflowing with Kleenex, "Do I want to know?"

Relieved that I am not on the receiving end of a tongue lashing, my nervous energy causes me to snap, "Keep your eyes on the road," I thankfully am able to remove the dress over my head quickly and scramble into his t-shirt. Great! In less than three hours, the man has already seen me half naked. He probably thinks I'm a sex-crazed nymphomaniac who is dying for his attention.

I stare at the rigid line of his shoulder and neck and realize he is upset. I say in a small voice, "I'm really sorry for—"

"Let's not talk about it," he abruptly cuts me off. We spend the rest of the car ride in uncomfortable silence.

I am so caught up in my musings and embarrassment, I fail to realize we are pulling into a parking lot.

"Where are we?" I ask, slowly adjusting back to reality.

"How can you not know where we are? Gene and Jude's," he catches the look of confusion on my face as I stare at the run-down hot dog joint, "Gene and Jude's, this place is an institution. Best dogs in Chicago."

"That place has the best hot dogs in Chicago? Really?" I ask with a skeptical arch of my brow.

***

Twenty minutes later, with a mouthful of hot dog and gorgeous, greasy fries, I declare, "Oh my God! These are the best dogs ever." We had spread out the food on the back of his trunk. My hip leans against his back bumper, and my eyes are closed so I can better savor the culinary ecstasy.

He stares at me and starts chuckling, "you have an onion on the tip of your nose," I feel him come closer, "Here, let me get it."

I open my eyes and find him staring at me intently, I feel him shift even closer and I immediately tense up, "I have hot dog breath," I blurt out.

"Me too," he murmurs as he leans in.

He kisses me and I let him. It is... wonderful. It has been so long since I've been kissed. I just stand there and get lost in the sensation of him, his warmth, the smell of his cologne, the feel of his cheek against mine.

We come up for air and I watch in fascination as his cheeks flush a light pink and he appears out of breath. Have I done that?

"Let's go," he says abruptly and heads back to the driver's side of the car.

"Go where?" I ask, suspicious. A few hot dogs and a nice kiss doesn't mean I want to... you know. Well, *of course* I do want to do that, but I also want to take it slow and savor this new delicious feeling of wanting someone and being wanted by him.

"Let's just drive, Maya. I just want to sit next to you and never stop driving," he says as I slide back into the passenger seat.

I understand his mindset. No destination, no obligations, no responsibilities, just us, the open road and wherever it will take us.

"I'd love go for a drive, Eddie," I say, snapping my seatbelt into place.

He entwines his fingers in mine, and we take off into the peach-tinged sky, the sun sinking into the horizon behind us. I feel the strangest emotion—hope.

CHAPTER 12

I TURN THE KEY INTO the apartment slowly around 2 in the morning and try to sneak in without being detected.

"Where have you been, missy?" Angie sits on her kitchen counter with a pickle in one hand and a jar of peanut butter in the other. *Ick, I can't wait for this baby to come so I never have to smell that combination again.*

"I—I—I was out," my eyes register her mussed hair, smeared makeup and the fact that she still has on last night's dress, "And where have *you* been, missy?" I mock her in return.

Her eyes light up and she shoots me a mischievous smile, "You want to go first, or should I?"

We both start to babble:

"We held hands all night long..."

"On a Ferris wheel and saw the fireworks, they were timed to classical music and it was— "

"The most beautiful night of my life— "

"So spectacular and he smelled so good— "

"We couldn't stop talking about everything, our hopes, our desires, our dreams—"

"and he was the perfect gentlemen, kissed me on the cheek, held out the car door, told me I was— "

"different, unique, and he liked how he felt around me."

"I think I'm falling—"

"head over heels! The best part is, I'm able to—"

"Finally be myself! It felt so natural. Like we had been talking to each other our whole lives."

We both finish out of breath, grinning like idiots at each other.

"Oh, shit!" she says as she stares at me.

"We're going to get really stupid, really fast, aren't we?" I ask in reply.

She nods, "I can't help it, and I haven't felt this way in so long, that I don't want to hold back. I'm all in."

I agree. "Let's just enjoy this feeling without worrying about it. Let's just be happy."

"We deserve it. We finally deserve guys who are decent." We head off to bed, both giddy in our euphoria, high on the multiple possibilities that now lie before us.

***

Two weeks later, those possibilities have contracted, shrunk, and disappeared, leaving behind a bitter reality. Eddie hasn't called me back.

"Maya, you got a second?" Professor Wiseman calls to me just as class ends.

I nod and make my way over to his desk.

"Hey, your article on the Arab spring from a women's perspective was very enlightening. We've all seen the news and the protests, but the continuous inequality of the sexes in the region hasn't been outlined in such a detailed manner," he turns his head back to the papers he's grading.

I smile, pleased at his comment, "Thanks, um... I was able to get in touch with Hannah, who lives in Egypt, through Facebook, and she was kind enough to answer some questions and also get me in touch with her friends."

"Very nicely done. I actually called you over because our intern at *The Tribune* got appendicitis and can't finish out the school year. We don't want to lose our spot to Northwestern, so we're trying to fill it before they notice," he leans back in his chair and eyes me, "Do you think you're up for the challenge?"

My head is swimming. *The Tribune* has been around since 1847; I am going to be an intern at the most prestigious newspaper in Chicago. "Oh my gosh, I'm so flattered Professor Wiseman, that's amazing. I can't believe I'm your first choice," I gush.

"You weren't. Hudson, Coleman, and Hathfield all turned it down. Hudson because he doesn't agree with the right-wing, xenophobic policies of *The Tribune*, Coleman because he's got a gig at the Red Eye, and Hathfield just got a boyfriend and doesn't want to spend, I quote, 'that much time away from him,' which leaves you. All of you have strong writing skills, but overall that is the order in which you all were picked."

I stare at him, unsure how to respond, trying to muster up the same enthusiasm as before. I say, "Well it's still very flattering to be the fourth runner-up. Thank you for considering me."

"You will take on the role of Christine Yamasaki. Here is her schedule, her list of duties, and her nametag. Be there Monday at 8am."

I look down at the nametag in confusion, "Sir, I'm sorry, you want me to wear her nametag?"

"Right, what part of taking on her role was unclear? We can't let them know that Christine has dropped out, they'll retract the internship and award it to Northwestern."

"But couldn't we explain that we're just switching it over to me?" I ask.

"Oh, gee, why hadn't I thought of that? Look, Khan, this is a deal the College has set up with the paper before I got here. It's stupid, it's archaic. We withdraw an intern, we forfeit our turn for the year. They may not even grant it to us next year for breach of contract, etc. I just need you to be Christine for a few weeks. Once January hits, we can switch it over." He cocks his head to one side and looks me in the eye, "can I count on you to get this right?"

I smile uneasily, it seemed so easy... except, "Well sir, I don't exactly look like a Christine Yamasaki."

"Well, that's kind of racist, don't you think? Anyone questions you, you tell 'em you're freakin' Tiger Woods. You can be any race you want to be. Believe it, be it, and own it."

I nod again; words just fail at me at this point. I slowly walk out of the classroom and look to the heavens for an answer. How in the world am I supposed to act like a person I have never met before? Won't they notice that a girl with a Japanese surname now looks very Indian?

I straighten my shoulders. I can do this. From now on, I am going to put all my focus into my schooling and building up my career. I have no time for men who don't call me back. I mean, the fact that Eddie hasn't called in two weeks pretty much means that I will never hear from him again, right? Unless he was in a terrible accident or something where he can't move his fingers and his larynx ruptured so he can't use voice command on his phone. It would have been easier if he had given me his number. But maybe that was also another smart move on his part, because I may have gone psycho-stalker chick on him.

I re-lived that evening in my head. Had I said something wrong? Was I too eager? I thought it was fascinating that he owned his own IT consultation business. His company did the computer upgrades for all the colleges in the Chicago Loop. He had started the business with a friend in his last year at DePaul. As a joke, they upgraded the software on the computer labs, because the current software was too outdated for what they wanted to do. I haltingly told him about my life, being a pre-med student at UIC and then dropping out to work with my dad. I omitted a few details (okay, a lot of details). I mean, I didn't want to scare the guy on the first date, right?

Towards the end of the night, neither one of us talked much. Or actually, he started talking less and less, and after receiving several monosyllabic responses, I gave up and sat in silence next to him. We had driven over to North Beach and watched the waves wash over the shore. I guess words weren't necessary. The sound of the water, the breeze, and the smell of the sand was all we needed. Maybe words would have pierced the perfection of the moment. Looking back on it now, he probably wasn't savoring the sand, the stars, and the moon; he probably regretted that he had brought me out and was contemplating how to safely back away without anyone getting hurt.

I cringe when I remember how I had tried to sneak in another kiss before leaving his car and how he had backed away. Was he being polite when he had kissed me the first time? Was I that bad of a kisser? Had I turned him off indefinitely?

I sigh. He had seemed so nice and normal. Maybe he could sense the disjointed being I was and didn't want to be bothered. I don't know and I don't care. I have more important things to do, like impersonating Christine Yamasaki.

***

"Hey, M," Van greets me in his languid surfer voice as I walk into the bookstore, "so, like, next Saturday, I got this show I'm performing at. You mind covering my hours at the bookstore?"

"What are you performing?" I say, shelving anatomy books.

"Vietnamese gangsta' rap," he says.

I laugh until I look at his face and realize he isn't joining me. "Seriously?" I ask.

He looks hurt, "Can you fill the slot or not?"

"I'm sorry, I wasn't trying to be mean. That's awesome that you rap and you have a show. Are you part of a group, or is it a solo act? What do you rap about?"

His face becomes unreadable and he looks down at his phone. I realize I've lost what little connection we had. Feeling horrible, I blurt out, "I have to impersonate a Japanese girl on Monday and I have no idea how."

He swivels his face back at me, "What?"

I quickly explain what went down with the professor, "so now I have to be Japanese, otherwise Columbia loses their placement at *The Tribune*."

"Dude, that's like the craziest shit I've ever heard. But you know, Christine might be like fourth-generation Japanese and not really know much about her own culture."

I agree. "But I don't want to be caught with my pants down."

"I could help you out. I know some stuff about Japan. Maybe we could write down a list between the two of us, you know of everything you should have in your arsenal in case they like test you, or something?"

I shoot him a grateful look, "Thanks V, and of course I'll totally cover for you Saturday night."

He smiles shyly, "Hey you wanna hear a verse I'm working on?"

"Absolutely."

He starts beat boxing and I join him (for moral support), "Yo, yo, so check it—uh-uh. There was this pretty girl I know/she was a lost soul for sho/Putting on faces/Trying to change races/Her face always full of woe/I try to tell her, "???c h?nh phúc," life's too short to give a fuck."

I throw my head back and let out a laugh. I had my very own Vietnamese rap lyric. How cool am I?

***

"Christine Yamasaki, you're going to be late for your first day," Angie yells towards my room.

I had been practicing being Christine all weekend. I purchased a Hello Kitty notebook. I dressed like a harajuku girl (complete with ripped panty hose, plaid mini skirt, polka dot shirt and lots of eyeliner), ate sushi, drank green tea and hot saki (not in that order, I did not need to get the runs). I watched the Tom Cruise movie, "The Last Samurai," (courtesy of Van, who let me borrow it) and picked up a few Japanese phrases, 'Arigatou', (thank you), 'Sayonara' (goodbye), 'Toire/yakkyoku wa doko desuku? (Where is the bathroom?). Oh yeah, they could put me on a plane and fly me over to Japan and I would probably blend in with the natives (If you disregarded the fact that I am probably a few shades darker and a few inches wider than the average Japanese girl).

Christine may have been born and raised in Chicago, Illinois. She may not even know she has a Japanese surname. But Maya Khan pretending to be Christine Yamasaki *is* going to know her Japanese history. No one is going to trick me into forgetting my brand-spanking-new Japanese heritage. Where's Mount Fuji, you ask? Why step this way, I would be happy to show you.

I take a deep breath and look at my reflection in the bathroom mirror. I say with precise determination, "I. Am. Christine. Yamasaki." And no one is going to tell me otherwise.

"You ready to do this?" Angie hands me a bowl of Cheerios and a copy of today's *Tribune*. I have been trying to bone up on that as well. Didn't want to run into a writer or columnist and have no idea who they were.

"I, Christine Yamasaki, am ready to do this."

Angie shakes her head and shoots me a sympathetic glance. "Don't be too hard on yourself if you get caught. What they're asking you to do is ridiculous."

I shoot her a death stare. "I won't get caught, because I. Am. Christine. Yamasaki."

Angie sighs and looks out the window muttering, "The shit this girl gets into."

***

"Welcome to *The Chicago Tribune*, how can I be of help to you today?" the receptionist greets me, her blonde hair swinging with every bouncy syllable.

"Hi, I'm," I swallow, as all of the words I had practiced, suddenly get stuck in my throat, "Christine Yamasaki, the intern. I'm supposed to be meeting with Barb Bennett, do you know what floor she's on?"

As soon as the receptionist registers the word intern, her perky demeanor instantly vanishes and a look of bored disdain washes over her face, her eyes hone in on the latest copy of *Vogue* on her desk and she says dismissively to me, "5th floor, interns use the service elevator located in the back."

I nod and attempt to smile at her but she doesn't bother looking up. How nice, I think I've made a friend.

"You're late," Barb barks at me the instant I walk through the door. I'm actually 15 minutes early and I'm about to disagree with her, when I notice the blond haired, green-eyed, golden God of a man standing next to her. He shakes his head at me and mouths the word, "Don't do it." Whatever words I may have said disappear into the wind because I can barely remember my own name. All I want to do is stand there for the rest of my life, and watch his lips move.

"Christine, hello Christine? Are you there?"

"Yes," I say, snapping back to reality.

"I need you to run out and get toilet paper for the executive bathrooms, you forgot to fill them on Friday. I refuse to wipe my ass with the cardboard shit they supply around here. And I also need you to make sure all of the copiers on this floor have toner and paper in them. Where is my vanilla Vente latte? Seriously? What have you been doing this morning?"

Barb Bennett has not looked at me during this entire diatribe, I am afraid to move for fear of her potentially not recognizing me. She finally does look up at me and says, "Well... are you going to stand there the whole day? Because I don't really like the drip dry method when I'm in the bathroom."

The gorgeous gentleman smoothly interrupts her, "You know what? I was just about to go to Starbucks, there's a CVS along the way. Why don't I escort our little intern over there so she can pick up the house ware goods and I can get you their latest macchiato cappuccino. I tell ya, Barbie, you'll love it."

Barb appears to blush. "Oh Simon, that's so sweet." As my face almost breaks out into a smile, she senses my sudden lack of fear and barks out, "I expect you to be back in ten minutes."

I nod curtly and follow Simon out to the elevator. I notice that he's allowed to use the main elevator.

"So, Christine, why don't you tell me your real name?" He asks as we wait for the elevator to come up.

My breath hitches and I say with a squeak, "What do you mean? I am Christine Yamasaki."

"Darlin', you're a lot cuter than our last intern. So why don't you do both of us a favor and tell me the truth?"

I stiffen and debate about whether or not I should tell him. But he already knows and hasn't turned me in yet. I really have no choice. "Okay," I say reluctantly, "I'm a student at Columbia College. Christine got appendicitis and can't finish out the school year. I'm here as her substitute until the semester ends, at which point you guys will turn over this coveted position to a very deserving boy or girl from Northwestern," I quote Professor Wiseman's words.

Simon throws back his head and laughs, "Are you kidding me? That's hilarious. And you know the sad part is, no one here will notice. They're all too busy running around with their heads up their ass to even bother looking at the intern." He chuckles as we both enter this elevator, "well, now I need to know your name."

"Maya, Maya Khan," I whisper, "Please don't tell on me. I really will do a good job here, I promise. I am a very hard worker."

"No doubt, Maya, no doubt. Well, I know your secret and I will keep it. So if I ever need you to keep a secret of mine, I hope you'll be as accommodating."

I'm not quite sure what I am agreeing to. Feeling trapped, unsure, and fearful, I smile at him and nod uncertainly. "Sure, I want to be helpful to everyone here."

We both stare at the lit up numbers on the elevator wall, "I bet you do, Maya, I bet you do." He murmurs.

I sneak a look out of the corner of my eye at his mane of honey blonde hair, the square jawline, and his built shoulders and sigh inwardly. Why do the good-looking guys always know they are good looking, and why do they use it against women like a well-oiled machine gun?

Eddie's face flits through my mind. I realize sadly that I miss him.

CHAPTER 13

RUSHING TOWARDS MATISHA'S CLASSROOM, I almost get knocked down by someone trying to leave. I can *not* be late again. Matisha has made that very clear. I would have been here on time if I had left as scheduled. I hadn't counted on Barb keeping me an additional thirty minutes so that I could file away newspaper clippings from 1985!

"Oh, I'm so sorry," I blurt out. I feel a hand on my shoulder and I continue to babble, "I'm such a klutz, I didn't see anyone trying to come out."

I'm met with silence. I finally look up and find myself staring into familiar hazel eyes. The entire horrible morning melts away from my memory. He has come back! My heart leaps with joy. He has come back to Columbia to see me. I knew I wasn't wrong—we did have a special connection that night.

"Eddie, you have to be more careful," I hear Matisha trill from within the classroom. That's odd. How does Matisha know Eddie?

I watch in confusion as Matisha comes out to the doorway and slips her arm around Eddie's waist. My tongue suddenly becomes glued to the roof of my mouth. "Oh, it's just Maya. Well, you're lucky it wasn't anyone important," she says with a false laugh.

I look at Eddie again, asking him silently what is going on. Except he isn't meeting my eyes. He's staring down at Matisha, jaw clenched.

"Eddie, have you met Maya? We used to go to high school together and now she's a student in my class. How wild is that? Yikes—imagine having to relive college at our age, huh? Maya, have you met my fiancé Eddie?"

I can't move. I can't look at him. I can't even think. So I try to stare solely at Matisha. Except I do see his cheeks take on this ruddy color, it couldn't possibly be embarrassment—what does he have to embarrassed about? I now understand why a deer would stand in the middle of the road watching the headlights of an on-coming car rush toward it. Horror and fear have a way of draining away reason and freezing up every single muscle in your body.

I raise my lips into what I hope is a smile and say, "Congratulations to both of you." I then will my feet to walk away from them. I see his lips move, but I can't make out the words. White noise is rushing through my ears and I struggle to sit in my chair upright.

I can't look at Matisha's smug face or his contrite one.

It was one night, Maya, one silly hot-dog-laden kiss. It didn't mean anything. Don't cry, don't you dare cry in front of them.

***

"Crap and shit, shit and crap," I rant to Angie. "If I'm not filling up the bins with toilet paper, I have to ensure that there's enough bottled water in the fridge to keep everyone hydrated. I haven't written anything since I've been there. I haven't even been allowed to touch a computer since I've been there. 'Oh, Christine, you're done with that crap? Well here's some shit you haven't gotten to. When you're done with that shit, please take care of this crap we haven't gotten around to doing since 1862! Ugh—I thought it was going to be glamorous and educational. A donkey could do what I do."

Angie nods dreamily from the couch. Her feet are stretched across Antoine's lap. He is giving her a foot massage. "Damn, is she always this fired up?" he asks her out of the side of his mouth.

"Usually," she sighs contentedly.

I realize uncomfortably that I've been talking about myself for the last thirty minutes. "So, how are you two?" I ask begrudgingly.

"I'm good. We have an appointment with the doctor next week. Antoine will be going with me," Angie replies with a purr of contentment.

"I got a b-ball game with your boy Eddie tomorrow, other than that I'm straight."

Angie sits up abruptly and shoots Antoine a hard look.

"My boy Eddie," I repeat, "why are you playing b-ball with my boy Eddie?"

"He seemed cool that night at my grandma's birthday party, he slipped me his number and told me he played. So I set up a game for this week."

My eyes bug out of my head, "You had his number the whole time? This whole time that I've been wondering why he hasn't called me? You had his number. Did you know he was engaged too? Did both of you know? Were you guys laughing at me?" I say. I am so angry. I'm surprised I haven't sliced them in half with my laser glare.

"No, I didn't know he was engaged. We're dudes, we don't talk about stuff like that. As for having his number, Angie thought it best—" he ends on a grunt as Angie kicks him in the stomach.

I swivel my head towards her, and she sighs. "Ma-ya, I liked Eddie, I did. I thought if he liked you, he would call. I didn't want you chasing after someone who wasn't interested. I didn't want you to call him and get hurt. I swear, Antoine and I did not know he was engaged."

"Well," I say after a pause, "If I'm not playing b-ball with Eddie than no one in this room gets to play b-ball with Eddie."

"Hold on, how am I supposed to get a partner at this hour?" Antoine protests.

"I don't know and I don't care. But I'll be damned if he's your partner. Unless you want both arms chopped off in the middle of the night, I suggest you make other plans," with that I turn on my heel and stomp away.

***

"Hey Chrissy-pants, how you doin'?" Simon sits on my desk and sidles closer.

I shoot him a reproving look, "Fine, Simon, what can I do for you?"

"So… I have to hand in my article by 4pm today to the layout people. I'm planning to hand them a dummy article that will fill the space instead. You see, I know for a fact that the printers don't start production 'til around 7pm. So, I need a resourceful little intern who can switch out the articles around 6:30ish. I know it's cutting it close, but I am waiting on this hot quote that is literally going to make or break this article. You feel me, Chrissy-pants?" he shoots me what he believes is a charming grin, but all it makes me want to do is bare my fangs at him.

"I'm sorry, Simon, but I have to leave at 5:30. That's my schedule."

He looks down at his coffee, "Oh, well, that's a shame Maya—oops, I mean Christine. Maybe Columbia chose wrong when they thought you were a team player…"

I can't believe this. The man is going to use my stupid secret against me for everything. He has an all-semester pass, from a hang nail to breaking and entering into the print room. I take a deep breath and chant internally, *a few more weeks. The semester would be over in a few short weeks.* I shoot him a serene smile. "I just remembered I'm meeting a friend this evening, so I guess I'll be in the area. Your request shouldn't be a problem."

His smug face gets impossibly smugger. "I knew I could count on you." He walks away whistling.

My phone vibrates with a call from an unknown number, "Hello," I whisper and crane my neck around the office to make sure no one is looking at me.

"Maya." I hear Eddie's voice on the other line and nearly drop my phone in surprise, "Maya, are you there?"

I regain my voice and say softly, "I'm here."

"Hey, look, please don't hang up on me. I need to talk to you. I know what I did was shitty, but I can explain. Can I meet you tonight? Coffee, dinner, drinks? Anything."

"Well, I'm going to be at *The Tribune* pretty late. I can meet you after 7, I guess." Why am I agreeing to this? I want to yank my tongue out and wag my finger at it.

"I can meet you there. They have a great restaurant, Howells & Hood, located in *The Tribune* Tower. You gotta job at *The Tribune*? That's awesome."

"No I'm just a lowly intern as well as being a lowly undergrad student," I say caustically.

"That's still impressive," he says awkwardly.

"I'll see you then," I don't wait for his reply and hang up the phone.

I look up to see Simon staring at me, he flashes me a wink. My stomach gurgles in fear.

***

It's 6:30. I don't have Simon's article and it's 6:30. What am I supposed to do? I have been circling the break room and the bathrooms for the past hour trying to look inconspicuous, but my nerves are stretched to the max. If Barb saw me on the floor and questioned me, the truth would burst out of me faster than Usain Bolt dashing towards the 100 meter mark.

"Geez, would you stop looking so serious? I'm not asking you to negotiate Israeli-Palestinian peace talks here. It's just a little article switch." Simon holds up his USB drive and I snatch it from his hand.

"I'm doing this, but consider us even. I won't be doing this again," I whisper at him fiercely.

"First of all, if you ever run any kind of con, you shouldn't whisper. It actually makes you look more suspicious. Secondly, I completely understand that this makes you uncomfortable. I won't ask you to do this again. Promise," he holds up two fingers. "Scout's honor."

"Well, now I only have 20 minutes to get this done," I reply, irritated.

"Well, I suggest you get a move on then. Scooch. I'll check in with you later."

I make my way over to the print room located in the basement of the building. Peeking in through the double doors, I see a few guys sitting around looking at crossword puzzles and sipping coffee. My professor's voice echoes in my head: *Believe it. Be it. Own It.*

I sweep into the room, all apologetic smiles and fluttering eyelashes, "Hi, I'm so sorry. Last-minute update by the art department. Barb sent me. Can I just review the layout and input the latest graphic? It's a flower instead of a leaf." I roll my eyes. "Those kooky artists."

They barely blink. "Sure, computer's over there. Make it snappy, we're going to turn on the machine in about 5."

I blink, surprised at how easy that was. Oh gosh, the heady sense of accomplishment takes over, and I realize that I can take over the newspaper right now and replace all the articles with the words, "Maya Khan rocks. Eddie Holden sucks balls. Matisha Zeniya sucks turnips." Yeah, I would use the word "suck" a lot. Like Columbia College could *suck* it for putting me in this position.

A buzzer snaps me out of my reverie, "Lady, you moving or what?" the guy in the overalls asks me.

"Yes, I'll just be a second," I smile at him confidently.

I input the USB drive and pull up the layout. Oh gosh, navigating Adobe In-Design is no joke. Every time I delete something, the columns expand or squish together. I hear someone clearing his throat in the background. I quickly delete Simon's old article and replace it with the latest. Saving the changes, I turn around and smooth my hands over my hips to cover up the fact that they've been sweating. "All done," I say cheerily. "Thank you so much, you've been an absolute peach."

I rush out of there before they can ask me any further questions.

***

"Maya," I see Eddie's hand wave at me from the table he's sitting at. Just as I make my way towards him, I'm interrupted by a lion's mane. Blond, golden, high-lighted locks almost whip me in the face.

"Did you do it?" Simon asks.

I sigh and look at him, "Yes, can you please go away and leave me alone now?"

His face breaks out into a grin, revealing perfect porcelain veneers, "Oh, Chrissy-poo, I could kiss you. In fact I think, I will." Before I can stop him, he grabs me by the upper arms and lands a big, sloppy kiss all over my lips.

"Mmmmmpph," I spit out in response. "That wasn't necessary. We're even, remember? No kissing needed."

He continues to keep his face close to mine. "Admit it, you secretly want me."

I balk in response, "Not even close, and if you don't get your face away from mine, I will bite your nose off." I pause as his head snaps back in disbelief, "Oh, here's your USB drive." I tuck it in his shirt pocket and walk away from him.

I arrive at Eddie's table and notice his face has taken on an ashen color. He doesn't meet my eyes, "Maybe this wasn't a good idea. I didn't realize you were busy."

I don't understand what he means, and then I notice him looking at Simon who has decided to sit at the bar. "Oh that?" I scoff, "that's just you're typical ego-centric journalist who thinks the world revolves around them. This building is full of 'em."

"Really? And do you all go around kissing each other?" Eddie asks with an edge to his voice.

I don't appreciate the tone of his voice and my hackles rise a bit, "Yes, we do actually. And when we're not doing that, we all secretly get engaged to one another and then take unsuspecting fools out on romantic evening drives and forget to tell them we are, in fact, engaged!" I practically spit out the last few words. A few heads turn to look at us. I sink down in my chair uncomfortably.

"I wasn't engaged."

"I think Matisha would disagree."

"*At the time*, I wasn't engaged at the time. Not that it makes a difference now, since you have clearly moved on."

I attempt to shrug my shoulders dismissively, "Moved on from what? Nothing really happened. It was just one night." My heart clenches inside, no way would he catch me pining away for him.

He eyes me warily, "Yeah, I guess it was. Stupid of me to even bother trying to explain. But I feel I should."

"Yes, let's clear up your conscience, shall we?" I lean forward, forcing him to back up slightly.

"Matisha and I had been on and off for roughly three years. She had her work in Afghanistan and was trying to complete her Master's degree," I roll my eyes in response, he made her sound like she was freakin' Mother Theresa. He pauses a bit disconcerted, "a—and I've been trying to build up my business, get my finances in order. We recently got back together. But I knew it was just a matter of time before we broke up again. I think she enjoys the making up part, so she creates these fights to up the ante and drama and then we get back together and it's like a scene out of those corny rom-com movies, where we promise we'll never fight again and declare our undying lo—"

"Hello folks, is there anything we can get for you this evening?" our waiter thankfully interrupts Eddie.

"Tequila," I say, pounding a fist on the table, "I need a lot of tequila tonight."

"Just a Sprite for me, thanks," the waiter discreetly floats away, leaving me with a lovelorn Eddie.

"Okay, let's get to the part where you meet me," I say, willing the pounding in my head to stop and trying my best to absorb his words.

"So, in my haste to avoid the makeup, break-up cycle, I suggested we get married. She refused. I was hurt. A few days later, we met up and both mutually decided that it wasn't going to work out. We actually parted as friends. I was on my way out of the building when I met you at the computer lab. So that is why I thought I wasn't engaged when I met you."

The waitress mercifully put down five shots of tequila. I thank her profusely as I throw the first shot down the hatch like there is no tomorrow. "And when *did* you get engaged?"

"That's the funny thing, she called me the Monday after our date—the one between you and I. Said she had changed her mind. That we had this history and companionship and she didn't want to throw it away."

I snort in response, "Sounds super romantic."

"I'm sorry, I should have called you afterwards and explained myself. I knew you were in her class, I saw her name on your essay. I knew you would find out eventually, I just didn't know what to say. I had a great time that Saturday, you were like a breath of fresh air and you were so fun to be around—"

"Please stop, I don't need you to build up my self-esteem. You explained yourself, are we done here?" It hurt hearing his explanation. There was no stupid closure to this thing. I still had an open wound and he had poured salt all over it. I needed more tequila to disinfect the wound. Enter shot number 3 for the night.

"Yeah, we're done," Eddie says sadly. "I hope you're happy with him," he nods toward Simon, at the bar, who currently has his head nuzzled in between the breasts of a buxom brunette.

I laugh haltingly, and then an evil thought popped into my head, "Yes, it's a very open relationship. Actually might be a threesome later," I slurp up shot number four and five.

Eddie knocks over his glass in surprise, "A threesome? I never—wow."

"Oh gosh, I'm feeling dizzy," I say swaying slightly as I stand up.

"Can I drive you home? Or will you be going with—"

"Nah, we'll meet up later and, ya know, do sexy-sex stuff. But yes, you can take me home. I dun wanna take the train," I hiccup loudly.

Eddie throws some bills on the table and grabs me by the elbow to steady me.

I like a man with an assertive touch. Who am I kidding? I like *this* man.

We thankfully drive in silence. He knows where I live, which is good, because I currently can't remember anything other than the fact that I luuuuurve tequila.

***

"I'm going to walk you up. You seem unsteady," he says as we pull in front of Angie's apartment.

"Psshhh, I'm shhh-fine," I assure him, my words slurring only slightly.

He comes around to my side of the vehicle anyway and opens the door for me. *What a gentleman.* I smile up at him dreamily. Engaged or not engaged, I still want him. *Ugh, first Damascus and now him. Do I have a thing for men who are unavailable? I dunwanna, hiccup, answer that right*

*now. You and your judgmental thoughts need to leave me alone.
I'm a grown woman. I can lust after anyone I wanna lust after.*

He walks me up to the front door and I turn
around to thank him, except his lips look soft and
yummy in the moonlight, so I kiss him instead. To my
surprise, he kisses me back. And it's as wonderful as I
remember it. I love his cologne and the way I can rest
my head on his shoulder and continue to kiss him.

We pull apart both breathing heavily. "Eddie, I
know you're engaged. But pick me instead. I would
never break up with you for the fun of it. I like you.
And if there's even a glimmer of doubt that you may
not love Matisha, then don't go through with it. Choose
me! Be with me!"

He stares at me taken aback. I can't believe I've
said it either. *Oh God, how utterly humiliating. Did I just beg
him to be with me?* Mortification makes the tequila twitch
in my stomach. Oh no, the twitch has turned into a
slosh. I can feel it gaining momentum, there is a tsuna-
mi tequila tide churning within me. I try, I try to stop it
by holding my breath and swallowing profusely, willing
it to back down. But it's climbing up the walls of my
stomach, through the lining of my esophagus, and there
is nothing I can do. The tequila has a will force of its
and as much as I attempt to warn Eddie with my eyes,
he is too busy looking at his shoes, so I do the same
except I also bend over and throw up on top of them..

CHAPTER 14

"My head has little people in it with little hammers that are trying to chisel away at my brain," I moan to Angie in the morning.

"I have a feeling the hammers are going to change to machine guns after you see this," she shoves *The Tribune* in my face.

"Why—what happened in the news?" I say, my eyelids still half closed, skimming over the words. I inhale sharply and my eyes snap open in horror as I stare at the thunderously large headline in bold black ink that declares, **"Why can't I poop? Simon Blythe's bowel and bladder diary."**

"Ohnononononono, this isn't happening," I moan in horror.

'It's Day 1 and I think I'm shitting raisins... at least it looks like raisins. There's no smell. Or maybe there is a smell but because it's my poop, I can't smell it.'

I suck in large mouthfuls of oxygen and gaze at Angie in wordless horror, "What have I done?" I wheeze with what I sincerely believe is my last breath.

"They may not know it was you who did this. Don't walk in looking guilty," Angie advises, sticking a piece of her pop tart in her mouth.

"Simon will know. It's his bowel and bladder diary. The whole world knows his poop schedule. I'm going to get fired from my internship. And then I'm going to get expelled from Columbia and then I'm going to get fired again from the bookstore. It'll be a pink-slip domino effect. "

"You. Know. Nothing," Angie emphasizes each word slowly, "Serves that jackass right for bullying you into something you didn't know how to do. It's his own fault the world knows he can't poop for three days after sex."

"What? Really?" I ask in horrified awe, "Is that even possible?"

"Oh yeah, paragraph 7 really gets down to the nitty-gritty. I personally would never do the man after learning all this. His sex life is going to shrivel faster than his penis."

"I think I'm going to be sick," I whisper.

"Don't throw up on my shoes, these cost me a pretty penny at DSW. You have to go to *The Tribune* today, no excuses. You're going to look Mr. Simon Blythe in the eye and act like you have no idea what happened. You are just a dumb intern. Dumb people get away with stuff all the time. Look at George Bush; we got into two wars because of that jackass. And whenever anyone points it out, we all go, 'oh well, you know, he was an idiot.' Oh, and wear something cute. That green-yellow thing kinda matches your skin color." With that, my sage-Yoda clambers out of the apartment in her three-inch heels and her bouncing basketball-like belly.

***

"How in the world did this happen?" Barb barks out at all of us, "I have been getting calls all day from the CEO and the advertisers. Who transferred Simon Blythe's poop journal entries onto the layout page? No one leaves this room until I get an answer."

We all shift in our seats, nervously eyeing one another. I can feel the moisture pooling underneath my armpits. Where is Simon? I thought he would be here, screaming at them to stone me in the courtyard or something. But he is absent, and in his place is a sickly silence.

Barb's cell phone shrieks wildly, thankfully diverting our attention. She shoots us all a glare and answers it. She lowers her voice and covers her mouth, even though her voice is muffled, we catch a few entrails of the conversation, "Yes, they're all here except for Simon... well he's always been—no I can't right now... what? Why?...fine, but this has to stop." She snaps her phone shut.

"You can all leave, we're going to handle this situation in a different manner. Our team will review the cameras and see if anything unusual occurred last night. This will hopefully alleviate some of the ridiculous lies you are all planning to tell me. Now go do something useful. Earn that paycheck," she ends on a growl, as if she resents the fact that her staff isn't willing to work for free.

Upon hearing the word "camera," my body decides to simultaneously freeze and perspire. My spine and tailbone go frighteningly numb while my face and hands start sweating. Beads of sweat drip down my forehead and catch on my eyelashes. I think I have swine flu. Actually, I would love the swine flu. Anything that would lay me up in a lovely hospital bed for the next three weeks would be heaven. It would hopefully allow enough time for the whole poop scandal to blow over.

"Yamasaki, Yamasaki, can you hear me?" I am jarred out of my musings by the sweet, scratchy bellows that emit from Barb's throat.

"Yes, I can hear you. Sorry, I was just thinking about what happened."

"Yeah, well, it ain't your problem. I need you on the fifth floor. Our astrology lady passed a kidney stone, so she won't be in for a while. We need someone to run the lines."

"Run the lines?" I stare at her blankly. For once it would be nice if people just told you what they expected from you, instead of having to decipher code words.

"Write the little blurbs. It ain't hard, and I'm not going to pay our actual reporters to do this. You read *Cosmo* and *Seventeen*, right? It'll be a no-brainer. Now scram, I have better things to do then explain to you what your lucky numbers are."

I shoot out of my seat and trot up to the fifth floor like a giddy school girl. I *love* astrology. I live my life by it. I get along really well with Aquarius's. Not a big fan of Capricorns—which explains my strained relationship with my mother as she was born under the month of the Goat.

"Yamasaki, hey Yamasaki," The voice that I dreaded hearing all morning booms behind me. My stomach muscles clench, and I can feel the blood drain from my head to my toes. I turn around to see Simon waving wildly at me. As he makes his way towards me, I take a step forward. I can do this, I am going to be professional and courteous. I am going to apologize for my mistake. Except he looks so mad. His skin is flushed an unnatural reddish purple color. I take a startled step back and then another. Screw this—I don't want to be fired now. Not when I finally get a chance to actually write for the paper. I turn tail and run. I can hear him shouting "Yamasaki!" and then "Maya!" but I pump my puny legs and rush toward the elevators. Tripping into the elevator, I desperately push the buttons trying to get the doors to close.

"Hey, wait—I need to talk to you," I hear him say as the doors practically close in on his nose.

"Sorry, I have to go. Very busy, we'll catch up." I say to his left nostril as the doors thankfully shut close, and I manage not to take his nose out in the process.

CHAPTER 15

I TRY TO SHAKE OFF my escape; hopefully he won't be looking for me in the Life & Style section. Barb usually has me in the basement, filing folders. This is going to be so much more exciting. I make my way over to the managing editor's office (conveniently labeled Managing Editor) and tentatively knock on the door. "Come in," I hear a hard, flat female voice answer.

I walk in and see a very stylish woman in her late thirties radiating contained anger. Everything about her is harsh angles and pointy tips, from her spiked hair and high cheekbones down to her black pointy Christian Lacroix pumps. Her eyebrows furrow in a deep V, "Yes?" she says. A single word, a command for me to explain myself.

"Hi," I squeak, "Barb sent me up here to help complete the astrology section."

Her mouth turns down (not curves, just slashes down), "You're not an intern, are you?"

I desperately want to say no, but I have a feeling I have exceeded my lie quota for the day, "Yes, I'm an intern from Columbia College. My name is Christine Yamasaki."

"Of course you are. Why would this be easy? So now we have to set you up with a user ID and password and explain our layout, instead of Barb sending me what I originally asked for, which was to spare one of her many other reporters who could put together a blurb for me in 10 minutes tops. Thanks, Barb, thanks a lot," the managing editor rolls her eyes at the sky and looks at me with resignation. "Go sit at one of the empty desks. I'll have one of the girls explain it to you. Because we have time for that when we're extremely short staffed," she mutters the last sentence under her breath.

I'm at a loss as to what to say, so I nod my head vigorously and paste on a weak smile, "Great! Sounds good, I can't wait."

I collapse onto an empty chair wearily. For once, it would be nice if someone actually talked to me like I am a human being. I am tired of feeling like a nugatory toad all the time. Yes, I am young, yes, I am at the bottom of the totem pole, but I am a person with feelings. Would it kill people to spare a smile? To dispense with one word of kindness? I constantly have to put a mental shield up. Anytime I put the shield down, somebody throws a jab or an accusation my way. I have to watch what I say and do. I have to exude professionalism and courtesy towards others, but no one else is obligated to display those same qualities back to me. And that just plain sucked.

***

"Christine," I hear a voice say behind me. I turn around to see the Managing Editor smiling at me.

"Hi," I smile back, trying to curve my lips up to the same angles her lips were at. I don't want my smile to be too big or too small. I am trying to go for the Goldilocks of smiles.

"I wanted to say, great job today. I read your blurbs. I thought they were really funny and as accurate as a horoscope column can ever hope to be. I don't even know if I properly introduced myself earlier. I'm Trish," she extends her hand, and I shake it timidly, waiting for the other shoe to drop. Waiting for her to tell me what I've done wrong. Her voice steamrolls over my thoughts, "I know I wasn't easy on you this morning, and I wanted to apologize. It's just been stressful being understaffed and spinning 10 plates at the same time. But you probably know how that is. Being an intern here, going to school, and probably juggling a part-time job too, huh?"

I nod, "Yeah, it's a crazy schedule. But I do love the newspaper; I think it's an amazing place to work. I never imagined I could be a part of something that touches so many people every day."

She looks around the office and nods slowly, "Yeah, I sometimes forget that. It is pretty cool. If you ever need anything, let me know. You really helped a lot today, more than you can imagine. I hate putting the horoscopes together. I think it's the most useless part of the newspaper, they should cut it out along with the classified section of men seeking women and vice versa."

"What?" I say aghast, "No way, that's like the best part of the newspaper. That's how I was hoping to find my future soul mate. I'm actually considering responding to "86-year-old SWM, almost-perfect man if i wasn't surrounded by dumb nags.""

She looks startled and then laughs, she has a very pretty laugh actually, husky and warm. And somehow during that laugh, she kind of loses all her harsh angles (but not totally). She looks more approachable, so I hesitantly ask her something I've been pondering all day. Something that's been nagging at the back of my mind. "Trish, let's say someone was asked to replace an article at the last minute, in the printing room. And that someone gets a USB drive from this journalist who asks her... er this person to switch this article. Is it possible for her… I mean this person to input the wrong article in the newspaper?"

Her face gets very serious very quickly, and I instantly regret opening my mouth. *I'm such a sucker! She says one nice word to me and I turn into her lap dog.* "It depends on what's on the USB drive. If there are several articles or documents, then it's possible to choose the wrong one, I suppose," She pauses, "Is there something you want to tell me?"

I shake my head, "No, I uh, I don't know enough right now. I have to look into it… or my friend has to look into it for another friend."

She meets my eyes and then says, "That article today on Simon Blythe was the funniest thing I have ever read. I can't stand that man. He is the biggest, egomaniacal talentless hack this newspaper has. And everyone kisses his ass because he almost got nominated for a Peabody award for some stupid NPR skit. I almost peed my pants reading about how he can't pee. Whoever is responsible for that is the coolest person in the world."

I break out into a relieved grin, "How do you know him?"

"I used to be married to him," she says grimly, as if he were some kind of disease she had and gotten rid of.

My mouth has dropped open in shock.

She continues, "So, if someone needed to talk to someone about how they may have accidently been manipulated by Mr. Blythe, there is someone on this floor, a managing editor, who may understand what that person went through. Seeing as how this managing editor lost 3 precious years of her life to that slimy, smarmy, jackass."

"That's good to know," I say in a small, relieved voice. Trish smiles again, and this time I see a bit of savage triumph in it.

She winks at me, "I'm here for you, Christine.

CHAPTER 16

I HOVER OUTSIDE AN OFFICE, in front of a set of gorgeous glass double doors. The glass actually has computers etched within them, old Macintosh Apple computers. I can go in, I need to go in, but I'm losing my nerve. I don't want to seem like a stalker, but I need IT help, and I know—knew—someone whose business is in IT.

The door swooshes open, "You are wearing me out with your pacing back and forth. Come in and sit down. Have a cup of tea, you can then decide whether or not you want to go back out and continue pacing," I hear a silky British accent and trip over myself trying to get a look at the man with the posh voice.

Warm brown eyes framed by long black lashes twinkle back at me. I take in the rest of his face. He has smooth chocolaty-brown skin and curly black hair, a lock of which falls carelessly across his forehead. Oooh, cute. I mentally shake myself. I don't have time for this. I am here on serious business.

Finding my voice, I answer, "Sorry, I'm looking for Eddie, I don't want to bother him. So I was, uh… waiting for him to leave the office. I figured that would be the best time," I swallow, my throat has suddenly become dry. Why can't I ever talk to nice-looking men normally? They are people too.

"Well, I suppose that's one approach. He's actually in the middle of something, maybe I can help you. I'm his business partner, Raj."

"Oh, you're the friend that started the business with him. The one from DePaul?" I ask excitedly, already knowing the answer, but for some reason wanting to insinuate that I know Eddie and I'm not some strange stalker chick at their front door—although those two items aren't entirely exclusive.

"Funny, you know a lot about me, but I know nothing about you, Ms...?"

"Maya, Maya Khan," I thrust out my hand, expecting to shake his. He looks down at it bemused; he then takes my hand, raises it to his lips, and gives it a soft peck. Oooh, the British are coming. I can feel a small invasion of butterflies invade my nervous system.

"On second thought, I *have* heard about you, Ms. Maya Khan, and I would be delighted to help you out," he takes me into his office. Everything is chrome, glass, and stainless steel. Shiny, hard, and uncomfortable. I sat on a swiveling white bar stool, and he sits behind his glass table on a silver ottoman with no back. Trying hard not to swerve left or right, I haltingly tell my tale of woe.

"So, I don't know if he set me up or if I actually did it myself. I believe there was only one file in the USB drive, but now I'm not sure of anything," I sigh melodramatically, trying to convey the aura of a damsel in distress. I peek over at him. Did that type of girl excite him?

Raj looks at me thoughtfully. "You need to see if you can get your hands on the USB drive, that would be the easiest place to look to see if there was an actual article on there, a legitimate one. If that option isn't available, we can go into the printing room and into the computer where you downloaded what was on the USB drive onto the hard drive. We have software that can detect what was downloaded."

"Really?" You do?" I ask excitedly.

"Yes, but the second option isn't fool-proof; we could miss something. The best thing is to get the USB drive. See if you can meet with him and find out where the USB drive is."

I shake my head in disagreement. "There is no way I am talking to that man again. He hates me. Why would he want to deal with me?"

"Well, based on everything you tell me, he's a guy that constantly needs his ego stroked. Meet with him, apologize, play humble, and try to get what you need. Because if he did what you think he did, that's very cruel and should be brought to someone's attention."

"Hey Raj, Mathisa and I are going to get a bite to eat, you want anything?"

I am so wrapped up in my conversation with Raj, I forget that I had initially come here to get Eddie's help. I wince and brace myself before turning around. I look up and see Raj watching me with knowing eyes, catching my wince.

"No, I'm fine, I was actually in the middle of a case with my newest client."

"Oh, that's great," Eddie says, I hear a smile in his voice. The smile disappears as soon as I turn around.

"Maya?" Matisha and Eddie both say out loud in confusion.

Eddie is quicker to recover, "What are you doing here?"

Matisha continues to scowl first at Raj and then at me.

"Well, Matisha mentioned that you had an IT consultation firm, and I had a quick question about—"

"It's a confidential matter, and I'm handling it," Raj interrupts me smoothly.

"I never told you what Eddie did," Matisha is quick to contradict me. Of course she didn't tell me that, but what could I say? Your fiancé told me what he did for a living when we made out in his car a few weeks ago? And I googled where he worked today because I'm pathetic and wanted to be near him—which, by the way, is not the case here. I have a legitimate, valid excuse for seeking him out. And if I get to smell his cologne as a bonus for when he helps me out, so be it.

"In class the other day, you mentioned that your fiancé had his own IT consultation firm." This actually is kind of true. Since Matisha had gotten engaged, every sentence began with, "My fiancé this, or my fiancé that." Like when one of us asked her when an assignment was due, she would answer with a smug, "My fiancé hates when I work over the weekend, so why don't you take an extra week and get it to me next Monday," It would be a lot easier on the ears if she would just walk around with a neon sign saying, "I win, I'm engaged!"

Matisha recovers quickly and points out to everyone in the room, "Yes, Maya is a student in my class Raj. Isn't that the most adorable thing you've ever heard? We went to high school together—"

"I think we all know the story," I quickly interrupt; I'm not in her class now, which meant I thankfully don't have to listen to her belittling me in public, "I was just leaving, actually. So all three of you can go to lunch together."

"Or you can join us, Maya, round us out to an even foursome." Raj stands up and walks around his desk to stand in front of me.

I cannot go to lunch with these three. For one thing, I might end up sticking the fork in Matisha's eye instead of my entrée.

I open my mouth to decline, but as usual, Matisha beats me to it, "Well we are also going to the post office to mail out our invitations—"

"Oh, wow, for the wedding, already? How fast, I mean punctual, I mean efficient with time," I am blabbering. I can't imagine Eddie married. I can't imagine him pledging his life to be with someone else, when I still think of him as "my" Eddie. We shared a passionate kiss—that had to *mean* something. Screw them and their measly three years together.

"Oh, not the wedding, not yet. No, these invitations are for the engagement party. The wedding is still 6 months away. Six months of hard labor ahead. Like building a mini Taj Mahal, except, of course that Eddie and Matisha are building a wedding party and not a mausoleum," there is a dark edge to Raj's voice that I don't like, a mocking quality that comes across as slightly mean.

"Well, I guess losing your best friend to a girl isn't much fun. But I don't think Matisha has cooties. Not that I know of," I laugh awkwardly to cover up the fact that I sound like a 4-year-old nitwit. They all stare at me with unblinking eyes.

"So, let's let the two love birds go to the post office while I convince you to be my date for the engagement party," Raj turns to me and does the twinkly, smiley face thing again. But I have a feeling his performance isn't meant for me.

"What?" Matisha demands before she can help herself, "Raj, it's a small affair, we've a very specific number of guests allowed. Not that we don't want you there, Maya. But, you understand."

"Eddie told me I could bring a date. Maya is going to be my lovely plus one."

"Oh," I prepare to make an excuse, "with school and the job at the book store, plus my assignments. I'm swamped." No way am I witnessing a whole party celebrating the fact these two are engaged. I'm not a masochist.

"Maya, you should come. It'll be fun," Eddie says the words softly, as if he's blessing our date.

Ugh, who is he, my dad? It would serve him right if I ended up—what's the British word for it, snogging? Yes snogging—his friend in front of him.

"It's in three weeks. Wear a tight dress, I like a girl in a tight dress," Raj purrs in my ear.

I smile weakly at all of them, "I have to check my schedule. Can I get back to you all?"

Matisha's lips have flattened into a line, "Yes, well if you can't make it, let us know so we can invite guests who will actually appreciate the effort we've put into this."

And before I can help myself, I say with defiance, "On second thought, I'll re-arrange my schedule. I'll be there. I wouldn't miss it for the world."

"Great," Matisha says with a tight smile.

"Great," Eddie echoes with a quizzical brow.

"Great," repeats Raj, looking like the cat that swallowed the canary.

CHAPTER 17

"I CAN'T BELIEVE YOU are going to their engagement party," Angie says as she takes the remote away from me and changes the channel.

"I don't want to watch the "Biggest Loser," I moan.

"Shut up, this inspires me to, you know, be better and work out and stuff," Angie retorts, stuffing an Oreo into her mouth. "Now how can you go to a party where you slept with one of the affianced?"

"I didn't sleep with him," I protest, "We just kissed a few times… and it was wonderful," I say dreamily, smiling at the memories, "Besides, they invited me. It would be rude of me not to go."

"Oh, it would be rude of you not to go, huh? Are you planning on sharing your tonsil hockey excursions regarding Eddie to Ms. Matisha before or after you scarf down the free food?"

"I mean, I can't really force the conversation on her. If it doesn't come up, it doesn't come up," I say stiffly, "It's never going to happen again."

"Not until the next time you get drunk and slobber all over him. That poor man stuck between two crazy Indian chicks," Angie mutters to herself.

The doorbell rings, interrupting the witty remark that was about to make its way out of my mouth. Angie rises to answer it the door. "Hey Baby, how you doin'?" I hear a very familiar and unwanted voice. No, no, no!

This isn't happening. She is in such a good place right now. She doesn't need this.

***

The clomp of work boots makes its way down the hallway, and I look up, dreading what I am about to see. Tyrone. In all his FUBU finery.

My stomach clenches in red-hot anger. What is he doing here?

As his eyes meet mine, he throws me a knowing smile and yells to Angie, "Still 'Captain Save-a-Hoe', huh?"

"Actually, I pay my share of the rent, unlike the hoe she was saving for two years," I say pointedly back at him.

"Oh look, the kitten has teeth, how sweet. Still running away from your family or whatever, huh?" He turns his gaze away from me, back to Angie, "Man I'm starving. Angie, you wanna fix me something to eat?" Angie haltingly enters the living room, her face has taken on an ashen complexion, "Damn, I didn't see it in the hallway, but you sure got fat," Tyrone laughs at his own observation.

"She didn't get fat, you moron, she got pregnant. Because of you. And no, she's not going to fix you something to eat, because you need to leave. Like right now."

"Oh really? You're telling me to leave my girl's apartment. Are you going to make me, shorty?" Tyrone starts getting close to my face. My hands ball up in fists. I am completely willing to punch him in the face.

"Yeah, sperm donor, I'm going to make you leave." I retort back, "And she stopped being your girl the minute you went to New York."

"Who went to New York? Aw shit, was that what I told you, Angie? Damn, my bad, I was actually chillin' at Trey's house. Trying to wrap my mind around this whole baby thing. But I'm good now. I'm ready to have this baby, girl. You, me, the whole family thing. It's gonna be wonderful."

"Get out before I call the police," I say in my most threatening voice.

"Maya, stop," Angie interrupts me, "Maya, I think you should leave."

Stunned, I gaze at her with my mouth open. "Angie, you can't be serious. He left, he ditched you. You're seriously not buying this are you? He's just trying to mooch off—"

"That's enough. I don't need you to judge me or us. Thank you for everything these past few months, but I—I need to talk to Tyrone and settle some things."

"Okay, I agree," I nod and sit back down on the couch. It is going to be very sweet watching Angie kick this loser's ass to the curb.

But she isn't having it, "I need you to leave. He's the baby's father, we have to figure out how we're going to handle being a family."

I stare at her, "What? I thought I was your family," I say in a hoarse whisper.

She looks away.

I cannot lose Angie after everything else I've already lost. I didn't want to be set adrift again. She is all I have left.

Tears are leaking out of my eyes and I impatiently wipe them away, "Okay, okay, I won't judge. You wanna be with Tyrone? Fine, I won't say anything. But don't tell me to leave. I have nowhere to go. I—I—I'll stay out of your way. It'll be like it was before and—

"You'll land on your feet Maya. You always do. Please—just go," she pleads, her voice breaking. And I know that I've lost her. Tyrone has won again.

I go to my room and hurriedly pack my stuff in my trusty duffel bag. I have become an expert on leaving the scene quickly. I brush past Tyrone and say nothing to Angie on my way out. She slams the door behind me. I should walk away but I can't, I turn around and rap on the door hard. She opens it warily,

"I get it. He has your number. But you are going to miss me and you are going to need me. And I will always be there for you. Always. No matter what. So when this ends—and it will end—do not be ashamed to call me. You are my sister," I whisper fiercely. Her face crumbles in front of me and tears start streaming down. Before she can say anything, I turn around and quickly walk away, before I start pleading with her to let me stay.

CHAPTER 18

I HAVE NOWHERE TO GO. Again. Wandering aimlessly, I end up back at the Columbia campus. Maybe I can spend the night in the lounge area and get my act together in the morning. I pass the bookstore and see Van shelving away books. I walk in, needing his calm West Coast energy.

"Maya, what are you doing here?" he pauses to ask before heaving a calculus textbook onto the highest shelf.

"Mmmm… just walking by. Need help?" I ask.

"Sure," we work in silence. He hums quietly while I concentrate on breathing in and out, my mind drifting back to my first encounter with Tyrone.

***

Two years ago, Angie had been seeing this new guy and was elated. He had sent flowers and chocolates to the salon. He was constantly showering her with little gifts—earrings and knick-knacks. She was completely enamored and she wanted me to meet him. His friends were having a get-together one night and she begged me to come out and meet him. I protested and reminded her of my curfew, "I have to be home by 10pm." It was so embarrassing to tell people, I had just stopped going out altogether. She claimed that didn't matter. She just wanted me there for 5 minutes, "You have to meet my future husband, After all, you're going to be my maid of honor." I reluctantly agreed and concocted a creative story so that my parents would think I was out helping the homeless instead of going to a party on the south side.

I showed up early. I always showed up early because I always left early. I walked into the club, which had about three girls staring at their nails and flicking their hair over their shoulder, looking bored and detached. I whipped out my phone and frantically started texting Angie when a guy walked up to me.

"Hey sweetie, can I buy you a drink?"

"No," I smiled apologetically, "I'm not much of a drinker."

"Oh, then how about a hot chocolate?" he asked.

That actually sounded really good, "I would love a hot chocolate," I said with enthusiasm.

Where are you? I texted Angie, as the guy went up to the bartender and requested my drink.

My phone vibrates back, *stuck in traffic, be there soon.*

I looked up and saw the overtly friendly guy bring me a hot chocolate, "You have really pretty eyes," he said, handing me the hot chocolate and tucking my hair behind my ear.

Ugh, I should have refused the hot chocolate, he now thought he could touch me. Where was Angie? "Thanks. My boyfriend should be coming any minute." My eyes flickered towards the door meaningfully.

He snorted, "Well what your boyfriend doesn't know won't hurt him. Why don't you and I go to the back and get to know each other a lot better? Because girl, your ass is—"

"Uh—I have to go the bathroom. Really small bladder, sorry, gotta go." I hurriedly shuffled to the bathroom and spent ten minutes washing my hands. When I finally looked at myself in the mirror, I made a vow. If Angie was not on the floor when I walked out, I was going home.

I made my way back out and was staggered by the large number of people that had entered the little hole-in-the-wall in my absence. I weaved through the throng of booty shakers and was relieved to see Angie's braids bouncing energetically, "Hey you," I said, standing next to her, "About time you showed up, the creepiest guy—"

"Maya, there you are. Meet Tyrone, my boyfriend," the man next to her turned around and my heart sank. Tyrone was the creepy hot chocolate guy.

Tyrone and I looked at each other, both of us filled with a mutual distaste for the other, neither of us telling Angie of our initial encounter.

***

"Earth to Maya, hello, Maya," Van waves his hand in front of my eyes.

"What? What happened?" I snap out of my reverie.

"Um, the store's closed. You can go home now," I look at Van and the tears start welling up before I can control them, "whoa, Maya, what's going on?"

"Angie kicked me out. Her boyfriend is back and she asked me to leave and I don't know where to go or what to do. I'm sorry, I'm not trying to dump this on you. I don't need you to do anything. I just—I'm so lost." I end in big hiccupy gulps while Van fumbles around his pockets, digs out a tissue, and passes it to me.

"Hey, chill. We'll figure this out, no need to panic."

"Having a place to live is a big deal, Van," I wail and blow my nose loudly.

"Of course it is, and you can totally stay with me." I shake my head, "No I can't. Your girlfriend would not be happy, and I don't want to be a third wheel again."

He pauses and looks at the ceiling fan, "You know my parents own a restaurant in Rogers Park, they have an apartment that they sometimes rent out. I can check with them."

"Really?" I say warily, "How much is the rent?"

"I'm sure they can meet your budget, but they're really strict, they don't allow girls to have guys over—"

I roll my eyes and snort, "Trust me, I could string a pork chop around my neck and not get a nibble... from a guy that is."

"No loud music," he begins the list.

"I'm as quiet as a church mouse, plus I'll hardly be there."

"No talking about politics or sex,"

"Done. Believe me, I don't really know a lot about either topic," I say vehemently, which causes Van to blush and smile.

"I'll give them a call tomorrow. But tonight, you stay with me. End of conversation," he puts his arm around my shoulder and gives me a little half hug before hauling me on my feet and walking me out.

"Thanks, Van," I whisper. He squeezes my shoulder in reply.

***

Van's girlfriend is a petite little thing whose family hails from Thailand but later settled in Iowa as farmers, of all things. She loves to talk and has an infectious giggle that reveals the most adorable gap between her two front teeth.

"Van texted me the details, you poor thing. That's the worst, when your girlfriend dates a guy you hate.

My own girlfriend back in Iowa did that to me, and I haven't spoken to her since, I mean that's the worst type of betrayal—"

"Babe, we're starving, how about we eat while you tell us your thoughts on Maya's situation?"

Lawan flutters around the kitchen and procures two take-out containers, "Your mom delivered these earlier."

"Awesome, have you ever had Vietnamese food, Maya?" I shake my head, as Van continues to talk, "I don't mean to brag, but my mom is like the best cook in the world. You're in for a treat."

Oh, he isn't lying. The rice is moist and fluffy, and the beef lemon curry is spicy, fragrant, and refreshing. The spring rolls are crisp and delicious. My taste buds are experiencing mini-orgasms of joy, and I am practically weeping with happiness.

"Oh my gosh, that was the best thing I've had in ages," I say, wiping my mouth and getting up to do the dishes.

"You're our guest, stop it," Lawan admonishes before picking up both our plates and heading to the kitchen.

"Please, it's the least I can do," I stand next to her and dry the dishes as she washes them.

"It's nice to have a girl to talk to sometimes," Lawan remarks.

"Yeah, nothing beats a good girlfriend," I say wistfully. Thinking of Angie, wondering what on earth is making her stay with that scum bug.

CHAPTER 19

"MAYA, I NEED to talk to you," An angry voice barks into my ear.

"Antoine, it's 5 in the morning, what is your problem?" I murmur groggily into the phone.

"Are you with Angie?" he asks me. Now that the sleep is receding, I hear the agitation in his voice. I don't know what to say, so I sigh.

"Maya, who is with Angie? She hasn't been picking up my phone calls all evening. What is going on?"

"Antoine, you gotta talk to Angie, I'm not the right person to be involved here."

"Be involved in what? I would love to talk to Angie, but she isn't responding, so you have to tell me, otherwise I'm going to lose my mind."

"Tyrone is back at the apartment. She kicked me out," I say flatly, swinging my feet over the couch cushions and straightening out my neck. The sofa is a lot smaller than it looks, but I am grateful it's not the student lounge.

Antoine is quiet on the phone and my heart squeezes for him in empathy. "Do you know why he's there?" he finally asks.

"Something about figuring out how to move forward as a family, it was really weird, I mean, he didn't even go to New York, he was in town the whole time just avoiding her. I can't believe she actually wants to be with him. It makes no sense when she's clearly falling in love with..." my mind starts to creak into gear, "Antoine, why would she be with him?"

Antoine clears his throat, "I'm not sure, maybe they're just talking. I don't know. I need to speak with her. If you talk to her, can you let her know that?"

"Definitely," I click off the phone and review last night's events in my head again, this time without my own emotional breakdown coloring the scene. Angie hadn't been happy to see Tyrone. The way she timidly walked into the living room with her ashen face—those are not signs of a woman in love. Those were signs of a woman who is really distraught and unhappy.

I sigh and punch in another number. A voice on the other end says, "Jesus Christ, do you have any idea what bloody time it is?" said in a British accent, even pure annoyance comes off sexy.

"Sorry to bug you, Raj, but I have a question."

"Mmmm... call me when I've had a decent cup of coffee. I have no answers right now."

I hear a women's voice in the background grumbling, "who the hell is that?" I hear Raj shushing her.

"Raj I didn't know you had a girlfriend," I tease him, "Do I know her?"

"I don't have a girlfriend," he says abruptly just as the female voice whispers "oh my gosh, she's everywhere."

Raj speaks louder to cover up his female companion, "My office hours are listed on my card, Maya. Use them appropriately," and then I hear the dial tone. Well that wasn't very polite. I expected better from the British. I bet Kate Middleton wouldn't have hung up on me like that.

***

153

Today is a brand new day. I am going to do my work honestly, I am going to be kind to every living thing. I am going to be grateful for my blessings. I repeat the Reiki chant over and over in my head, as I sit in Simons Blythe's ginormous office with a bran muffin and a Vente latte. I need to charm the man into giving me his USB drive once again.

As I see his shimmering blond head make its way through the throng of cubicles, I cringe. I quickly amended my mantra, *I am going to be kind to every living thing—even if they don't deserve it and even if it kills me.*

"Simon, I brought you a snack," I say with a determined smile, holding up the baked goodies.

"Maya," his eyes widen in surprise, "Well, it's about time you groveled out an apology, you almost cost me my job, you know." He grabs the bag and the latte out of my hand (without a thank you) and proceeds to chomp down on the muffin.

"Did you tell anyone it was me?" I ask in a small voice. I peer up from beneath my eyelashes and try to convey fragility.

He looks over at me and sighs, "No, everyone deserves a second chance. But I did you a huge favor, so you owe me one in return, got it?" Little flakes of muffin fly from his lips, and I try not to recoil in disgust.

I instead open my eyes wide and force myself to convey gratitude and delight, "Oh wow, Simon, thank you so much. You are the best!"

"Don't forget the other favor you might owe me. Man, this latte is the best," he pauses to savor a sip. I smile and pat myself on the back for not spitting in it. It might have a tiny, tiny laxative in it. But that is just me helping to ensure that he continues to have interesting poop episodes to write about. See how kind and generous I can be?

***

"He has to be up to something. The Simon Blythe I know would always have a fall guy attached to his mistakes. You got off way too easy," Trish leans in and whispers, "Did you get the USB drive?"

I shake my head no. "You're right, it doesn't make sense. But I have to keep letting him think that I'm super delighted and grateful he still likes me."

"Ugh, how do you not throw up?"

"Years of practice, plus I have an iron stomach."

"Sooooo…" Trish pauses, "there is a psychic convention this week at the McCormick Place, and I need an eager young reporter to cover it. Check the place out, gather some quotes, get me an article containing 250 words. Something funny but that doesn't make fun of people. Whoever writes it gets their own byline."

My mouth drops open, "Oh, pick me, pick me, pick me." I flap my arms in the air wildly.

"Of course, you're my favorite intern," she pops another Skittle in her mouth and washes it down with bottled water. The woman subsisted on Skittles, Smarties, and smart water.

"I'm the only intern, you know," I point out.

"The only one worth knowing. Don't let me down."

"You got it boss!" My first byline… as Christine Yamasaki. Sigh.

***

"Right, now this is a more civilized hour to disturb a man," Raj says polishing off a croissant and sipping his cup of coffee.

"It's practically noon. I've been waiting for almost an hour," I protest.

"Dear, I own the company, so I set the hours and today I set them at," he glances at his Cartier watch, "11:53am."

"Okay, is there a way you can look up a shifty individual?" I try to keep my voice clipped and business-like.

Raj quirks an eyebrow, "We own an IT consultation firm, luv, not a detective agency."

"But could you do a background search or something?" I press on, desperate to hear what I need to hear.

"Is this regarding the USB drive? You need me to dig into Simon Blythe or something?"

I shake my head, "No, another shifty individual. I want to know business dealings a friend of a friend is involved in."

Raj rolls his eyes at the ceiling and says, "I need a bit more info than that, luv. Sorry, I've got a call in a few. You can show yourself out, right?" he doesn't bother looking up as he reaches for his phone and starts dialing.

Feeling dismissed and a little stung, I leave his ice cube office and shuffle slowly out the door. If I look pitiful enough, maybe he'll change his mind and decide to help me. Halfway through the lobby I realize he won't be calling out my name so I resume my normal stride.

"Hey Maya, back again, huh? Raj helping you get what you need?" Eddie greets me with a binder under his arm and a tablet in his hand. Jabbing at the screen, he glances up and shoots me a smile. My stomach flutters in response.

"Kind of. I have this second request which isn't technically IT related so he can't help me out."

"Oh, sorry to hear that," Eddie says distractedly.

Before he is about to walk away, I impulsively say, "It's about Angie. Her ex is back. I think he's up to something seedy and I want to find out more about him. He's getting in the way of her and Antoine being together. And I really think Antoine is the right guy for her. I don't want to stand by and watch her mess up her life like this." I pause for breath and watch him process all of my jumbled thoughts.

"Maya, it is her life," Eddie says gently, "You can't decide what's best for her."

"Yes, I can. She needs me. She just doesn't know she needs me yet"

He closes his tablet, "Why don't we go into my office?"

As cold as Raj's office is, Eddie's is the exact opposite. Warm earth tones permeate the room, from the mahogany brown desk to the sprawling, dark red Persian carpet. His brown leather armchairs with matching ottomans face a crackling fireplace. I want desperately to sink into an arm chair, sip a cup of hot cocoa, and have Eddie massage my feet while he tells me over and over again what a fool he's been and how he will love me forever and forever if I will only give him a second chance.

"So you were saying about Angie?" Eddie snaps me out of my fantasy.

"Err... Angie and, um, Tyrone. Tyrone is the guy I'd like to find out about. She's been with him for almost two years. In all that time, he's never had a job, but he always has the latest cell phones, sneakers, clothing. You name it, he's got it."

"You don't think he could be—ahem—a... dealer?" Eddie ventures.

"I don't know, but I need to know, because if Angie is truly going to start a family with this guy and their future includes jail, well then, she needs to be aware of that possibility."

"Look, I'm not an amateur sleuth or anything. We download software, not people's dirty laundry, but let's do a cursory search on the net and see what we can come up with. Do you have his last name and birthday?"

I nod. Yup, I remember his birthday from a year ago, when Angie tried to put together a surprise party for the buffoon and he never showed up. So there we were with confetti and party blowers and no guest of honor.

"Alright, Tyrone Whitehead, let's see what you have contributed to the world." Eddie types the name into the computer.

"Not a damn thing," I snort.

Eddie looks at me reprovingly, "You aren't a forgiving woman, are you?"

"I can forgive some things, depending on how truly sorry the individual is," I hold Eddie's eye a second longer than necessary. I know, I know, he's getting married. But I can't help myself!

Taking a deep breath, I stare at the screen and try to focus on why I'm in his office. For Angie's sake. *Although I could totally lock the office door and take Eddie in his super sexy, ergonomic, executive, leather chair.* I have to get a grip. I realize I'm beginning to sound a little bit like a rapist.

"There's about a dozen Tyrone's. Any of them look familiar?"

"That one," I point to an individual on the second page of the search screen. He's wearing his Bears Jersey with a drink in his right hand and another woman in the crook of his left arm.

Eddie clicks and then double clicks and furrows his brow in concentration, after a moment he seems to remember something, "Hey, aren't you the one majoring in journalism?"

I swallow unsure what to say, "Um... I'm still learning. But you're doing a wonderful job teaching me."

He grunts and continues searching while I stare at my nails and wonder if I should get a manicure. I've never been into manicures; I always manage to smear the polish before it dries. Matisha always has perfectly manicured nails, I wondered if Eddie noticed that type of thing.

"Got it!" Eddie says triumphantly.

"Yay! He's a drug dealer?" I say, unsure if that is cause for a celebration.

"Nope, amateur porn dealer and sometimes porn star."

"Oh, ew! No, him? Really?" I say, aghast.

"It gets better. Recognize anyone on here?" he swivels the screen over to me and I shield my eyes with my hands.

"You have to move your hands to see this," Eddie says, grabbing my wrists and trying to pin them down.

"Nope, I don't have to do anything. You can't make me." We both struggle until he finally pins my wrists down and I'm forced to stare at the screen.

I see what looks like a massive coil of braids and then a female voice saying, "Oooh, yes baby, yes, come for mommy!" My face goes numb and my vision goes black. That voice belonged to my dearest, best friend of twelve years. Angie Wesley.

My face falls. "Turn that off," I say.

"Um... I'm trying, there doesn't seem to be a stop button on this thing."

We are both subjected to Tyrone and Angie's cries of ecstasy. I place my hands over my ears and shriek, "Turn it off, turn it off, turn it off!" while Eddie fumbles with the mouse and then the keyboard, trying to force it to stop.

The door bursts open, Matisha and Raj stumble into the office, both looking wind-blown.

"What is going on in here?" demands Matisha.

"I'm just—um, helping Maya with an investigative story she has to do for school." Eddie ends up yanking the plug out of the outlet and shutting down the computer altogether.

"Oh, for God's sake, we're an IT consultation company Eddie, not Maya's glorified babysitter," Raj says with sudden vehemence.

"I'm sorry, I didn't mean to bother either of you, both of you," I say, edging to the door slowly, "I should go. I'm so sorry"

"Wait—Maya, we should talk. Don't do anything rash," I hear Eddie say as I bolt out of their office.

I hear Matisha angrily say, "Why on earth do you keep helping her?" I shut the door behind me before I can hear his meek response. Screw them, screw the whole lot of them. And screw their stupid engagement party, too. I was done dealing with fake, flakey people who constantly lied to one another.

CHAPTER 20

"ANTOINE, ANTOINE, I need to speak to you now," I say to him as he walks by with a clipboard in his hand.

I had taken the train to the clinic where he works. I need someone's advice, someone who also cares about Angie. Maybe between the two of us, we can figure this out.

"I have a break coming up in 10 minutes, can it wait until then?"

I nod and my phone vibrates. Simon Blythe has just texted me: *Need that favor. Now*

I text back: *In class. Can it wait until tomorrow? Major mid-term paper due.*

I receive his text back: *Barely. Be at The Tribune by 7:30 tomorrow morning. Otherwise today might be your last day as an intern.*

Really? Were the threats really necessary? *Got it. More than happy to return the favor.* Jackass!

"What did you want to talk about?" Antoine says as he stands next to me. I gesture for him to follow me. We walk outside and sit on a park bench. The October weather is a bit nippy but still nice.

"Do you love Angie?" I ask Antoine bluntly.

He raises his eyebrows taken aback and then stutters, "Y—yeah, I guess I do."

"Why?" I demand.

Antoine starts to blush and rotate his shoulders uncomfortably, "I guess it's the way she carries herself.

She just has the bearings of a queen. You know? The way she walks and smiles and moves. I love being around her, I love the way she makes me feel."

I nod, this is good. So good. But now I am going to ruin it by revealing something deeply personal and really bad.

"When Angie started dating Tyrone two years ago, it was the first real relationship she had ever been in." I begin. Antoine nods in understanding.

"When people start relationships, they sometimes do things they wouldn't normally do to impress the other person. They buy them cars knowing that it might ruin their credit; they get tattoos, even though they hate needles. They're on that adrenaline, euphoric rush of being in love. It's an emotional high. LSD users feel the same way... right before they jump off a building," I pause to gather my thoughts. "When Angie met Tyrone, he was an amateur porn star. I think because Angie was in love and wanted to impress him, she may have made a sex tape with him."

Antoine jumps up from the bench and starts pacing, "You're wrong, that's not the Angie I know"

"I saw the tape, Antoine. I recognized her in it."

His eyes widened. "It's on the internet? Are you kidding me?"

I exhale slowly and try to be patient. "I think Tyrone is using that video as leverage against Angie. The video was made long before she met you, long before she knew how stupid it was."

"You know this for a fact? She told you?" Antoine asks me.

"No, I researched it and put two and two together. She doesn't love Tyrone, Antoine. She loves you. She practically glows around you. I never saw her that happy with Tyrone. It's the only explanation that makes sense. I mean why else would she kick me out? She's probably scared that he'll tell me or that I'll find out."

"She's 6 months pregnant! What on earth is she thinking?" Antoine drops his head in his hands and groans, "You know at 5 months, the baby has eyebrows and eyelids. We were picking out names, Maya."

I pat his shoulder awkwardly, trying to comfort him, "She's not thinking. She's got fluctuating hormones and a really bad guy potentially blackmailing her."

Antoine stands up and shakes his head, "I can't deal with this. I'm sorry. I wish her the best, but if she's going to choose that bum over me, well then, she deserves him. Good luck with everything. I know you're trying to be a good friend to her, but I'm out." Antoine starts walking back to the clinic.

"That's it??" I yell after him, "You just told me you love her, and now you're done? Well, that's real loyal of you."

He turns around and walks towards me furiously, "Sorry, but I didn't know that my girlfriend was a former porn star; forgive me for being a little bent out of shape here. She should have told me."

"Well, I've known her for twelve years and she didn't bother to tell me either. She's probably ashamed and expected this type of reaction from you, from both of us. What happened to her being a queen and you loving the way she moves and stuff?"

Antoine takes a deep breath, "How do you know it was just once?"

"Because that's all I could find on the web," I had researched it on the train ride over. Eddie is right: I am majoring in journalism. It is time I practice the research techniques I have seen in school. "He makes really bad '70s-type porn. Complete with disco ball and polyester pant suits—I mean, for the 5 seconds that they bother having clothes on. The date of the video is two months after she started dating him. She must have been trying to impress him."

Antoine shifts his weight and flexes his knuckles, so I throw down the gauntlet, "Look, I can't convince her on my own. I need your help. We both agree she needs to leave this guy. As her friend, you should see this through. Whatever happens afterwards is between you two. But can you really live with yourself knowing you did nothing and let her stay with that scumbag for the rest of her life?"

"It's her life!" Antoine protests, "You can't control it. What makes you think you're doing the best thing for her?"

"Because she looked so damn sad last night. She cried, Antoine. She never cries."

Antoine sighs and looks at the ground. An eternity later, he finally looks up at me, and nods. "All right, I'll talk to her with you. At least to find out the truth. I can't promise that I'll tell her to leave him or something. They might belong together."

I smile, relieved, "They don't, but thank you so much for agreeing to this." I stand up and give him a quick hug. "She works at the salon tomorrow from noon to 8. Let's give her a surprise at the end of her shift."

Antoine nods in agreement.

***

"No boys, no loud music, no sexy-sex, no political topics, no fighting, and no boys." Mr. Nguen wags his index finger at me as Van groans in the background.

"Da-aad, she gets it. Stop embarrassing her," Van says, covering his face with his hands.

"No, Van, its fine," I smile at Mr. Nguen, "My parents were also very strict. I am very familiar with these rules, thank you so much for letting me rent out the apartment." We were standing in a loft-like space above ThucPhamTot Restaurant. There are no barriers dividing the areas between the gorgeous wooden walls and golden wooden floors. In one corner is a toilet with a sink, in another corner is an old stove pipe oven and a deep basin sink. A microwave sits in the middle of the room. The space is warm, airy, and fragrant with spices. I love it. Sunlight streams in through two large windows. I would be perfectly content to crawl into a ball by the window and nap the afternoon away.

"$500 due by the 5th of every month. I don't like late payments," Mr. Nguen, "Because you are a friend of Van, I waive the security deposit."

"Dad, it's a storage space above the restaurant, you store cans of fish sauce up here. It's hardly the Ritz," Van protests.

"Van, I'm fine. Thank you both so much."

"Did you have dinner yet? My wife and I, we sometimes cook too much food. Maybe you and Van can join us for dinner?" Mr. Nguen brown eyes soften as he looks at his youngest son.

"Uh—no Dad, I gotta get going. Tons of homework and stuff," Van starts to walk away.

Mr. Nguen's face never falters; his eyes never lose their smooth glacial stare. But I feel the air leave his body a little. Maybe I am missing my own dad or trying to butter Mr. Nguen up, but I instinctively grab Van's elbow as he walks by me and say, "Actually, Van is helping me with some homework later. So we'd love to join you for dinner."

Mr. Nguen breaks out into a small smile, "Good. Long time, my wife and I haven't had dinner with the family. My other two sons have moved away. One works in Dubai as an engineer and the other is in Boston as a heart surgeon."

"Oh wow, that's impressive," I remark, looking at Van. His eyes are glued to the ground. He walks with a heavy slouch, feet dragging across the floor.

"But Van also very good artist. My wife and I see his show in Harlem Avenue. Very impressive too."

Van jerks up to look at his father, obviously surprised by his father's observation.

"You saw the show?" he asks.

"Yes, we walked through your um... what is the name? Exhibit? Yes, exhibit. Fine work, very fine work." Mr. Nguen pats Van on the back as we make our way downstairs.

I hold back, letting them walk ahead of me for a moment, and I smile when Mr. Nguyen automatically smoothes the cowlick on Van's head.

My father used to pat me on the head after I would get into heated arguments with my mom. I'd usually lock myself in my room and refuse to eat her cooking. He would make me an egg sandwich, and considering he never cooked anything, this was a big feat. He would come in my room, and I would gobble up the sandwich because by then I was starving. He would sit on the edge of my bed and listen while I wailed about how deeply unfair my mother was and how she didn't understand anything. Then he would pat me on the head and say, "well when you have a family of your own, you can make the rules." He would then walk out of the room and expect me to make up with my mother. Those were his problem-solving skills. Listen, nod, pat patient on the head, offer the patient a nutritious meal, and hope the rest resolves itself. I laugh softly. I want so badly to contact them, but what would I say to them? I live above a Vietnamese restaurant and I'm taking college courses with kids who are almost 10 years younger than me? *I need time. I will contact them soon; I just need a little bit more time.*

***

I enter Simon's office reluctantly. I have a plan of sorts, but I have no idea what he is going to throw at me. I breathe a tiny sigh of relief when I see the lights are closed. Good, this means he isn't in yet.

"You're late," he barks, causing me to jump and bump against the door. He swivels his chair around and narrows his eyes at me, "Can I trust you, Maya?"

"Do you need to trust me?" I squeak out in return.

"What I'm about to ask you to do is extremely confidential. I know you are an ambitious young woman who wants to succeed. So, yes, for this project I need to trust you. Can I do that?"

Thank God I grew up in a household where lying was a necessary skill. I look Simon in the eye and say, "Absolutely, Simon. You can most certainly trust me," I am proud of how my voice comes out. Strong, steady, and reassuring. I would completely believe me.

He smiles, "Good," he places a small black box with little clips around it in front of me. "I need you to tap Mayor Emanuel's phone."

My eyebrows shoot up against my hairline. "Um... why? I—well—I don't know how to wiretap a phone."

"It's simple, you go to their house, find out which wire is the telephone wire and put this little bad boy around it."

"Uh, I have to get into their house first, right?" I can't believe I am engaging him further, "Plus, isn't this illegal?"

"Well, how do you think they got Blago or Gov. Ryan? This is what the big boys do, Maya. You going to write horoscopes your whole life?"

"Um... well I've only been an intern for like 5 weeks," I protest, "I want to help you Simon, I really do, but I can't do this. I'm sorry."

He looks down at the device and sighs, "It's a shame, *Christine*, I liked you, I really did. Tough about you being dismissed from the internship like this. So suddenly and with no recommendation."

I swallow. My throat has suddenly become unbelievably dry, "Why don't we do it together?" I venture.

"Uh, no, kid. I gotta reputation. I can't be skulking around people's sewer systems trying to locate a phone wire. You, on the other hand..." he stops and looks at me with his eyebrows raised.

I nod slowly. I need time to process this, but I also need him on my side while I processed it. I wrap my fingers around the little bug, "Got it. You can count on me, Simon."

He smiles at me smugly, his canines gleaming in the sunlight.

I walk out of his office slowly and make my way over to the Life & Style section. I love interning at *The Tribune*. I don't want this taken away from me. On the other hand, I'm pretty sure what Simon is asking me to do is illegal. I look at the clock on the ceiling and my head starts to throb. It is 8:00am. I have to get through the whole day and then talk to Angie about her sex tape. But what I desperately need is a nap.

I send Trish and Barb a quick e-mail letting them know I'm not feeling well and scuttle out of the building. On my way out, I catch Simon in the hallway, where he gives me a thumbs up sign and hisses, "Go get 'em!" which leaves me feeling nauseous. I desperately need to go home. I desperately need my bed.

I love my new bed. Technically, it's Van's old bed. But it is wonderfully firm and soft in all the right places, and I have placed it right by the window so the sunlight hits it just so. It makes me feel like a decadent beach bum. I walk over to it wearily. I should be at school, I should be at work, I should be at *The Tribune*, but I needed to lay my head down for a few minutes... just a few minutes.

***

Something is vibrating against my head. I wish it would stop—it's making my head hurt. I groaned awake. "Hello?" I croak into the phone.

"Maya, where have you been? It's like 8:30, I've been calling you," I bolt upright at the sound of Antoine's voice.

"Where's Angie?" I ask.

"She left, I didn't want to go in on my own. We had a plan, where were you?"

"I was," I sigh and glance at my delicious bed, "sleeping."

"What?"

"I wasn't feeling well, so I lay down and lost track of time, I didn't think I'd sleep this much."

"Yeah well... so now what?"

"We could go to the apartment," I say tentatively.

"I thought we wanted Angie alone so we could talk to her reasonably," Antoine says. He's right, he's being logical. The problem is, I just didn't have time to catch Angie alone. With school, work, and the internship, my free time had been carved down to nothing.

"I know, you're right, Antoine. But we don't have much time between the two of us, so why not just surprise her? What's the worst that can happen?"

CHAPTER 21

THIRTY MINUTES LATER, FOUR police officers are at Angie's apartment, escorting both Tyrone and Antoine away. Angie is standing in the corner of the living room, arms crossed, eyeing me with absolute disgust while Tyrone is shouting, "That's right, trying to keep a brotha' down. Always trying to keep a brotha' down!" The black police officer who handcuffs him rolls his eyes in response.

What's the worst that can happen, right? Let me fill in a few details leading up to this not-so-ideal scene.

***

Antoine and I knock on Angie's door (as politely as possible), and she answers it. Mascara stains are smudged on her cheeks, her lower lip is trembling, and she's wearing a hideous puce-colored dress.

Her eyes widen when she sees Antoine. She whips her head at me and hisses, "What do you think you're doing?"

"We needed to talk to you, and you haven't been taking Antoine's calls," I say.

"Right, most guys would take that as a hint," she says sarcastically.

"I'm right here, Angie. You still can't talk to me, baby?" Antoine intones from behind me. His voice is deep and caressing. No way am I going to let Angie lose this guy for that bum inside.

"Let us in. We can talk like adults. This can all be handled in a perfectly civilized manner," I say, trying to use the professional, grown-up voice I'd heard Trish use in the newsroom.

Angie can't look either one of us in the eye, "This isn't a good idea. He's not in a good mood."

"I frankly don't care what mood he's in," I hear Antoine shift behind me. "I need to talk to my girl-friend, *Angie*. The one I picked out baby names with, the one I picked out baby furniture with. You remember her? You owe me an explanation."

Angie sighs and lets us in. Tyrone is lounging on the sofa watching Floyd Mayweather beat someone to a pulp. He glances up at us and snaps at Angie, "Hey, didn't I tell you I don't want company tonight?"

"We came here to speak with Angie, not you," I say in a calm, measured tone.

He rolls his eyes at me and then notices Antoine, "Oh is this the nurse-friend you were talking about? I didn't realize he was a guy. Prob'ly cuz real men ain't nurses."

"Real men also don't speak to women like that. Real men don't knock women up and then go hide like a little bitch because they can't deal with the consequences of their actions," Antoine spits back at him.

Oh boy. The testosterone level in this room has just shot up. Angie chooses to stand in the kitchen safe-ly ensconced behind the island while I stand between Antoine and Tyrone. Heat radiates between the two of them, I open my mouth to speak but Tyrone beats me to it.

"Who you calling a bitch, Nurse Ratched? At least I don't run around wiping people's asses." Tyrone clicks off the TV and stands up.

"We came here to calmly talk about what is in the best interest for both Angie and Angie's baby—" I begin and try to gesture for both men to sit down.

"Naw, you just run around licking people's asses, don't you Big Buck. Yeah, you're Big Buck and you come ready to f—"

"Angie you told this she-man what I do, I swear I am gonna tell your momma what a—"

"She didn't have to tell us, you're all over the Internet, you and your little buck," I say nastily and then wish I hadn't as he bears down on me.

"What did you say to me?" Tyrone shoves me against Antoine.

"Tyrone, don't!" Angie yells (still safe in the kitchen).

"Oh, you're one of those guys, huh? You into hitting women, Tyrone? How about you pick on someone your own size, Big Buck?" Antoine swiftly lifts me up and places me behind the sofa, while I sputter. He turns around and clips Tyrone in the jaw.

Tyrone head snaps back, when he comes to, he slaps Antoine across the face.

"Did you just slap him?? Pussy move!" I yell.

"Maya, get back here!" Angie shouts at me.

But I am getting into it. "Get him, Antoine, rip his tonsils out. Step on his toes," I jeer.

"I am going to pull your hair out, you little conniving—" Tyrone threatens me as Antoine lands another hard blow to Tyrone's mid-section.

"Go, Antoine, Go! Beat that sucka' to the flo!!" I cheer, waving my arms wildly in the air.

I hear Angie shouting behind me, "Yes, I'd like to report a domestic disturbance, there are two men fighting in my living room. Please send someone to restrain them as soon as possible."

"No, don't tell them to come," I turn around and tell her, "Antoine's winning!" and then something bangs against the back of my head and the world goes black.

***

When I regain consciousness, four police officers are at Angie's apartment escorting both Tyrone and Antoine away. Angie is glaring at me.

I touch the back of my throbbing head gingerly. "What did I miss?"

"Gee, well, you put my ex-boyfriend in a room with my current boyfriend and they started pounding on each other. Did you not see this coming?" she asks sarcastically.

"I've been injured, be kind to me," I say, wounded by her callous remarks.

She grabs her purse and heads to the door.

"Angie, wait—we need to talk," I get up suddenly, and the room begins to tilt, "whoa," I sit back down and clutch at her coffee table.

"Maya, are you okay?" Angie walks over to me and places her hand on my shoulder.

I take a deep breath and wait for the pounding in my head to recede, with my eyes still closed, I blurt out, "Angie, I know about the sex tape."

Angie goes completely still; I can't even hear her breathe.

"How did you find out?"

"I saw the expression on your face when Tyrone came back. You weren't happy, and I saw how you were with Antoine. He made you laugh; you two had this insular love bubble thing going. I was so happy for you," I pause and I see her looking at me with utter confusion, so I continue. "It made me wonder why you would stay with Tyrone. I mean, there had to be a reason other than that 'wanting to be a family' crap. So I dug into Tyrone's past and his profession came up, and within his website, you... uh... came up also."

"I'm on his website?! He swore that video was going to stay private, that's the only reason I put up with his shit," Angie explodes. She jumps off the sofa and kicks the coffee table, turning it over, "Dammit, Maya! Why couldn't you leave this alone? Why do you have to meddle in my business?"

"Because he was blackmailing you, Angie! He was holding you back! I know you're angry, but you can't be angry at me. I'm trying to help."

"I didn't ask for your help, Maya," Angie snaps at me.

"You're being an idiot," I say furiously. "You have a good thing with Antoine. Tyrone is an abusive asshole. You couldn't raise a cactus with him, let alone a child."

Angie sighs and sits back down, "You don't get it, Maya. You've never embarrassed yourself like this. You've never degraded yourself for a guy."

"Uh—have we not met?" I grab hold of her hand and gently nudge her to sit down. "What part of working in a brothel, purchasing a Navigator for a married man, and having the hots for an engaged guy sounds intelligent and admirable?"

Angie lets out a little giggle. "Wow, well, when you put it that way, you're a mess."

"You're a bigger mess," I shove her playfully.

We both stare at the overturned coffee table. After a pause I say, "You could get revenge you know."

"What?" Angie asks.

"You could get back at Tyrone. He distributes porn illegally. He completely ignores the little FBI

175

warning that comes up before the movie starts." She starts to shake her head, but I continue on, "You can also press charges and say that he blackmailed you. You can say you did not give consent to have that video loaded on the website. They call what he did to you 're-venge porn.' Illinois recently enacted laws against it."

"Oooh, look at my journalism major friend," she teases me.

"Angie, there's a whole list of unforgivable things he did to you. You can go down to the police station tonight, make a statement, make sure that video never sees the light of day again. If you would like, I can also slip a big dude named Bubba $20 to ensure that Big Buck gets gang raped tonight."

Angie starts coughing but manages to say, "Maya, I had no idea you were so vicious."

"I don't like when people mess with my Angie, plus he shoved me."

"I'll give my statement, but I don't know about the other part."

"I swear, Angie, sometimes you can be such a softy," I pout.

***

"There's my lady, come to bail her man out. About time, you know I missed the match tonight, thanks to your annoying-ass friend."

I glare at Tyrone and open my mouth to speak, but Angie squeezes my elbow.

The police officer opens the gate and nods to Antoine, "Wingman, you're out," Antoine looks up in surprise and slowly gets to his feet. He saunters out of the holding cell with Tyrone close behind him.

"Just Wingman, no one has claimed you, boy," The officer shuts the door on Tyrone's bewildered face. I snap a photo with my phone.

"Ma'am, no photos, please delete that," the officer warns me.

"Oh, I'm so sorry. It's just that today is one of the happiest days of my life. I had to capture this special moment," I grin at Tyrone who scowls back in return, "But I completely agree and will follow protocol," I walk over to the officer and delete the photo in front of him (after quickly e-mailing it to myself first. Journalism 101 in action here, ladies and gents).

"Yo, Angie, what the hell?"

"Oh, baby, I'm sorry, I only had enough money to bail one guy out. And I figured between the two of you, the guy that wasn't blackmailing me, abandoning me, and insulting my friend was the right choice."

"Girl, you wait 'til I get out of here, I'm going to have a real serious talk with you." Tyrone shakes the iron bars in frustration, while Angie just laughs in response.

"You're going to have to get out first. With the list of charges I'm pressing against you, that's going to take a while," Angie loops her arm around Antoine and marches out of the room proudly.

"Say hi to Bubba for me," I say, waggling my fingers goodbye. Payback is a nasty business.

CHAPTER 22

"I NEED TO SPEAK with you," I say as I lean over Professor Wiseman's desk, my chest heaving in distress.

He looks at me tiredly. His tie has a coffee stain on it and his fingertips have ink residue on them. "What's this about, Khan?"

I have tossed and turned all week regarding my Simon dilemma, and I figure the only person who can help me is the one who got me into the scenario in the first place. Professor Wiseman will know what the ethical answer is. I spill the whole story about Simon.

"...so I have the bug, and I don't know what to do now," I finish up.

He rubs his hand over his face and leaves an ink smudge along his jawline. "I see, well, that is a pickle," he finally replies.

I nod and eagerly await his answer. I know he will have the perfect solution to this. "Listen... err, can you write all this up for me? Everything he's asked you to do. All the stuff that you think falls into a grey area. It'll give me a clearer understanding of how to proceed."

"Oh," I say, a little disappointed, "Sure, I can do that. It's just that I have to go in tomorrow and he's going to want a progress report."

"Just keep stalling him until I mull this over. I'll get you an answer by the end of the week, I promise."

"Thank you, Professor Wiseman, I'm so relieved. I've been carrying around this unbelievable amount of guilt. I keep replaying the scenarios in my head and wondering what I could have done differently to prevent this from happening."

"Well err… no need to get emotional. It'll work itself out. Just give me that list soon."

"I'll get it to you within the hour," I smile at him, glad that it is all out in the open. "I knew coming to you was the right thing to do. I feel so much better now."

Thank God this whole thing will be straightened out by the end of the week. My life will finally go back to being normal. If not normal, then at least the threat of being constantly blackmailed will be dispelled.

***

"What do you mean, I'm being fired?" I say, mouth open in shock.

Barb looks at me not unkindly, "It has come to our attention that you have been posing as Christine Yamasaki, when you are in fact Maya Khan. I admire your gumption, girl. It was an opportunity and you took it. Unfortunately, it's also a bit of a risk. You got caught, and now we have to let you go. We grant one internship a year, and it wasn't granted to you."

"But my professor asked me to pose as Christine Yamasaki," I protest, "You can call him. Please, he'll explain everything."

"Did your professor also ask you to switch out articles and replace the front page of *The Tribune* with Simon Blythe's poop saga?" as I open my mouth to protest, she holds up a finger to silence me. "Don't deny it. We have video footage showing you down at the print room changing the layout. Apparently under orders from me," her biting tone stings a little.

"Simon asked me to switch out the articles, it wasn't my idea," I know I sound desperate and my story seems far-fetched. But I haven't done anything wrong. I can't be getting fired for following orders, can I? I just got my first assignment. Trish and I are friends. I am actually starting to view *The Tribune* as part of my future.

"I'm sure he did, dear, now let's not make a scene. I'm afraid you have to leave the premises now. I would escort you out myself, but I have a meeting to get to. Bruno here will make sure you find the exit okay."

I can't believe this! They are treating me like a criminal. Bruno yanked my chair out from underneath me, forcing me to stand on shaky legs. Barb stands as well, "I really am sorry to see you go Chris—er... Maya. Trish said you were very good at writing the astrology section. I thought you made a nice addition to our team." *No, no, no! This can't be happening. They can't get rid of me without hearing my side of the story!*

I stare at Barb, beseeching her to re-think this, "Please don't do this! If you could just speak to my Professor, he would tell you—"

"I'm afraid I don't have time. One last piece of advice, you're a student and an intern, so you can recover from this, but when you are in the professional world, people won't be as forgiving. Deception against your colleagues is a deadly thing to do in this field," with that she turns on her heel and walks out the door.

I miserably walk alongside Bruno in the historic hallways. Rounding a bend, I accidently bump into Trish, "Jesus—would you watch where you're going?" she exclaims, staring down at her shirt, which now has a coffee stain on it.

"I'm so sorry," I say, horrified.

She freezes and then stares at me. Her face turns to granite, "I. Can't. Believe. You. Lied. To. Me," she spits out each word. Her icy tone chills me to the bone.

"I can explain," I protest, "Can I call you? Or talk to you outside of work?" I look at her beseechingly.

"No, you cannot call me. I thought we were friends. I trusted you. I stuck my neck out to get you that assignment because I saw talent in you. And the whole time you were playing me," her voice is low, controlled, and absolutely lethal.

"It wasn't like that—I swear. I didn't have a choice. I wanted to tell you the truth."

"I don't want to hear it. I have work to do. I am now short staffed—again! I hope you're happy." She brusquely brushes past me, hitting my shoulder hard.

"Oww!" I say after her, "Trish, I never meant to hurt you. I swear." I call after her. All I get in return is the sound of clipped heels echoing off marble floors. I hang my head and meekly walk out the double doors of *The Tribune.*

How could I have lost this? I'm finally good at something, and it is being ripped away from me. I reach for my phone and call Professor Wiseman. It goes straight to voicemail.

What on earth did that man said about me? Something isn't adding up here, and it isn't due to my lack of math skills..

CHAPTER 23

"I DON'T WANT TO go to this thing," I sigh at my reflection. "I'm sorry I ever agreed to it," I haven't smiled since the day I got fired. Even with the permanent frown, I have to admit that my dress is stunning. I have been hitting up the thrift stores pretty hard, and I finally found a gorgeous white strapless number with black leaves embroidered across the bodice. The corset tightens around my waist and then puffs out in a princess skirt that ends asymmetrically mid-calf. Black leaves are also embroidered on the bottom edge of my dress. I feel like an ethereal fairy princess.

"Come on, Maya, you aren't going to let Matisha win, are you? Show Eddie what he's missing," Angie bends over in front of her mirror and pushes her boobs up so that they almost spill out of her bodice. I take a look at the stretched out fabric and pray that it holds better than my leopard print dress did. We don't need another wardrobe malfunction on our hands.

"How are you invited to this thing anyway?" I ask her.

Touching up her lip gloss, she twirls her hair with her fingers, adjusting the ringlets, "Well, Eddie and Antoine are friends. Eddie checked in with him after the whole Tyrone incident. Wanted to make sure your ass wasn't in any sort of trouble. Then he invited him to the engagement party."

"You know they said this was an exclusive affair. I almost didn't get invited, and then I come to find out they are inviting every Tom, Dick, and Harry that crosses their path," I mutter to myself.

"Doll face—I can assure you, I am no Tom, Dick, or Harry. Every party needs a little Angie factor. Shazaam!" She does a little shimmy in front of the mirror and catches my eye in the mirror. "You need to smile, you look like you swallowed a lemon."

I grunt in response.

***

Eddie and Matisha's engagement party is being held at the Chicago Botanical Gardens. Thank God Antoine has a car, otherwise Angie and I would be taking the train. We pile into his rusty 1973 Ford Mustang, tucking our dresses around us, grateful for the heat against the November chill. Overnight the sidewalks and grassy turfs have become covered in white frost.

"Wasn't Raj supposed to pick you up, Maya?" Antoine asks, shifting the gears in his car.

"He hasn't contacted me in weeks. I don't even know if I'm still his date," I shiver and wrap my shawl around me tighter.

"Well, then, in that case, I am the lucky fella with two gorgeous dates tonight. I hope you save me a dance, Maya." As Antoine speaks, Angie leans over and kisses him on the cheek.

"That's very sweet of you, Antoine," Angie purrs.

"And if you want to leave early—" Antoine begins.

"Who's leaving early? Uh-uh, I haven't been out in ages. Tonight we're going to dance, eat free food, and drink alcohol-free champagne. I didn't buy them a toaster oven for nothing,"

I mewl in protest.

Angie turns her head around and stares at me. "Suck it up. I am so tired of you whining about that internship, about how hard your classes are and how you don't have a man. Get yourself a new man tonight, or I swear, the next time you open your mouth, I'm going to shove a boiled egg in it."

I nod back meekly.

The ballroom is magnificent. Icy blue cloth covers the surface of the multiple round tables. Blue hydrangeas are placed carefully at the center of each table. A big band is set up at the edge of the dance floor. I feel as if I've walked into a winter wonderland.

"Hello, darling, glad you arrived safe and sound," I hear a smooth British accent intone in my ear.

I turn around and muster up a smile, "I'm your darling, now?"

"Of course you are. Sorry I haven't called, my cell has taken a beating and it's taking forever to get a replacement. You look exquisite by the way. Is that Givenchy?"

I hear Angie snort behind me, "Um… it's an original piece. These are my friends Antoine and Angie," I turn to introduce them.

"A pleasure to be in the company of such beautiful women," Raj lifts up Angie's hand and kisses the back of her knuckles. I hear her emit a high-pitched giggle that I've never heard before.

"Oh, charmed I'm sure." *Did she just curtsy?*

"Waddup, dude? I'm Antoine, Angie's boyfriend," Antoine breaks in brusquely and grabs Angie by the waist, just in case there is any misunderstanding whose woman Angie is.

Raj gives him a tiny nod back and turns to me, "Shall we dance?"

I nod and place my hand tentatively in his, "Lead the way."

Raj is quite the nimble dancer. As he whirls me around the dance floor, I catch glimpses of Eddie and Matisha walking throughout their party. Smiling, waving, and greeting guests, they look like the perfect couple. My heart flutters when I look at Eddie. He looks particularly handsome tonight. His tall build fills out the charcoal black suit splendidly and the icy-blue tie makes his hazel eyes even more vivid.

I can be his friend, I try to convince myself. I want to be his friend. I want to get over this silly little crush I have. Except when I see him stare adoringly at Matisha, I realize I don't have a silly little crush. What I feel for him is much deeper. I realize with dawning horror that I am completely, utterly and wholly in love with Eddie...and he has no idea. I stumble on the dance floor, stepping on Raj's toe by accident.

"You look about as miserable as I feel," Raj mutters in my ear.

I glance back at him, startled, "What do you mean?"

"Have you ever wanted something so badly, knowing you'll never attain it?" As Raj speaks, I catch sight of Matisha whispering something into Eddie's ear. Eddie kisses her cheek in return and my chest starts to ache.

I abruptly break eye contact and turn back to Raj, "What do you want, Raj?" I ask trying to read the man in front of me.

"I thought I knew, but now I'm not so sure," I hold my breath as he leans forward, but before his lips can land on mine, I feel a finger jabbing me in the shoulder blade.

"Mind if we cut in?" Matisha asks with a hard smile.

"Uh—no, of course not," I say, my eyes blinking rapidly in shock. Am I really going to let Raj kiss me? Do I even like him?

I transfer into Eddie's arms and determinedly stare at his clavicle. I can't look at him. If I do, I might end up saying things I'll regret. Instead, I savor his arm around my waist, the touch of his hand on my hand, the smell of his cologne mixed with the scent of his soap. I am utterly seduced and bereft all at the same time, and the man hasn't even spoken a word!

"You look really pretty," the words rumble up from his chest and fall from his lips.

"Thank you." *Darn it! Why did I make eye contact?* "You too," I blurt out before I can help myself. "I mean, congratulations to you and Matisha. The party is beautiful. You two did an incredible job."

"Most of it was her doing," as he tilts his head over to Matisha, we notice both Raj and Matisha arguing heatedly. Eddie sighs and shakes his head, "They've never gotten along. But recently, they've been at each other's throats every time they're near one another."

"They both have very distinct personalities. Neither one seems the compromising type," I say diplomatically. We both know what I'm not saying—they are both bat-shit crazy.

"I'm glad you came," he says, giving me a slight twirl.

"I'm not," I answer truthfully, and then think better of it, "...feeling well. I think I should get something to drink. I'm a bit light headed."

"Can I help?" Ever the courteous gentleman.

"No, please enjoy your party." I stagger away from him and head over to the open bar. Still feeling uncomfortably warm after drinking a tall glass of mineral water, I make my way out to the garden area. The November chill actually feels refreshing.

How am I going to make it through the rest of the night? The man I love is going to marry a woman I hate. How can he not see how vile she is? How can he not see that he belongs with me? I am nicer, kinder, a better listener, and, of course, extremely humble. Well, I guess if you take in the whole picture, I am also a 26-year-old girl-child who hasn't yet gotten her life together. Matisha, on the other hand, has a career, a car, and really professional-looking suits that make her look like a grown-up. She holds a Master's Degree in woman's studies and has tenure at Columbia College, while I just got fired from an internship and can barely hold down a part-time job. I also have the attention span of a gnat and am wearing really tight shoes that are hurting my feet tonight. Oww.

Low, angry voices interrupt my yearning for Eddie, and I realize that Raj and Matisha have taken their argument outside. I toy with the idea of wandering back in and giving them privacy, but what are they so angry about all the time? Pretending to stare at the poinsettias wrapped in plastic, I inch closer to the voices.

"I cannot believe you almost kissed her in front of me," I hear Matisha hiss.

"I can't believe you are going to marry him in front of me," Raj counters.

"We've been over this. I love him. He is a good man. You are just a dog that sniffs after any bone he can find."

"Really, luv? You didn't mind when I was sniffing the bones between your legs last night."

Wait—what? I feel the hair stand on the back of my neck. I must have misheard.

"You're disgusting. No gentleman would ever bring that up."

"And no lady screws her boyfriend's—excuse me—fiancé's best friend. But there you have it. Two screwed-up ships passing in the night, and all that jazz," I hear Raj sneer.

"I really hate you," Matisha snaps. "Stay away from me and that little tramp who's trying to be me."

"Oh Maya's the tramp?" You really need to look up the definition of that word darling."

"Fine, maybe she isn't a tramp, just a loser who wants my life. Do you see how moony she gets around Eddie? It's nauseating."

I stumble away and find my way back inside the party, unsure of what to do. Oh God, what are they doing? And am I really that sickeningly obvious when it came to Eddie? Even Matisha knows I'm carrying a torch for him?

"Maya, Maya, are you okay?" I stare at the hand on my shoulder, unsure who it belongs to. Eddie's face slowly comes into focus, "you're chilled to the bone. Why don't you sit down and I'll get you something warm to drink."

I sit docile, unsure about what I'd just seen or heard and whether or not I should bring it up to Eddie. "Here we go, a hot cup of coffee ought to warm you right up."

"Thank you," I murmur, staring into the dark depths of the cup.

I hear him sit next to me, "You want to tell me what's bothering you?"

I stare at him, trying to memorize the flecks of yellow in his hazel eyes, the tiny scar above his right eyebrow. Will he believe me? Or will he think this is another desperate attempt on my part to seduce him? *A really pathetic attempt*, I think wryly to myself.

"Eddie, did I ever have a chance with you?" I ask him instead, staring into his eyes, trying to ascertain if he feels a flicker of something for me.

Unfortunately, he looks away before I can gauge anything, "Maya, I tried to explain at *The Tribune*. This isn't really the time or the place."

"But we had something, didn't we? Even if it was for a few moments. I'm not crazy, right? You felt it too, didn't you?" I press on, completely demolishing any dignity I have in the process.

"What do you want from me, Maya?" Eddie asks me, his voice low, his eyes glued to the floor.

Everything, my heart screams. *I want everything from you. The house, the kids, the mortgage, the dog, the picket fence, I want the rest of your life, and I want to give you the rest of mine. I want to be your best friend and your lover. I want to fight about who hogs the covers at night.* My mouth re-arranges itself and instead I say, "How about the truth? Why are you marrying her?"

"I love her, Maya. What we had was a special night that was *fleeting*. Nothing more, nothing less. I'm sorry if I ever led you to think otherwise. What I have with Matisha is solid and real, that's the foundation that we are building our lives on," he looks up and around me, deliberately avoiding any and all eye contact with me. "You know, I should check to see where my fiancée is. I do hope you feel better." He abruptly stands up and walks away.

I nod and place a hand over my lips to stop them from trembling. Have I just lost his friendship too? The closer I try to get to him, the more I end up pushing him away.

***

The plates are being cleared away, the floor is being swept up, and still some couples linger on the dance floor—Angie and Antoine are one of them. He has one hand on her belly and the other encircling her waist. It looks like he is slow dancing with both her and the baby. I stare at them wistfully. Don't get me wrong—I am happy for Angie, of course I am. It would just be nice to have a solid, masculine shoulder I could lean my own head on.

I look over at the bar and see Raj staring morosely into his whiskey glass. Straightening my shoulders, I walk over to him determinedly.

"I'll have what he's having," I say to the bartender, casually draping my arm around Raj's shoulder. As the bartender places the whiskey in front of me, I whisper in Raj's ear, "I know about you and Matisha."

Raj jerks his shoulders slightly and takes a sip of his drink, "Fair enough, I know about you and Eddie."

"There's nothing to know," I say, trying my best to look composed and not distraught when Eddie's name comes up.

"No drive to North Beach? No sweet, summer kiss?" Raj registers the shock on my face, "Yes. Sweet, loyal, loving Eddie does tell me everything. Unfortunately, some of it has been to his own detriment."

"Why—?" before I can get the question out, Raj cuts me off.

"Face it, sweety, you and I both belong to the dirty mistress club, whether we like to admit it or not." Raj raises his glass and clinks it against mine, "Here's to us," I inadvertently take a sip and toast our mutual self-loathing.

"You have to tell him. You're his best friend," I say.

"You think I don't know that? You think I don't hate myself for feeling the way I do?"

"So why do it?"

"I think… I love her."

I start choking and Raj hits me between the shoulder blades—hard! "I'm okay, please stop," I sputter, "hitting me just makes it worse." With tears in my eyes, I start to laugh hysterically. Two men are in love with Matisha and I can't even get one sorry slob to ask me out.

Sobering up, I dispense with one last word of wisdom, "If you are truly his friend, you should tell him. Who knows, maybe you'll even be able to salvage your relationship. As a wise man once said, 'Bros before ho's my friend, bros before ho's.'" With that, I slide off the barstool and walk away.

CHAPTER 24

"TRISH, TRISH, hi, it's me Christ— er, Maya," I wave my arms wildly at Trish as she begins to enter *The Tribune*.

Trish stares at me and then flicks her eyes back to her phone. Well... that's progress.

"Hey, I have punchkis for you, they're like really fancy Polish donuts," I say, running up to her and waving the pink box underneath her nose.

"I know what punchkis are. I don't eat carbs, and honestly, if you keep hanging around here, I'm going to have to file a restraining order against you."

"Can I please tell you my side of the story? I didn't mean to lie to you. It was all a big misunderstanding. I really, really liked working here and working for you."

"Too little, too late, Maya,"

As she slams the door behind her, I hurriedly yell out, "I think Simon might be up to something illegal."

The door swings back open. "You have 10 minutes."

We settle in at the Artists Café down the street, and I've managed to convince her to try the custard-flavored punchki. As she licks the powdered sugar off her lips, I launch nervously into what I hope is a convincing tale.

"Professor Wiseman asked me to be Christine Yamasaki. He told me she had appendicitis and that if I didn't take her place, there would be hell to pay, and

Columbia would lose its position at *The Tribune*. The internship would be handed over to Northwestern and Columbia would lose face."

Trish raises her eyebrows in disbelief.

"I know it sounds crazy, but he had her ID card, her schedule, everything. How else could I walk around with those items? I asked if I could be an intern under my own name, but he was very assertive when he said that I was to only go by the name Christine Yamasaki."

"Get to the point YamaKhan—or whatever your name is," Trish whips out her phone and starts texting.

I realize I'm running out of time so I start speed talking. "So anyway, on my first day, Simon immediately knows I'm not Christine. He tells me that he won't tell anyone as long as I do him a favor in return. A week later, he asks me to swipe out one of his articles from the layout. Unfortunately, I pulled the wrong file and accidently printed his poop diaries all over the front page," I hear her snort. Encouraged I plow forward, "So Simon is furious but still adamant that he needs my help, only this time he wants me to bug Mayor Emanuel's phone. When I went to my professor about this, he told me he would take care of it. Except the next day, I arrive at *The Tribune*, and I'm fired," I pause for breath. "I think I was setup, but I don't know how or by whom or even why."

"Bring me Yamasaki." Her fingers click over her Blackberry; she doesn't bother looking at me.

"Did you hear the part where I said he was planning to tap the mayor's phone?"

"I can't trust you until I have a second source confirming your story. Right now that person is Christine Yamasaki." She puts the phone away and takes a sip of her iced tea.

"I don't know where she is or if she even exists," I protest. "How am I supposed to pull that off?"

"You're the journalism student. If you still plan to take this profession seriously, that's something you have to figure out on your own."

I slump back in my chair. I really thought she would believe me. I mean, we were kind of friends for half a second.

She gets up and looks down at me, her face sympathetic, "I want to believe you, Maya, I really do. But we're in a business where there are people like Jason Blair and Janet Cooke. I can't just take your word against Simon Blythe and this Professor Wiseman. You have little to lose, while they have their entire careers at stake here. Find me Christine, and then we'll talk."

I nod slowly. No problem, I could find Christine Yamasaki. How hard could it be?

***

"There are 53 Christine Yamasakis in the Chicago tri-state area. That's assuming she's even in the Chicago tri-state area. She could be one of the 30 Christine Yamasaki that lives in Hawaii and is now there to recover after surgery or she could be in Birmingham, Alabama. Wild horses couldn't drag me to Birmingham, Alabama. Or—or—here's another thought. Maybe she doesn't exist at all. Maybe Professor Wiseman made it all up and now no one will believe me, not even my almost-friend Trish," I stamp my foot in irritation.

"She's doing that thing again where she talks without breathing," Antoine whispers out of the side of his mouth to Angie while he massages her feet.

"Let her get it out of her system. It's good for the plants—they get their daily dosage of oxygen," Angie murmurs back with her eyes closed.

"I can hear you," I snap at both of them.

"Honey, why don't you just go to the registrar's office and see if there is a Christine Yamasaki registered to your school," Angie says.

My mouth opens and closes like a guppy fish, "I was just about to do that. It was on my to-do list."

"Um-hmm, I know it was," I hate Angie when she is all smug and happy. She's a lot more fun to kvetch with when she's crabby and miserable.

***

"Sorry, you do not have the authorized privilege to access that information." The girl with the purple hair pushes her hipsters glasses up her pierced nose and looks down at me like I have a third eye.

"It's for an article that I'm writing, I just need to get a quote from her. We were in class together but she got ill and I lost her number. It's really not a big deal, if you think about it," I try smiling, twirling my hair, and rolling my eyes. I am the picture of sweet and innocent. Unfortunately, the girl is completely missing my act because she's too engrossed in her Instagram account.

Grunting an expletive, I turn away and walk over to the bookstore.

***

"Hey Maya, how are the new digs?"

I smile at Van, glad to see him, "Awesome, I have dinner with your parents on Wednesday nights. They are so talented. I love that your dad plays the Ɂàn nguyɁt and your mom sings!"

"Yeah, I guess they're pretty great."

"So do you need any help with anything? I have a lot more free time if you need me to cover extra hours," I sigh and lean against the bookshelf for support. When I don't get the attention I'm looking for. I sigh louder and end on a whimper.

"What happened now, Maya?" Van teases me. "Pray tell, what disaster has befallen you today?"

"Well, since you asked..." I relay my conversation with Trish. "But now I can't access our registrar's records."

"I can ask around if you'd like. There are only 50 Asian kids in this whole school, if she's one of them, she won't be hard to find," he continues sketching in his notepad.

"Thank you. Please call me as soon as you find out. I think my potential career depends on it."

The phone rings, cutting off our conversation. We wave our goodbyes, and I leave the store.

CHAPTER 25

HAIL IS COMING DOWN HARD against my window. I pull the pillow over my head trying to drown out the noise, but it's no use. I can't freakin' sleep, and I have an exam in the morning. Maybe if I open the window a crack, it won't be as loud. Hmm… that's odd, glancing outside, I can see no hail. But what is causing the racket? I open the window, stick my head outside and get lobbed in the mouth with a pebble. "Ow!" my head snaps back. I check my lips to see if they're bleeding.

"Maya, is that you?" I hear someone whisper loudly.

I see a tall Waldo-like shadow out on the street, "Eddie, is that you?" I half-whisper, half-yell downstairs.

"Can I come up?" he asks.

"I'm not allowed to have boys up here," I whisper.

"What?" I hear him shout.

"No boys allowed," I yell down.

"Please, it will only be a moment. I don't know where else to go."

"Fine, I'll let you in." I hurry down the back stairs, anxious and hoping that Mr. and Mrs. Nguyen do not hear my late night guest.

Silently, we both creep upstairs. I hold his hand to guide him and try to ignore the thrill his touch brings me. *Engaged, he is engaged*, I repeat to myself.

"I'm so sorry. I didn't mean to put you out. But I'm a wreck. I can't, I can't think," Eddie paces back and forth within the confines of my tiny storage compartment.

"Eddie, you're scaring me. Why don't you sit down?" I say.

He nods and looks around. Right, I don't actually own a chair. The only thing he can sit on is my bed. I gesture for him to take it. I try to be the gallant one, so I stand in front of him wearing my flannel pajamas bottoms and Hello Kitty t-shirt.

He collapses on my bed and puts his head between his knees, I hear him gulping for air.

"How did you know I was here?" I ask.

"I went by Angie's and she told me. I hope I'm not intruding," his head is still between his knees so his muffled words sound like, "iwenbyshetolmeintrudin."

"What's going on, Eddie?" I ask to the back of his head.

He finally looks up. "Raj is sleeping with Matisha."

I take a step back, "How did you find out?"

Eddie emits a bitter laugh, "He comes into my office after work and tells me he's in love with her. Oh, and he wants to marry her."

"Oh my gosh—what did you do?" I ask, horrified. Surely Raj could have found a more tactful way to spring this on the poor guy. Like maybe a haiku written in cotton candy?

"I thought he was joking, I played it off and started laughing, only he wasn't laughing. They've been having an affair for two years. Behind my back, laughing at me, playing me for a fool," he agitatedly runs his hands through his hair, and I notice the bloody knuckles.

"Eddie, you're bleeding," I grab his hands and turn them over.

"Oh, yeah, I... punched him," he pauses, "he didn't fight back. I think that made it worse. How do you fight someone who doesn't fight back?"

I go over to the basin and run a towel under warm water. Walking back over to Eddie, I wordlessly wrap his hand in the warm towel.

Eddie groans, "I can't even bring myself to call her. I know I should. But I can't even fathom what she is going to say. God, I feel like the biggest idiot."

"No, no, you are the kindest, nicest person in the world. You are not an idiot," I get on my knees in front of him, so that we are eye to eye. I take a hold of the hand that isn't bruised. "Listen to me. They are in the wrong here. They betrayed your trust. They don't deserve your friendship. This isn't a reflection of you—umph—" before I can finish my sentence, Eddie is kissing me hard. His hands are in my hair, on my face, underneath my shirt. Before I can think or even comprehend what is happening, he pulls me off the floor and onto the twin-size bed.

"I-uh—I don't think this is a good idea," I begin to say.

"I know, humor me anyway," and then his lips are on my stomach, moving their way up.

"Wait—you should stop. I mean you're in pain," I grab his lips and they become fish shaped between my fingers.

"No pain," he chirps between them. He shakes out of my hold and begins to kiss my neck, "I don't wanna talk anymore. Please don't ask me to think tonight." Oooh, his fingers are doing things they shouldn't be doing. As he softly bites my earlobe, I shiver and become completely lost in the smell, taste, and wonder of Eddie. Mmmm...

***

I wake to the sound of birds chirping. Smiling dreamily, I look at the pillow next to mine. Instead of seeing Eddie's face, I'm greeted with a note and a lily flower. I open the note, "Dear Maya, I'm so sorry for last night. I hope we can still be friends."

The hazy, pink bubble of happiness that I am floating in immediately pops. Friends? He hopes we can be friends? We had mind-blowing, epic, earth-shattering sex last night and he wants to be friends. I inhale sharply, oh my goodness. Maybe I thought it was good sex, but it was actually horrific for him. Could we have had completely altered experiences last night? Is my idea of mind-melting his version of mundane?

My phone rings, snapping me out of my tailspin, "M, it's Van."

"Hey, V," I say morosely.

"Sorry to wake you, I found your girl. She lives in Old Town."

"Ugh, okay. I need coffee first. Can you text me her details?"

"Sure... you okay? You sound out of it."

"Yeah, I just woke up... and I had sex with Eddie last night," could I keep nothing to myself? I mean, he is my landlord's son.

"Whoa! At my parent's restaurant?"

"Well, above the restaurant," I say defensively, "I wasn't like doing him on the kitchen counter or anything."

"So why the crabby attitude?"

"He left me a lily flower and a note that says he hopes we can be friends. Is that what guys say after bad sex?" I hold my breath in anticipation. The rest of my day hinges on his answer.

"Sex is kind of always good for a guy. Even when it's bad. It's like pizza, even when it's cold it's still tasty."

"So, even though my pizza may have been cold, he still should have had a good time?"

"Pretty much. Um... I think you should focus on checking out this Christine chick for today."

"I know, I just really like him, V."

"I know M. But worrying about something you can't change isn't going to help you."

We hang up, and I twirl the flower in my hand, breathing in its sweet scent. *What are you thinking, Eddie? Am I anywhere near your thoughts?*

***

"Maya. Maya, do you have a moment?" Matisha stops me after class ends.

I freeze, unsure where to go. "Er... not really. I have a story I'm chasing for Journalism class."

"This will just take a second. How was the exam?"

"You tell me," I awkwardly laugh. "I think I did well, I've been studying all week."

"That's nice," she says distractedly, "You haven't run into Eddie lately, have you?"

I swallow and shake my head no. "Engagement party was when I saw him last. Beautiful, by the way, the party was beautiful. Hope you liked our toaster oven."

She smiles wanly, "Yes, thanks. Now, if I could just track down my fiancé."

"Is he with Raj?" I venture. My hands flutter nervously around my neck, I think Eddie may have left a small hickey last night. I thought I had seen it when I rushed out the door this morning, but hadn't given it a second thought until now.

"Raj and I are no longer speaking to one another," she says darkly. "Well, if you run into him, let him know I'm looking for him, would you?"

"Of course, you two make such a lovely couple." *Why did I say that? What is wrong with me?*

Matisha raises a supercilious brow, "Of course we do. That's why we're getting married."

Clamping my own hand over my mouth before any other sounds can be emitted, I quickly trot out of the classroom.

***

"Christine Yamasaki?" I am greeted with the door resoundingly being shut in my face. I bang on it, "I know you're in there. I just want to talk. Look, it's important, I was an intern at *The Tribune* after you left, and I recently got fired."

I stare at the grainy wood. I've just clambered up three flights of stairs in heels. My body is still deliciously achy from last night and can't handle this much exertion. I knock on the door again, this time half-heartedly. "Look I'm just trying to get your side of the story. I think we both may have gone through a similar situation."

The door is yanked open, the hinges scream in protest, "You don't know the first thing about my situation, princess!" Hostile eyes stare at me from underneath a fringe of blue-black hair.

"Christine?" I ask tentatively, "It's so nice to meet you, my name is Maya—"

"Did anyone see you come up here?" She darts her head out of her apartment and looks up and down the corridor.

"Um… no," I say. "Oh wait, maybe the elderly Italian couple. I came up with them."

"No witnesses, I can't have witnesses," I hear her mumble, "Get in here and next time don't loiter in the hallway."

She grabs my elbow and tugs me into her apartment; I stumble before entering into the black hole. Seriously, there is no light in here, and I am freaking out a little bit. She could be the female Jeffrey Dahmer, and I just came into her apartment willingly. What kind of nimrod am I? I hear the scraping of a match, and a flame illuminates her face. Oh my gosh, she is going to set me on fire! Taking a quick step back, I trip on her carpet and fall against some cushions. Somewhere near my right ear, I hear a cat hiss at me. Startled and shaken, I get back on my feet quickly. Only then do I realize that she is crouching down to light candles. She swiftly blows the match out.

"Sorry, I, uh… forgot to the pay the electricity bill last month."

"No worries, do you want to go to a coffee shop or something? Sorry to ambush you like this."

"No coffee shop. I'm comfortable in my own space." Space that apparently smelled like damp clothes and cat urine, "But I don't want you here, you should leave."

I smile to cover up my discomfort. "Okay, well, I won't be long. I just had a quick question regarding your time at *The Tribune*. I know you left because you had appendicitis and I was wondering if you noticed anything funny about Simon Blythe while you were there."

"Appendicitis? Is that what they told you? I definitely did not have appendicitis. Those bastards set me up."

"By those bastards, who are you referring to?"

She stares at me, assessing me, my clothes, my shoes, "Why don't you tell me, princess? You're the one who got fired and tracked me down. I have a feeling you have a few suspicions of your own."

"Okay, I am far from a princess," I say, irritated by her snobby calculation of who I am. "What does the name Simon Blythe mean to you?"

"Why should I trust you? I don't even know who you are." We both stand there with our arms crossed, eyeing each other.

I sigh, "Can we please do this sitting down? It's a long story, and I did a little bit of research. I was hoping I could share it with you."

"How do you know you can trust me? You're awfully naive for a journalism student."

"I don't really have a choice," I say, exasperated, "It's either trust you and get some idea of what's going on, or don't trust you and I am exactly where I started. No story, no proof, nothing to exonerate my name."

"Fine, go ahead, spill your guts, when you have no idea if I am working with them or not."

This gives me pause, "Are you?"

She laughs, obviously enjoying manipulating my deeply gullible and malleable mind. I am so confused, I can't speak. I had genuinely believed that if I showed up, we would bond over the mutual injustice that had been done to us. Instead, I am standing in a dark room, staring at this chick dressed all in black and surrounded by candles. All we're missing is the the creepy séance music.

I roll my eyes. Why on earth did I think this was going to be easy? "Forget it, I'm leaving. I thought we could bring them down together. I guess I was wrong. I'll have to figure something out myself."

"Good luck, Princess, you're going to need it," Christine smirks at me. "I have plans of my own for Columbia and *The Tribune*."

I look around the dark living room and wonder if she had dead bodies buried underneath the couch. Is that what she means by having her own plans? "I understand you don't want to work with me, but I'm still in the class taught by Professor Wiseman. I have access to information you don't anymore. We could work together. You might even need me."

"I doubt it, you're a liability. You're too trusting. And honestly, no one will take you seriously if you walk around with that puppy dog complex of wanting to be liked, no matter what the cost."

"I do not have a puppy dog complex," I say stiffly. "Look, if you change your mind. Here is my number, give me a call. We both want the same thing."

"I doubt it," I hear her mutter under her breath. She looks up and says in a louder tone, "Good of you to leave your number. Sure you don't want to leave your social security number and birth date while you're at it? Better yet, just give me your home address and I can drop by."

I shut the door behind me and step back into the hallway, which is thankfully filled with sunlight. *Ugh, could it have gone any worse?* My memory briefly flits over to what Jeffrey Dahmer would have done... okay, it *could* have gone a lot worse.

***

After that scintillating conversation with the real Christine Yamasaki, I decide to scuttle back over to campus. I need to dig up research on both Simon and Professor Wiseman. If I am going to be a serious journalist, I need to learn how to do my own research and not rely on others for once. I walk down the hallway and catch Eddie escorting Matisha out of her classroom. Her head is tucked into his shoulder and he is whispering something in her ear. Ugh. No! Not again.

"Eddie!" I say loudly and with false cheer. "What are you doing at Columbia?"

"I just came to see Matisha. We have some things we needed to discuss," his eyes are darting all over the place. Everywhere except at me.

"Right. Of course, well I'm sorry to interrupt. But I have that file for Raj and I can't get ahold of him. Can I give it to you instead?"

"Sure, can it wait—?"

"No, it can't wait. I definitely need to give it you to you now," I bite out each word.

"It's okay, babe, I'll meet you in the cafeteria," Matisha gives him a watery smile and slowly shuffles away.

Babe? He is her babe now? Eddie follows me as I lead us into an empty stairwell. Closing the door behind us, I smile sweetly at Eddie and recite his love letter to me, "Dear Eddie, I'm so sorry for last night. I hope we can still be friends," he winces at my sarcasm. "So, did you realize in the morning that you were just using me for the night? Or did you plan it all along?"

"Maya, I'm sorry. I planned to talk to you. But I had to talk to Matisha first and figure out the facts."

"Are you two back together?" I ask, my mind reeling. How can this be happening? Am I really going to get rejected for another woman—again?

"I don't know yet. We were just about to have that conversation when you accosted me."

"I accosted you?" I scoff in disbelief, "I believe you accosted me last night... several times. So does your conversation with her require you to cradle her in your arms while she softly weeps out an apology onto your big, manly shoulders?" I jeer.

"According to her, nothing happened between her and Raj. She thinks he's just jealous of me and everything I've accomplished," he shrugs helplessly, as if to say, *It's not my fault, I'm super adorable and women fall madly in love with me.*

"Seriously? You have got to be kidding me!" I stare at Eddie, my mouth open in outrage.

"With all due respect, Maya, this is between her and me." Eddie tries to walk past me, but I grab his arm.

"No, it's not. Since you slept with me last night, you have brought me into this. Oh, and she's lying to you." I let go off his arm and stomp down the stairs.

"You don't know that," he calls down to me.

Fuming, I turn around and stomp back up the stairs, "Yes I do. I saw them at your engagement party arguing in the patio. Raj wanted to tell you and come clean. Matisha wanted to marry you and continue having the affair with Raj. As much as you may hate Raj right now, he at least did the right thing. Your former or current fiancée, however, is nothing more than a selfish brat who wants to have her cake and eat it too."

"You knew at my engagement party and didn't tell me?" Eddie asks. His voice breaks.

"Would you have believed me?" I ask. "You knew I had feelings for you. You knew I trusted you and you still... decided to move forward last night." I suddenly can't breathe. I take a deep breath, trying to get air into my lungs. "You know what? I don't care anymore. I thought you were intelligent enough to see through her, but since you really do love her, who am I to stand in your way?" My sanctimonious speech is interrupted by my phone ringing.

I answer it while Eddie glowers at me.

"Maya, it's me, Antoine. Come quick. Angie's gone into labor."

"How can she be in labor? She's only eight months along," I say, panicking.

"I know, she started having sharp pains this morning. I'm taking her to the hospital right now. I gotta go," I hear the sound of sirens before his phone abruptly drops off.

I stare at my phone, shaken. What does this mean? What had caused her to go into labor? She had been taking her vitamins. The doctor said she was in great shape.

"I'll drive you." I look up to see Eddie dangling his car keys in front of me.

"I'd rather take the train," I say flatly.

"I know, but she's your friend and this is the quickest way you can get to her."

"What about Matisha?" I ask, still waspish.

"I'll text her. She can wait." Eddie holds the door open and I brush past him, careful not to touch him.

CHAPTER 26

WE ARE STUCK IN THE worst possible traffic. We haven't moved an inch. The only reason I haven't jumped out of the car and taken the train is because there are gobs of snow coming down and I have no idea what direction to go in.

I cannot bear to look at Eddie. Instead, I stare at my hands on my lap and will myself not to cry. I feel like a wounded soldier who has just come out of battle; everything is battered and bruised and sore. I am aching with loneliness and pain, and the only one who can take it away is the same person who is causing it. The worst part about this whole situation is that I have no one to blame but myself. I knew all along he was unavailable, and yet I continued to pine for him like a lovesick teenager, vying for his affection. *Look at me, pick me. I'm prettier, funnier, more lovable.*

If only life had a map and you knew in advance the guy you were supposed to marry and spend the rest of your life with, there would be none of these mistakes with the wrong men. Kind of like an... arranged marriage organized by your meddling parents. My mind snapped the pieces into place—that's why they did it. They wanted to spare me the hurt and agony of falling in and out love. They wanted me to be with someone who would treat me well and be considerate of my feelings. Love is messy, feelings are messy. An arranged marriage would bypass that mess completely.

I think of Hamza. Would I have been happy with him? Sleeping next to his clammy skin, enduring his shaky touch on my most intimate parts? I shiver in revulsion just thinking about it. I would rather choose my own unhappiness than have it forced upon me by a third party. This basically resigns me to the fact that I am going to spend the rest of my life alone. I guess it is time for this spinster to start adopting cats and walking around in orthopedic shoes.

"We're here," Eddie says to me quietly.

"Thank you," I say as I climb out of the car.

"Maya, can I call you after—"

"No," I say abruptly as I shut the car door on his words.

***

"How is she doing?" I ask Antoine as I step into the hospital room painted a sickly green. There are tubes everywhere, and most are attached to Angie. I'm afraid to touch her.

"Resting. They've given her medication to help her sleep and delay the labor. But we haven't spoken to the doctor yet." He looks up at me, his face creased with worry. "Look, Maya, I'm sorry to do this to you, but my shift starts soon and I don't want her to wake up alone. Do you mind hanging around until I get off work?"

"Absolutely," I say. "You should get some rest too. Or at least something to eat."

"I'll try. I'll be back as soon as I can," he promises before bending down to give Angie a soft kiss on the cheek and leaving the room.

I settle in, open my laptop, and start to take notes. I can't think about Eddie and what I might have just lost. I can't think about my parents and how I have failed them as a daughter. All I can do at this moment is to try and salvage my newfound dreams of becoming a journalist.

Simon Blythe attended the University of Chicago, where he majored in journalism and apparently had aspirations to go into law. He studied under the fine tutelage of a Professor Robert Wiseman—well isn't that interesting? Professor Robert Wiseman had an up-and-coming career working at the *Washington Post* until he abruptly resigned in 1998 and went missing for two years. What happened then? When did they re-connect?

"Maya?" I hear Angie croak from the bed.

"Hey honey, how are you?" I close the laptop and walk over to her bed.

"Thirsty," she replies.

I quickly get a glass of water and hand it to her. She has dark circles under her eyes, and her forehead has a feverish sheen to it. "How are you feeling?" I ask.

"Sleepy, achy. How is the baby? Is the baby okay?" she grabs my arm.

"Yes, they managed to slow down your labor with medication. We'll know more once the doctor comes."

"Antoine?" her eyes dart around the room looking for him. I hate seeing her like this. Her skin has taken on a yellowish tinge while her hair hangs in clumps around her face. She would hate to know she looks like this, the girl who takes great pride in always looking fabulous.

"He had to go to work, but I'll be here until he gets back." Her eyes are starting to droop again, "Don't worry about a thing. Just get some rest. I'll be here when you wake up," I say soothingly. I pull the covers over her and smooth her hair away from her face. She snuggles deeper into the covers and starts to softly snore. I smile down at her, feeling maternal and nurturing. Why do people look so innocent and adorable when they're asleep?

"Stop watching me sleep, you weirdo," I hear her murmur to me.

"I wasn't, I was just checking if you had a fever," I snap defensively.

She snores softly in return.

I head back over to my laptop and continue to hunt for microscopic clues that lead me nowhere. My phone vibrates and a text pops up: *You still want to meet? -C.Y.*

I reply: *Yes, but I'm not in the mood for your broody angst. Either we work together as a team or not at all. No put-downs, no insults. No counter-productive B.S.*

The phone goes silent, and I fear I've lost her again. *Fine - meet you at The Purple Pig tomorrow. You're buying.*

I agree to the meet up and go back to digging up dirt. I am going to get reinstated at *The Tribune* or at least try to bring those bastards down a peg.

***

"Maya," I feel a hand shake my shoulder. I snort awake and open my eyes to see Eddie staring down at me.

"What are you doing here?" I ask him, while surreptitiously trying to wipe the drool from the corner of my mouth.

"Antoine asked me to check in on you, he's running late." He sits down in the other armchair opposite from me.

"How are you two even friends?" I ask, irritated.

"We're in the same basketball league. We hang out every other weekend. We're probably closer than you and Angie."

"I highly doubt that," I mutter.

"Look, I know you don't want to talk to me. Feel free to leave. I can wait for Antoine to get here."

"I promised Angie I would be here when she woke up, and I keep my promises. Unlike some people," the last sentence is muttered under my breath. *Yeah, I know I'm acting like an immature brat. But he did reject me for Matisha—again! I'm allowed to be a little testy.*

"Good, you two are here," Antoine skids into the room.

"Everything okay? Did the doctor say something?" I ask concerned.

"Everything is fine, more than fine," Antoine smiles widely and pulls out a black, velvet ring box from his pant pocket. "What do you think?"

There is a lump in my throat as he opens the box to reveal a beautiful princess-cut diamond ring. "Oooh," I exhale, "it's lovely."

"You don't think I'm moving too fast, do you? It just feels so right with her," Antoine is brimming over with nervous energy, while Eddie and I can't make eye contact with one another.

What am I supposed to say? I am certainly in no position to give advice. Eddie apparently feels the same way, because he pastes on a weak smile, slaps Antoine on the back and says, "It's great, man. Just great."

"Should we leave you two alone?" I ask and start to gather up my things.

"No, I want you here. Actually, do you mind recording it?" Antoine hands me his phone and I hold onto it with trembling hands. I hope they don't blame me for the shaky footage 50 years from now.

"Angie, baby, Angie, wake up." Antoine gently nudges her awake and cradles her hand in his.

Angie smiles dreamily at all of us, "Antoine, hi. Whachya doin' here?" Her words are slightly slurred.

"Angela Wesley, I knew from the moment I saw you that you were a force to be reckoned with. You are beautiful and strong and kind, and I am so blessed to have you in my life, which is why I never want to let you go." *Oh my goodness, he's getting down on one knee!* "Being with you has made me so incredibly happy. I realized today how fleeting everything can be, which is why I want to spend the rest of my life protecting you from all harm. I promise to love and cherish you for the rest of our lives. Angela Wesley, will you marry me?"

By now, tears are leaking out of my eyes, because it's so nice to see a man finally appreciate and understand Angie. A man who can do the right thing and isn't afraid to commit to a strong, independent woman. I realize in my joy I've inadvertently grabbed Eddie's hand. I hastily drop it like a hot potato. He gives me an odd look.

"Okey-dokey Artichokey!" Angie's voice comes out in a sing-songy voice, "oooh pretty shiny rock. Is that my shiny rock?"

Antoine abruptly stands up and looks at her completely bewildered by her response.

"I'll go get someone," I volunteer and scuttle out of the room.

When I return back with the nurse, I hear Angie lecture Eddie, "You and Maya should have little beige babies too! Because s-s-s-she's really in lurve with you, Eddie. And she's super bendy. Kicks my ass in yoga."

"Oh boy, I think somebody has gotten too high of a dosage here. Why don't I hang you up some IV young lady," the nurse proceeds to give us a reassuring smile, "She's just adjusting to the pain medication. She'll be fine once she sleeps it off."

"Right, it's the medicine that's making her say things that are completely untrue," I say a little too loudly, "nobody wants a beige baby in this room."

"I'm getting married," Angie squeals in response, "I'm getting a beige baby."

"Of course you are, honey, but how about a nap first," the nurse proceeds to shift the blankets around, hang up the IV and poke Angie with various other needles.

Antoine chuckles, "Maybe now wasn't the best time to declare my undying love."

"Your heart was in the right place, and now you have blackmail footage, should you ever need it," I say and hand him back his phone.

"It was a great proposal either way," Eddie chimes in, "I think we've all had a long day. I'll just take Maya home."

As Antoine nods and I sputter in resistance, Eddie calmly takes my elbow and steers me out into the hallway.

"Stop jerking me around. I can find my own way home." I say, shaking his hand off my elbow.

"It's late and I want to make sure you get home safe," his tone brokers no arguments, and I'm a little stumped.

I desperately want to ask him how his talk with Matisha turned out, but there is no way I am going to come right out and ask him. I stare at his profile as he deftly navigates the car across the snow-slicked streets. He catches me staring at him and gives me a half smile. I whip my head around and stare out the passenger side window. Chicago under a blanket of snow is truly breathtaking. I had forgotten how beautiful Lake Shore Drive can be. The steely grey water is slowly turning black as the sun sets behind us.

"Have you eaten?" He is met by my wall of silence. "Can I take you out to dinner? I'll pay." My stomach rumbles in approval. But I determinedly sit stone-faced and stare ahead. I hear him exhale beside me. Well he could run out of oxygen for all I care. I was not going to get suckered into another rendezvous only to find out 5 minutes later he was *still* in love with Matisha.

"Maya, I hope you change your mind soon. Because we do need to talk. Hopefully you'll get over this grudge you have against me."

Grudge? I'm not holding a grudge, I am just plain furious. I snap my neck from the window and stare at him, but there are too many words flying through my head, so I settle on a lady-like grunt instead. Hopefully that will show him!

He sighs in return and pulls the car up to the curb. Before he can say anything, I hop out of the car and slam the door shut behind me. Jerk!

CHAPTER 27

"YOU'RE LATE, PRINCESS," the dark one greets me.

"The trains are running late with the cold weather," I say in defense. Actually, I'm surprised by the cool, confident, and very pretty woman sitting in front of me. Outside the confines of her cat litter apartment, I can see that her black, silky hair falls to her waist, and her fringe of bangs no longer cover her almond shaped jade-green eyes. Her porcelain skin is slightly flushed from the cold.

"So, what do you have?" she asks, pulling on the straw in her glass.

"You first. You contacted me. What do you need from me and why? You were pretty clear that you wanted nothing to do with me."

She raises an eyebrow (dare I say in admiration?). "Touché. I guess you coming to the apartment reminded me that it isn't all about me. If they got away with doing this to you, that means they're going to keep doing it to other interns. We need to act quickly, bring it to their attention."

"I have an in. Trish the Managing Editor in the Life and Style section is willing to hear us out, but we need some proof. Our word against Simon's isn't going to be enough," I signal for a glass of water from the waitress.

"Which is why I have this." Christine pulls out a large manila envelope and pulls out the contents.

I also pull out my black binder. Together we piece together that Professor Robert Wiseman was fired from the Washington Post for illegally recording sources without their permission. He then re-located to Chicago, where he taught at the University of Chicago. Simon Blythe turned out to be his star pupil. Together they got rid of the U of C Hedge fund Manager who was mismanaging funds and pocketing most of the returns. They also managed to humiliate a dean who was having an affair with a student along with getting financial records that indicated the school was deeply in debt to a company that sold weapons overseas. They were a dynamic duo. Simon Blythe was a great 'Robin' to Professor Wiseman's 'Batman'. Simon then graduated. The groundbreaking stories subsided until they became nothing more than the expired yogurt in the cafeteria. This leads us to wonder, who is the investigator and who is the writer?

"This isn't enough," I groan and sink my head into my hands, "We have no proof that they did anything."

Christine muses, "Simon asked me to tap Mayor Emanual's phone last semester. When I refused, he ratted me out to Barb and told her about the other times I *did* bend the rules. He got me fired and expelled." She peruses another article by the odious Mr. Simon Blythe.

My mouth drops open in shock, "He asked me to do the same thing. I was trying to figure out how to answer when Barb found out I switched out the articles on the poop diary. I was quickly dismissed thereafter."

Christine chuckles, "So you're the reason we all know why Simon can't make love after eating black licorice."

"Oh gross, I didn't finish reading the whole thing. It was too disgusting," I shake with silent laughter as well.

"Look, we have enough information to at least get them thinking. It's going to have to be enough. Call your contact, set up a meeting. I'll be there to vouch for you."

"How do I know I can trust you?" I tease her.

"You can't." We've been sharing a plate of fries for the duration of this meeting, and she snags the last one, "But I was thinking about you coming over to my apartment and trying to put the story together. It was kind of brave. When I got fired and expelled, I curled up into a little ball and cried for days. It takes strength to reach out. I'm sorry I was so hard on you." I stare at her, shocked. I didn't expect her to even like me, let alone compliment me. She sees my surprise and rolls her eyes, "Now don't go getting all mushy or anything."

"I'm not getting mushy. But you do realize we're officially BFFs now, right? We'll go shopping, get manicures together, maybe have a slumber party and braid each other's hair," I trail off in a fit of giggles as a look of utter horror crosses her face and then it occurs to me. "Wait—that's it! We can't be the only one's they've used as patsies. There has to be more," I lean forward in my chair, excited by this possible angle.

We look at the class rosters for every semester that Professor Wiseman has taught. We notice a pattern emerging after his third semester at U of C. For every groundbreaking story, a student was expelled or suspended for unethical conduct. Christine's eyes light up with excitement, "Oh my gosh, we've cracked it! All we have to do is get everyone together and finagle a meeting with Barb and Trish. We can clear our names and put this sucker behind bars, or at least suspended."

I lean over and give Christine a big hug, as I lean back and open my mouth to thank her, her lips land on mine and stay there. What the—what? Oh boy! Uncertain what to do as I did not want to be rude, I let the kiss go on… and on.

We pull apart to the sound of people clapping around us. Self-conscious and feeling very awkward, I stare at Christine, "Um… I'm not…you know" I then shake my head and make nonsensical hand gestures.

Her lips curl into a smile, "Have you ever tried it?"

My eyes widen and I desperately don't want to continue this conversation, but I'm not quite sure how to extricate myself from it. She was my partner in crime three seconds ago and now she wanted to be my partner in bed? "No, that was my first kiss with a girl. I think I like boys," I finish off lamely. Why did I say *I think*? I *definitely* like boys.

"Well, you should think about it. I thought I was straight, and then I kissed a girl," she laughs self-consciously, "kind of like that Katy Perry song. Anyway, my first time making love with a woman was the most intimate, most tender type of love-making I've ever known. It changed my life," she drops her hand onto mine. "If you ever change your mind, I'd be willing to pop your lesbo-cherry."

My mouth is re-working itself to form shapes that make words, and I furtively try to remove my hand from her grip, "I very much appreciate the offer, and you're very pretty. This is nothing against you. But I'm straight, thanks."

"Okay, well, when you're sick of the boys who act like assholes. I'll be around." She starts to stuff the papers back into her book bag. "Let me know when you've got your contacts lined up, Princess. We can then set up a meeting with Barb and Trish."

I nod and watch her walk away. After she leaves the restaurant, I gingerly touch my lips. The words, "most intimate" and "most tender" echo in my head.

What would it be like to make love to a woman? Christine's body is lean, and she moves like a lithe cat. I realize I am curious to see what she looks like naked. Maybe we could compare breasts, and she could give me tips on how to get a flat stomach. Although the kiss didn't make me want to rip her clothes off, it did feel soft. Maybe if I were with a woman, I could finally be with someone who would understand me. I love to talk, she loves to deride. It could work...

CHAPTER 28

"YOU ARE NOT A lesbian!" Angie throws a pillow at me from her hospital bed.

"How do I know? I've never tried it," I point out as I dodge the pillow and continue to pace back and forth in front of her. "This could explain why I never seem to get it right with guys. Maybe I'm destined to be with a woman."

"You've also never tried cocaine, or heroin. You don't have to try everything in life to realize when something isn't right for you," Angie is now drenched in sweat from shouting at me. She takes a deep breath and settles back into her pillow.

"You know what, Angie, I'm sorry I brought this up to you. It's clear you are not as open with the homosexual community as I am. I feel sorry for you and your bigotry on the matter. I think I'm going to join the LGBT club at school and get some feedback from my fellow comrades on the matter."

"Just because I don't let strange women stick their tongue down my throat doesn't make me homophobic." She takes a deep calming breath. "Okay, let's try something else. You realize you will have to lick another woman's pussy, right?"

My body does an involuntary spasm in rejection, "Uh no. That's not true. We could have a relationship that's based on mental and emotional support."

"Yeah, that's called a regular girlfriend. You already have that with me. And trust me, honey, there are days when I think of breaking up with you. Today being one of them. But you are not gay. When a lesbian thinks of having sex with another woman, she gets moist at the thought. You aren't hot and bothered , you are squirmy and spastic. That means you are a straight woman who is tired of dealing with the shit dealt by other straight men. But you are definitely not gay... huh-ha-hoo!" Angie starts breathing heavily and gasping for air. Her tongue is hanging out of her mouth.

"Ang, Ang, you okay? Should I get a doctor?" All she can do is nod, her body starts to shudder and her teeth begin to chatter.

I run out of the room and shout for the nurse. A whole team of them rush into Angie's room. Before I can figure out what is going on, they are wheeling her out. I hear machines beeping and Angie screaming. I am absolutely terrified.

"Ma'am, are you her family?" one of them asks me. I nod, my heart in my throat. "You're going to want to come with us."

I rush along beside them as they hand me a pair of scrubs. While they set her up in the delivery room, I quickly don the scrubs. Rushing to Angie's side, I grab her hand and look into her wide brown eyes that are currently filled with pain. She gestures for me to come close.

"Drugs, give me lots of drugs," she whispers, "I don't want to feel a damn thing."

I shout this information to all of the other green uniformed people in the room and they give her an epidural. "Should I call Antoine?" I ask her.

"Don't leave me now, please. Just stay here and take my mind off the pain." She grabs onto my hand

and squeezes so hard that I feel bruises forming underneath her grip. I smile reassuringly and try to extricate myself, but she just grips on harder.

"Well, if you want to completely turn me off pussies, this is a great tactic," I say in between gasps of pain.

She laughs in between her contractions, "Maya, you are so disgusting. And if you take one look at my va-jay-jay, I will personally claw your eyeballs out."

Needless to say, I keep my eyes fixed on her face for the duration of the labor.

CHAPTER 29

LANGSTON ROBINSON WINGMAN WAS BORN weighing in at 5lbs and 3 ounces. A fighter, he came into the world screeching baby profanities, fists raised, cheeks red, and clearly displeased by the multiple people endlessly poking and prodding him. He quickly calmed down after he was swaddled in a light blue blanket and settled into the crook of his mother's arm.

"He's beautiful," I say with awe.

"That's my baby," Angie whispers, caressing his forehead. She looks up at me and squeezes my now numb hand, "Thank you so much for being here."

I smile and my eyes are a little damp. "I can't believe you're a mom."

"Oh my gosh, did I miss it? Is that him?" I turn around to see Antoine run into the room.

Angie beams and props up Langston to face Antoine. "Hi, Daddy," she says.

Antoine's eyes have unshed tears in them and he has to clear his throat several times before he can say, "Hey, son."

I can't help myself. I snap a quick photo of the beautiful, happy family. "Maya, you know my hair is a mess, what on earth are you thinking?" Is the thanks I get in return.

***

I am truly spent. I have nothing left to give. The world tends to gush over women who give birth, those freakin' womb warriors. But the true unsung heroes are the people on the sidelines—me. The ones who have to watch these women drip with sweat and shriek in pain. My ears are still ringing from the after effects. As happy as I am for Angie, I am also truly grateful that the spitting, pooping, screaming, shriveled, alien-like creature is not coming home with me, as I need to sleep. Note to self: Buy Langston a pacifier or some other baby gift. Like a true woman, the nagging sense that something is wrong pulls me back from the grey matter of the beautiful, unconscious dreamland that awaits me.

I realize I am unsettled. I want something I can't name yet. Contentment. Yes, that is the word for it. I want to be content. I am done reaching for its super-popular twin sister: happiness. Happiness is for the overachievers. But for the average C+ student such as myself, contentment will do just fine. Although showcasing Simon Blythe's true colors would be nice, and usurping Matisha just once would be wonderful, I will just settle for being at peace within my own skin. *Just sleep*, I scream at my brain, *can you please just go to freakin' sleep?* But no, my brain will not listen. It instead replays the past year in my head in slow motion. Every mistake, every embarrassment, and every bad decision.

This is me, I realize with dawning horror. I am not going to get any skinnier or smarter or funnier or better with men. I am going to go through the rest of my life in this skin with these thighs and the inability to make poached eggs. And I have to make peace with that. I have to realize that who I am is enough for my friends and for my family. If Eddie is too dense to realize what he is missing out on, that is his loss. I am tired of auditioning for people's approval. I have to speak to my parents and make peace with them... but not tonight.

***

I wake up disoriented and realize that no alarm clock has blasted me awake. I have slept in. I snuggle back into my pillow, delighted. Nothing awaits me today. I have no hours scheduled at the bookstore, no internship, and very little homework. Today is all about me. The first order of business is breakfast.

Settling into Elly's Pancake House, I order my favorite, the Very Berry Pancake special and a hazelnut latte. Popping open my laptop, I scroll through my list of individuals done wrong by Simon Blythe and Professor Wiseman. First up—Joseph Lytte.

Dear Mr. Lytte,

You don't know me. I am a student in Professor Wiseman's class. I recently lost my internship at The Tribune because I carried out instructions from the illustrious Mr. Simon Blythe. I was charged with acting inappropriately and not conducting myself in an ethical manner. Sound familiar? I know that I am not the first individual this has happened to, but I do hope I am the last. If you could please reach out to me, I believe we both have similar stories that would be of interest to both Mr. Blythe and Professor Wiseman's higher-ups. My phone number is 555-1234.

Sincerely,
Maya Khan

I hit the send button and go to the next name: Elaine Yellis.

"Maya Khan, my little lotus flower, what an honor it is to run into you here," the silky smooth tone of Raj Mugrati fills my ear.

I look up to see his twinkling eyes stare at me. The curly locks have been buzzed off, showcasing a very well-shaped skull. My eyes widen in surprise. He takes a seat without asking and proceeds to order a cup of coffee.

I continue to stare at him, bemused. "I thought you hated me."

He methodically pours two packets of sugar in his cup and stirs his coffee. Taking a slow sip, he stares back at me. The twinkle has been replaced with thoughtfulness, "I never hated you, Maya. I hated myself. I hated my own lack of balls for poaching my best friend's girl and not being up front sooner."

"When did it—how did it happen?" I ask without thinking, "Sorry if you don't want to tell me, you don't have to," I tack on hastily, even though I am dying to know.

A brief smile flickers over his weary features, "Matisha and Eddie have been together for as long as I can remember. I think they met their first year at college and were stuck at the hip ever since. I was happy running around campus and conducting my own sociological survey on women and their g-spots," he pauses meaningfully and looks at me.

Determined not to blush, I meet his eyes levelly and quirk an eyebrow, "Interesting."

"So we graduate, Matisha runs off to Afghanistan, breaking Eddie's heart. He and I try to put our business together. Anyway, we realize that there is some software in China that might be helpful to us, but one of us has to go in person to authenticate it and see if it's worth acquiring. Eddie is better at the permit and bureaucracy end of things, and I love to travel." He takes a forkful of my very berry pancake and I scowl in disapproval. He continues, "so off I go."

"Alright, get to the hot and heavy part," I say, impatiently. I still have 13 people to contact on my Simon Blythe sting operation.

"Patience, grasshopper," he says, continuing to leisurely sip his coffee, "So on my way back from China, I decide to surprise Matisha in Afghanistan. I take a roundabout route and meet her in Kabul. Maybe it was my getting dysentery in China or the jetlag, but I realize that Matisha is actually quite adorable and technically not with Eddie anymore." I let out a large belch in disgust. Raj does a double take, "Classy," he says in response. I nod and rub my stomach, satisfied with the breakfast, if not the company.

"Anyways, I wasn't planning on sleeping with her." I again emit a rude noise, expressing my disbelief. "I really wasn't. Yes, she was cute, yes, she and Eddie were not together, but I didn't want to be tangled up in that. So I decide to camp for one night, see what she's doing with her students. Maybe give her a donation and be off on my merry way." He pauses and continues to eat off my plate.

"You know, you can order your own food," I snap at him in irritation after he snaps up a particularly large strawberry. I may be full, but I had hoped to take some leftovers home! He silently continues to chew and sip his coffee, his eyes have taken on a faraway look.

"So then what happened?" I ask grudgingly, curious in spite of myself.

"Air raids," he says simply while my eyes bulge out of my head. "Overnight multiple school units turned into a chaos of burning buildings and screaming bodies. We woke up to flames engulfing the perimeter. Luckily, the children had gone home, but there were still school administrators and other volunteers who were in the area. We tried to get everyone, but I didn't speak Pashto or Farsi, so I ended up just shouting until I collapsed from the smoke inhalation. Someone managed to pull me into a jeep, and we went to a refugee camp for the night."

"Oh my goodness, what happened to Matisha?" I ask, my mind reeling from the images and the horror they had endured.

"Who do you think pulled me into the jeep?" he asks wryly. "Anyway, when I came to, she was sitting over me, and I couldn't help it, I kissed her. It was meant to be a 'thank you, I'm grateful to be alive' kiss, but it turned into a 'shit I almost died and you're a woman, let's have sex before the world ends' type of thing."

I interrupt with a laugh, "Look, I'm not doubting you, but you do realize some of this sounds like it was lifted from 'The English Patient.'"

He purses his lips, obviously displeased by my lack of swooning over his epic love story. "Anyway, it was supposed to be a one-off. Everyone knows that travel sex doesn't count as real sex."

"But?" I ask, because clearly it hadn't been a one-off.

Raj takes a deep breath, closes his eyes, and smiles dreamily, "It was amazing. I have no idea why. Maybe it was because we almost died together and there was still a fire raging 4 miles away. But I fell for her, and I fell hard," he opens his eyes and looks at me. "At that point, I didn't care if she belonged with Eddie or the Sultan of Sudan. I was hers. But she came back, resumed her relationship with Eddie, and I waited. Waited for the fights, the breakups, and I tried to be there for her, in whatever capacity she would have me," his eyes have gone bleak and I realize the glib, charming fellow has dissipated in the midst of our conversation.

"Oh Raj," I whisper, I realize he isn't a cold, conniving bastard but a victim of his own heart. "I had no idea."

He shakes off his own reverie, and I don't even wince when he finishes off my hash browns, "That doesn't excuse what I did. But now you know. So hopefully you won't spit in my face when I ask you for a favor?"

I jerk back, "Favor?"

He sighs, "They won't talk to me, Maya. Eddie hasn't shown up to work in weeks, Matisha hasn't returned my calls. I just need to connect to Eddie. If we can't work together, I need to know so I can move on. I have clients that are complaining because he hasn't completed his assignments on time. Please, I desperately need your help," he looks at me beseechingly.

"Raj, I'm sorry, I really don't want to be involved any further," I protest.

"Maya, I am grateful to you for telling me to come clean. I'm glad I did it. I can finally look at myself in the mirror. But I need to know what to do with my livelihood. If I no longer work with Eddie and Matisha won't have anything to do with me, well, I have no problem returning to London," he takes a gulp from my glass of ice water.

"Okay, now you're pushing personal boundaries," I say swiping the glass away from him. "Fine, I'll talk to Eddie. But he isn't exactly thrilled with me either. When he talked about getting back together with Matisha, I kind of let loose that I knew you two were having an affair at the engagement party," I wince in recollection.

Raj lets out a low whistle, "I would be deeply indebted to you, Maya," he takes a hold of my hand and kisses the center of my palm. I snatch my hand back and shift uncomfortably in the vinyl booth.

"Okay, but that's it. This is the last favor. I am done with the love triangle thing here."

"Don't you mean love rhombus?" Raj asks suggestively, "You know the only two who haven't sampled each other's nectars here are you and me—"

"And you've officially gone back to being gross and smarmy. I'll call Eddie. No promises." I leave to pay my check before getting suckered into anything further by Raj.

CHAPTER 30

"YOU'VE REACHED EDDIE, leave a message," I sigh into his voicemail and hang up. Chewing on my lower lip, I contemplate what to do next. It has been a few days since breakfast with Raj, and I hadn't gotten a hold of Eddie. I mean, I'm not worried or anything. He is an adult; he can ignore my calls if he likes. But he could also be lying in a pool of his own blood somewhere and no one would ever know. Fine, I am a *little* worried.

"Earth to Maya, hello!" I turn my attention away from Eddie's fate and over to Christine. "We need to get going or we're going to miss the speech."

Van stands on the sidewalk, looking decidedly uncomfortable in his powder-blue tux, pulling on his collar. He clears his throat, "Are you guys sure you need me here? I mean, I'm totally fine waiting in the car and picking you up afterwards."

"Don't be ridiculous. You know there has to be three people here tonight in order for this to work," Christine says curtly.

I don't blame Van; although I had enlisted his help and have a lot to gain from tonight, I too want to turn tail and hide. Readjusting my pantyhose underneath my black sheath dress, I looked at the Chicago Art Institute in trepidation. It is hosting The Ethics in Journalism Awards tonight. The entire building is lit up in purple, blue, and pink hues. Classical music is spilling out from the doors, and there is the light titter of well-spoken people doing well-spoken things like enjoying hors d'oeuvres and talking about their stock portfolios.

"You guys have the passes I made, right?" Van asks.

We nod; all three of us walk up the steps and hold our breath as the security guard inspects the passes thoroughly. After an agonizing 30 seconds, the guard finally lets us in with a brief nod. I break out into a big relieved grin and start to say "thank you," when Christine yanks me by my elbow and pulls me into the Institute.

"Alright, Van, you're on," Christine turns to Van for instructions.

Van looks a bit pale. After swallowing several times and taking a deep breath he finally says, "Okay, well, it's a bit different when you aren't a cater waiter at these things. But from what I remember, the stage is on the left-hand side, which is where the speeches will be made; the audiovisual room is most likely on the right-hand side. I think it's behind those gold double doors right there."

"Perfect, I will be near the stage. You and Maya can go head over to the audiovisual room," Christine looks at me and sighs. "Maya I told you to wear something that showed off a little cleavage tonight. You could pass for a Swedish nun in that outfit."

"I was going for classy elegance," I retort, affronted. *Swedish nun, my butt! Do Swedish nuns have a million little sparkles sewn into their dresses that shimmer under fluorescent lighting? I think not!*

"Well, we don't have much time, so if we're going to do this, let's get going," Van offers me his elbow and I gladly take it. We sweep through the room nodding and laughing, acting like we're having the best time. He's also kind enough not to mention that my forearm is covered in sweat, "This is where I leave you, kid," he whispers to me before heading off.

I pretend to stumble onto the security guard standing in front of the golden double doors. "Oh my word, I am so sorry about that," I say, glancing up and fluttering my eyelashes.

"Is everything okay ma'am?" he pauses while I continue to flutter my eyelashes, "Is there something wrong with your eyes? You need eye drops or something?"

"Well, aren't you helpful? I just think I'm a bit dizzy from the heat. Do you know where I can cool off?" I say, fanning myself while pulling on the neckline of my dress and attempting to push up what little cleavage I have.

"Well, the washrooms are around the corner, you could put a little cold water on your face." The man's face is wreathed in tired wrinkles, and he looks like he couldn't care less about the hot flash I am experiencing. I see Van out of the corner of my eye.

Panicking, I clutch at the security guard's collar and pull him towards me, "Ma'am, I'm going to have to ask you to let go. I really would hate to taze you."

"Officer, I'm so sorry, but I'm having a panic attack. That's what happens when I get in a crowded room full of people. You have a kind face, which is why I gravitated towards you. Do you mind doing some breathing exercises with me? It helps calm me down."

"I'm sorry, ma'am, but I have no time for that sort of thing. I have a job to do tonight, and you need to let go of my shirt." He finally pushes me off, and I pretend to stumble and fall. "Ah, hell! Are you alright, ma'am?" As he bends over to help me up, Van sneaks into the audiovisual room.

I slowly weave my way up, but still continue to sway. "Thank you very much, sir. You have been most helpful." I beam at him before sashaying away. I have done my part. I can now sit down and enjoy the night.

As I begin to sit in one of the metallic chairs, my phone begins to chirp. "Maya, ow, Maya, are you there?" I hear Christine say through the static.

"Yes," I whisper, "It's done. He's in. Where are you?"

"I'm in the ladies' room. Can you meet me there?"

Glancing around surreptitiously, making sure I don't see anyone I know, I carefully make my way to the ladies' room. Pushing the heavy door in, I see Christine lounging on the sofa in the waiting area in front of the stalls with her leg up. Really? She decides to relax now?

"What the hell are you doing here? It's almost time-"

"I twisted my ankle," Christine interrupts me. I stare down at her ankle. Sure enough, it's swollen to twice its normal size and has a big purplish-looking bruise on it.

"How did this happen?" I squeak.

"I thought I saw Simon, so I tried to run and hide behind a plant, but I forgot I was wearing heels. I tripped hard and then I realized I couldn't put my weight on it."

"Oh my gosh, we should get you to a doctor. Here, put your weight on me," I go over to her side but she stops me.

"No, it can wait. You have to finish what we started. You have to take over my part."

I shake my head vehemently, "No way, Christine, I will be terrible. We've all practiced our various sections, and you know no one can replace your delivery. Look, maybe this is God or whoever saying we should call it quits for tonight."

"No way," Christine shakes her head adamantly, "We've come too far. You gotta do this, Maya. For me, for you, for everyone else he has screwed over."

I swallow against my extremely parched throat. I know she's right, but a part of me wants to tell her that I'm not the brave kind. I'm more the quitting kind, the running away kind. Staring at her ankle, I realize that tonight I had to be the fighting kind. We've come too far to fail at the end.

I nod and whisper, "Okay. I'll do it."

We distantly hear a microphone being turned on and a voice saying, "Ladies and Gentleman, welcome to the 11th Annual Ethics in Journalism Award. We are here tonight to honor…"

"Get out of here," Christine shoos me out the door. I hurry out towards the stage.

I arrive on the floor just in time to see Simon accept his award. Can you believe the bastard nominated himself?

"Ladies and gentleman, I'd just like to say that I," his eyes focus on the teleprompter, "don't deserve this award. The truth is that I'm a fraud who uses young interns to do my dirty work for me," Simon abruptly stops speaking and looks away from the prompter, confused. The crowd starts murmuring. Simon shakes himself off, "I'm sorry, that's not the speech that I had prepared for this evening—"

"No," I say loudly, "But it's the speech you should have prepared, because it's the truth!" I walk up to the stage on trembling legs.

Simon's eyes widen as he recognizes me. "Security, we have a disgruntled former intern. I believe she needs to be removed from the premises. She poses a danger, not only to us, but to herself as well."

"Ladies and gentleman, Simon Blythe is a fraud, and the irony of him receiving this award is beyond belief."

The wall behind the stage comes alive with colors and music. The strains of the Knickerbockers' classic song, "Lies" begin to fill the room, and the first PowerPoint slide comes into focus.

My voice begins to waver, but I quickly clear my throat. "For every groundbreaking story that Simon Blythe has uncovered, an innocent victim is expelled or fired thereafter, usually under the guise of unethical conduct, when the truth is that Simon Blythe has exploited that individual, and after his story is in print, he discards them like yesterday's trash. Case in point: in October of 1989 at the U of C campus, Simon Blythe broke the story that the university was mismanaging funds. Shortly thereafter, Joseph Lytte was expelled from campus for lifting confidential financial records from the administrator's office."

"This is ridiculous! This girl is clearly having a nervous breakdown, someone please remove her from the premises." Simon 's eyes are wide with terror. His upper lip is covered in sweat. I have managed to walk onto the stage and am now standing next to him. I'm surprised he hasn't pushed me off the stage.

"Not that ridiculous," a voice in the crowd answers. A tall, red-headed man stands up, "I'm Joseph Lytte, and I can corroborate that the story is true." The low whispers have turned into loud gasps of disbelief, and a tidal wave of noise is threatening to overpower my presentation.

"And in 1991, he did a lot of bad things," I say, my voice shaking as I see policemen begin to storm the stage.

"Maya Khan, you are under arrest for disorderly conduct and trespassing," the police officer says to me before putting me in cuffs and hauling me off the stage. The last thing I see is Van's face gazing at me helplessly and mouthing, "What do we do?" I shrug my shoulders, too scared to answer.

***

"Maya Khan, I thought I told ya to stop comin' here. What is it this time?" A familiar voice gripes in my ear.

"Officer Rodriguez," I say, delighted, "So nice to see you again."

"I see you dressed up for the event," he says, indicating my shimmery black-sheath dress. Would a Swedish nun be complimented in that manner? I think not!

"I can explain everything," I say, prepared to launch my defense.

"No need, the charges were dropped. You're free to go."

"What? Wait, that can't be right! You see, I'm a journalism student now. And this is my first arrest in standing up for truth, integrity, and honesty against the corruption that festers in the world."

"That's very nice, Maya," Officer Rodriguez says, his eyes skimming over the paperwork, "You just need to sign this and you are free to go."

"You don't understand, Officer Rodriguez, I have a point to make," I say, stamping my foot petulantly.

"Dios mio, give me strength," he rolls his eyes heavenward. "Yes. I understand. But let's pretend this is the Hilton. Charges are like reservations. At this time, you don't have any charges, hence I cannot let you stay here. Do we got it?"

I nod my head, still miffed. I wish he would say something about how far I've come. I mean, my first arrest was for being a prostitute, and my second was for fighting crime. A little applause would have been nice.

Signing the papers, I wearily make my way out of the police station and am startled to see Trish.

"You never do things halfway, huh Maya?" Trish says, shaking her head and enveloping me in a warm hug.

I collapse into her embrace, "Am I banned from the city of Chicago?"

Trish pulls back with a wide smile, "No, not yet. Let's just say you got a lot of people talking and reviewing records. I'm not sure what the outcome will be. But they are definitely digging. Barb wants to see you in her office tomorrow morning. 8:00am sharp."

"I won't be late," I promise. I had finally pulled back the curtain to reveal the real Simon Blythe and I hadn't fallen flat on my face in the process. All in all, I would call that a good day.

CHAPTER 31

"WELL IT'S NICE TO see the real Christine Yamasaki," Barb peers at us from beneath her glasses, "Oh yes, I remember you now. I must say, Maya, you look nothing like her. How on earth did no one notice this mix-up?" Looking back down at her paperwork, I hear her mutter, "I guess everyone in this building is blind as well stupid."

I shrug my shoulders in response. Christine flexes her bandaged leg in front of me.

"Well, I thank you both for being here today. I commend you for your excellent investigative skills in uprooting a truly vile character in our journalistic midst. People like that give us all a bad name."

Christine and I both murmur our thanks as Barb pauses to sip her coffee. We've both been called into her enormous office. As we sit in front of her desk, I try not to squirm uncomfortably when she stares at me with her unflinching eyes.

"The thing is, I only have one open internship slot per semester, and I understand that both of you were unfairly swindled from the position. I'm afraid there just isn't room for two. Christine, are you still a student? When I checked with Columbia, they said you were expelled."

"I'm in the process of being reinstated; I should be back on campus this January."

"Yes, well, that is a pickle, as you've already been an intern with us, so I can't have you here in the spring," Barb looks down at her notes. "How about you work at the Red Eye part time? As an assistant reporter? Would that suffice? I'm afraid that's the best I can do."

Christine gives a small tentative smile, "That would be perfect. Thank you very much for taking the time to place me in another newspaper. I really appreciate it."

"It's the least I can do. Now, Maya, you can finish out the semester here, but beyond that I'm afraid I really can't commit to anything else. I'd like to place you in the metro department. I want to see what your investigative skills are capable of."

I swallow nervously. Do I have investigative skills? Well, I certainly can't correct the woman now, so I smile and nod and accept graciously. *Metro! Ick, that is the grossest department in the whole building. The entire floor smells like jockstraps and Gatorade. God, I hope I didn't contract athlete's foot or something.*

***

I sit and listen to the police scanners, which spew mostly static and various numerical variations. "Operator we have a 507 on the corner of Cicero and First Avenue." Luckily I had my police decoder trick-sheet in front of me. 507 meant public nuisance—not newsworthy.

It's the last day of the semester before winter break. I have managed to ace both classes. After Professor Wiseman's resignation, the T.A. took over, and it was like the entire debacle never happened. The college didn't issue a statement. No one batted an eyelash. One minute he was there, and the next he wasn't. Matisha, for whatever reason, also gave me an A on the final exam. The normal snippy, condescending tone in her lectures became subdued and much more bearable during the last couple of weeks. I tried to keep my distance. I still felt a little sleazy for sleeping with her fiancé, even though she wasn't exactly innocent in the whole scenario herself.

"Operator, we have a two-alarm fire at 1275 W. Devon Street. Fire and emergency vehicles are needed."

I jump and then freeze. 1275 W. Devon Street is my address—er, my parents' address. There is a fire at my parents' house! White noise roars in my ears. I can't hear or think. Everything swirls around me in slow motion. Standing on shaky legs, I wave over an actual reporter on the floor and offer a garbled explanation. He tells me to sit down and take a deep breath. Grabbing my jacket, he gently places it on my shoulder. "You don't have to come. I can tell you what's happening from the ground."

I shake my head, "No, I need to see my parents. I need to make sure they're okay." I had been avoiding them for far too long.

"I'll drive," he says, "You just keep breathing. You're looking a little pale."

I nod, unable to argue.

CHAPTER 32

IF ONLY I HADN'T WAITED. I should have called sooner. I should have seen them sooner. I was so determined to prove to them that I hadn't screwed up and just assumed they would be there when I *did* get my life in order.

"It's going to be okay, it's going to be okay," I whisper to myself fervently. Please let them be alright. They are the only parents I have. As much as I disagree with some of their philosophies, I have always loved them.

We park the car and I jump out, unsure what to expect or see. Plumes of smoke billow up into the sky from the roof of my house. My bedroom window is spitting out orange and red flames. There is a loud cracking noise before the second floor of the house collapses in on itself. I stifle a cry; my childhood home is crumbling in front of me. It is like watching someone die very slowly. Firefighters are already on the scene, blasting the area with their power hoses. Through the noise, the lights, and the chaos, I see her. Standing regally, she takes in the scene around her; one hand is clutching a rolling pin while the other one holds a cell phone.

I stand, glued to the ground beneath me, three feet away from my mother, yet unable to bridge the distance. Her eyes meet mine and she freezes. I wait for her to say something. I open my mouth, but no sounds emerge. I want to apologize, I want to hug her, I want to comfort her, but most of all, I want to wipe the soot from her nose.

Tears begin to well up in my eyes. I decide to take a step towards her when she lifts her face to the heavens and says in a voice loud enough to wake the dead, "Of course, she comes back to the house when there is no house left." She startles the firefighters, who lose their grip on the hose and point it—towards me! A blast of ice-cold water pierces my skin like a thousand tiny needles. I am gasping, sputtering, and squeaking in pain. The firefighters finally manage to get a grip on the device and turn it away and back over towards the house.

"Hi, Ma," I say as water drips from my eyelids over my knees and sluices into the inside of my shoes.

"Oh, now I'm your mother? For four months you haven't called or come home. I thought you had a new mother. Maybe someone who loved you more than I did…" she breaks off, her breath hitching. One lone tear runs down her cheek, and I have no idea if this emotional display is for me or for the folks milling around the street.

"Ma," I begin to say carefully, "I am very sorry I haven't been in touch. But you were making me do something I didn't want to do."

"Oh, it was me. I'm the bad guy here. I suppose you think your father is completely innocent in all of this?" she spits back at me.

I look around at the charred debris, "Where is Dad?"

"That son of a goat. He's at his practice, where else would he be? I am left alone to deal with the runaway daughter. The fact that Amir and Delia can't get pregnant. All the shame of this family. I have to deal with it alone," she pins me with her laser glare, "Do you know how much suffering I have had to endure in my life?"

I shake my head warily.

She doesn't bother to look at me as she rants on. "Of course not. Your life is easy. We brought you children here at a young age, so you could get a good education, be brought up in a good environment, and how do you pay us back? By turning your back on us. Going against all of our cultures and beliefs. That's the thanks we get. All of my children have been such a disappointment to me," she breaks off, sobbing.

Yep, this may have been the reason I haven't exactly been tripping over myself to rekindle the mother-daughter love affair.

***

Huddled in a blanket on the back of a fire truck a few hours later, I finally spot my dad making his way through the throng of people. The fire has died out, but the entire second story is burnt to bits. Ashes swirl through the air and land in people's hair like dirty snow. My dad stands next to my mother and places his hand on her shoulder. It's the most I've seen them touch in twenty-six years. They stoically stand side by side, watching the men clean up the gear around them. She whispers something in his ear, and I see his head jerk up and his eyes scan the area. I tentatively wave my hand and smile. He breaks out into a grin and then glances over at my mother. As she purses her lips in disapproval, he quickly tamps down the grin and assumes a more somber expression.

Sighing, I drag my feet over towards them. There she goes again, my mother dictating what my father feels and when to feel it. Any genuine connection I may have had with the man is constantly usurped by her approval or disapproval. "Hi, Dad," I say shyly, tucking my hair behind my ear and looking up at him, feeling like a little girl.

"Maya, I'm glad you're safe. Your mother and I have been very worried," he says. My mother snorts in response.

"I've missed both of you too," I say, politely ignoring her, "I've been busy. I've gone back to college and I have a job. I meant to come sooner, but the timing hasn't been right."

"Oh, now we don't fit into her busy schedule," my mother says, arching a brow at my father.

"I'm glad you're back in college. You can finally take over the practice when I retire—"

"Oh no, I'm majoring in journalism. I have an internship at *The Chicago Tribune*. I write articles." I'm met by befuddled silence, "articles that go into a newspaper," I taper off awkwardly.

He stares at me silent, unblinking. I can't tell if I've disappointed him or hurt him. Maybe both. "I see," he finally says and turns around to face the charred, skeletal remains of our home.

***

"And then, their perfect son Amir pulls up in his Prius and picks them up," I say, staring into Langston's golden brown eyes. "I am completely forgotten, like chopped liver. I'm standing on the sidewalk, when Amir throws me a half-hearted dinner invite. He thinks he's so cool, because he's an ecologist. Like studying the earth is difficult. It's been here forever. What's there left to study?" Langston coos in response, I love how this baby completely understands me.

"That's right, your brother Amir! Why didn't you call him when you ran out of your wedding? He could have helped you. Would you come over here and help me with this dang zipper?" Angie's muffled voice interrupts my story time with Langston.

I stand up and pull back the dressing room curtain. I am greeted with the vision of Angie surrounded by yards of white tulle, "Oh honey, you look beautiful," I gush.

"Thanks, these are the undergarments," she says wryly, pulling up the corset. "Help me zip this sucker up." I pull up the zipper gingerly, glancing at the $1500 price tag, not wanting to accidentally pull a stitch and have to take the Vera Wang knock-off home with me.

I take a step back and admire Angie's post-baby figure. The girl has bounced back to her size 6 shape *with* bigger boobs. If she weren't my best friend, I would probably hate her. She catches my eye in the mirror, "This is the one, isn't it?"

I nod, a tiny lump in my throat, "He's not going to be able to take his eyes off you."

She smiles widely, and I catch my breath. That is a smile of pure joy. There's no attitude, no smirk, no steely-eyed wariness, just pure bliss. "I can't believe how big of a deal his family is making it out to be. I thought we'd go down to City Hall after Christmas. But his sisters have totally taken over the whole thing. All I'm allowed to do is pick a dress."

"I'd say you got off pretty lucky." As she adjusts the folds of her gown, I ask casually, "So any guests I should be aware of at this thing? Anyone to avoid or look forward to?"

"No, I don't know if Eddie is coming. Stop beating around the bush and go stalk that poor man already," she responds. "Now get out of here so I can pay for the dress and feed Langston. I swear my boobs are about to explode."

"Oh ew," I crinkle my nose in disgust. "We are not the type of friends that talk about that sort of thing. Save that for the 'mommy and me' classes."

I head back over to Langston's baby carriage. He's drifted off to sleep. His sweet little head is tucked into a light blue cap, and he's softly sucking on a pacifier. *I want one, I want a baby*, I realize with a shock. My hormones start screaming at me, *We want a baby! Go out, get laid, and get one of those!* I stagger a bit and hold onto the countertop for stability. The truth is that I can barely nourish and shelter myself, so how on earth could I provide a livable habitat to a small tiny being that deserved only the best? My hormones weep a little. *How about next week?* they ask. I deliberately ignore them.

"So are you going to go to dinner at your brother's house?" Angie asks, coming out of the dressing room wearing her regular Apple Bottom jeans and Baby Phat t-shirt.

"I don't want to. They're all going to sit there and judge me and judge how my life sucks." Okay, maybe I am feeling a tiny bit insecure about how my life has turned out. I already constantly second guess myself; I certainly didn't need my family crawling into my head, making me third and fourth guess myself in the process.

"Maya, they're the only family you have. You've shown them that you don't need them to make it on your own. Let them see the new you, the strong, financially independent, educated young woman that you are." Angie smiles at the sales lady and indicates the dress that she would like to purchase.

"But that's the thing. I'm not any of those things when I stand in front of them. I still feel like the eight-year-old who got caught shoplifting chocolate from Mrs. McMillan's shop. I feel guilty and shifty and my insides get twisted all out of order. And then I feel bad that they feel bad for me or about me. It's awful. I think I have a syndrome or something. It's abnormal how much I hate disappointing them," Angie is paying for the dress and has tuned me out completely, so I turn to face Langston and continue talking to him, "I think I have 'over-empathy' disorder. I think that's when you feel what the other person is feeling to such an extreme that it overrides your own emotions. You feel what I'm sayin', Langston?"

"Would you please stop talking to my sleeping child? We still have to hit Nordstrom and Bebe. Nobody has time for your neurotic self-analysis today," Angie pushes Langston's carriage towards the exit.

"I may have come up with a new disorder and you're missing it," I call out after her.

"Another disease I can live without, I'm sure," she says over her shoulder before heading out into the bright, glittery mall. I reluctantly follow, tugging my lemon-meringue Maid of Honor dress behind me.

CHAPTER 33

"MAYA, I'M SO glad to see you," my sister-in-law Delia envelops me in a warm hug, "Your mother is driving me crazy," she whispers in my ear, causing me to chuckle.

"Delia, have our guests arrived?" my mother calls out from somewhere in the house. My brother and his wife live in a gorgeous eco-friendly home in Hyde Park. Everything within the house is recycled from something else. There are ginormous solar panels that capture the sun's energy and rain barrels that catch run-off water. They are gluten-free vegans who subsist on vitamin tablets, air, and rice crackers (provided that the rice is fielded by farmers who have organic farms and are paid fair wages). I *do* admire their commitment to the earth and to the people in it, but it's exhausting keeping up with their various causes. Anytime I engage in a conversation with them, I feel like a spoiled, narcissistic brat. Immediately afterwards, I desperately want a burger with two hefty chunks of gluten-filled bread on both sides. What's worse is that they take the time to patiently explain in detail how fifty million people are exploited everyday so that I can live a comfortable, cushy life. I have to insert toothpicks underneath my eyelids to stay awake for the whole diatribe.

"Maya's arrived... Mom," Delia tacks on as an afterthought.

"Well, tell her to come into the kitchen, this salad isn't going to cut itself. We have visitors coming," I follow the sound of my mother's voice into the kitchen. Naturally, my mother is in the kitchen. This is where I've seen her for most of my life. She has always been surrounded by spices, Indian music, and a pot or two of something simmering away. Today is no exception; on the stove are several pots bubbling over with various dishes. The smell of cumin, turmeric, paprika, basil, and coriander fill the air, "I can't believe you don't have a decent cheese grater, Delia. Honestly, how you two manage to feed yourselves is beyond me. No wonder my poor Amir is turning into nothing but skin and bones." I feel Delia stiffen beside me.

"Hi, Ma," I say tentatively, unsure whether or not she's still miffed that I chose to disappear on her for four months. My mother glances up and looks over my outfit (skinny jeans, tank top, and a black blazer with warm Ugg boots).

"Delia, can you please lend Maya a more suitable dress for the evening?"

"Who's coming?" I ask, not surprised that there would be guests. My parents love to throw big parties, invite all their friends, and reminiscence about the good ol' days of India. They then complain about how America is turning into a cesspool of bigots, fascists, and idiots and make grand plans about how they will all one day go back to the motherland and retire like kings and queens. If the conversations don't give you a headache, the cigars, overly strong colognes, and hair pomades surely will.

"Oh you know, some of our neighbors, they just want to make sure we're all right after the fire. You know, several people want to donate towards a new home. Isn't that sweet? That's what happens when you are an important member of the community," My mother says, her chest puffing out ever so slightly, "We told them that, of course, we have insurance and there is no need for all the fuss."

"Do we know what caused the fire?" I ask starting to slice a cucumber. Delia has mysteriously disappeared.

"Not sure, electrical circuits or something. Your father is sorting it all out. Here, come taste this," my mother holds out a wooden spoon, on it is a delightful morsel of lamb. I close my lips around the bite and close my eyes in response to the delicious spicy, savory flavor. My mother is an amazing cook, and I had missed her meals more than I care to admit out loud.

"Ma, that's fantastic," I say. The tender piece of meat had practically melted in my mouth.

She nods her head, satisfied, "Yes, I'd say that is done." Turning off the stove she moves onto the next dish.

I head back over to my end of the countertop and begin slicing up the tomatoes, red onions, and cilantro. I glance up and catch her looking at me. "Kind of like old times, isn't it?" she asks with a soft smile.

I nod my head, "A little bit." She goes back to humming an old Indian song under her breath and I stare at her wistfully. I don't understand her, I realize. I don't understand what makes her happy. I have been bending myself into pretzel-like shapes my whole life trying to present this façade of the perfect Indian girl for no reason. I can't make her happy. She is either happy or she isn't. The best I can do is respect her and respect myself.

***

"Reeny, Mina, Hamza, Abil, so good to see all of you. Oh, why did you stop and buy sweets? That wasn't necessary. Come, come, get in from the snow. Take your shoes off, put the coat away. Sit, sit. Food will be out in a second," my mother is in her element. Kissing her friends on the cheek, whisking away their coats, hiding the sweets out of the way (sweets she will later discard because she hates store-bought Indian desserts).

I am so caught up in the meet and greet that it takes me a second to recognize that all the people walking in the door are my former potential in-laws. As my eyes graze Hamza's, we smile at each other uneasily. I then do the polite, adult thing—turn tail and run.

"What is going on?" I whisper to Delia once we are safely ensconced in the kitchen again. She is plating the fish curry on a serving platter.

She shrugs her shoulders helplessly and looks at me with empathy—or maybe it's pity? "You know your mom always has a card up her sleeve," she walks quickly out into the dining room, her sari rustling with each step.

I try to discreetly pick the salwar kameez's pantaloons out of my ass-crack. Delia is much skinnier than I am, and the taffeta confection she has loaned me is hard to breathe, sit, or walk in.

"There you are, Maya, finally," my mother's blinding smile greets me as I walk into the dining room, and my heart clenches in fear. "Come, come, take a seat. Don't dawdle," she sighs in exaggerated aggravation and shoots a mischievous look at our dinner guests, who all titter out a laugh. I feel like I've walked onto a stage play and forgotten all my lines. I guess I'll be playing the dumb mute this evening.

"Well, as we all know, due to Maya's illness last August she was unable to attend her own wedding." There are murmurs of sympathy within the room, and I even get a few compassionate glances thrown my way,

"But as we can all see, she has made a full recovery and even lost a few of pounds in the process. So without any further delay, these two lovebirds are to get married at the end of January. Luckily, we were able to reserve the banquet hall in advance..."

I stand there, my mouth hanging open in disbelief. As my parents' friends and family begin to toast my upcoming nuptials, I contemplate whether or not I should walk out of the room, the house, and their lives forever. I know in my heart that isn't the answer. I shouldn't have run the first time. I should have stood firm and fought for what I believed in—myself. Once again, my parents are dictating my life for me, and I am standing here, allowing it. I have allowed them to get away with it for so long without fighting back; they just assume I don't have a mind of my own. Instead of correcting them, I had run away. Instead of fighting for myself, I had caved in wordlessly to the ridiculous engagement with Hamza. No wonder they believe they can railroad me all over again.

Over the noise of people conversing, laughing, and passing lamb chops and potato dumplings to one another, I clear my throat and shout, "There isn't going to be a wedding!" The conversational din dies down, and I see my mother gesturing me to sit down with guillotine-like hand motions. "I want to live a life with no regrets. I don't want to look back and be upset that I let other people dictate my path for me. Mom, Dad, I love you." My parents smile uneasily. "But you're going to die," they jerk back in shock, and I realize that may have sounded like a threat. "...eventually," I tack on hastily, "you're going to die eventually. And if I follow your instructions and get married to someone I don't love, I'm going to be stuck in an unhappy marriage and be pissed at my dead parents for making me live a life I don't recognize or want. I would rather be alone and trying to be happy than married and miserable. If you want me in your life, you're going to have to accept that. I am capable of making my own decisions regarding who I marry and how I live my life."

The room is silent. I can hear the crackle of the fireplace and someone clearing their throat. Then, onslaughts of screeches occur across the wooden floor as people push back their chairs. Hamza and his family abruptly rise and begin to walk out of the room. Hamza's mothers first walks up and wags her finger in my mother's face, "Really, Hemma, having your daughter humiliate our son once wasn't enough. You have to invite us over and smear the shame on our face some more." Hamza's mother flicks her eyes over at me, "You're nothing but a tramp. My Hamza is too good for you."

"You can't talk to my sister like that," Delia rises to defend me, "I think a lot of us at this table wish we had the courage she does."

In a final huff of clinking bracelets and swirling saris, Hamza's family leave the room.

"Honestly, Maya, you couldn't wait until after dessert? What are we going to do with all this food? I have a whole pot of rice pudding still boiling away," my mother throws her hands up in exasperation.

My father stands up and stretches out his back, "Like I've said to all of you, your whole lives. Don't do drugs, get good grades, and give back to the community. Be kind with your words and most importantly, be happy." His eyes land on my mother's, "Divorce can be a messy business."

She shoots him a dark look in return and says, "Of course, everyone blames the mother. It's always the mother's fault."

"Ma, I don't blame you," I begin to explain, but she waves off my words.

"Enough speeches, Maya, I understand."

"You do?" I say hopefully. Had I finally gotten through?

"Yes, of course. Hamza was too weak for you. It's obvious you need someone with a little more spirit. I think your Aunt Tilly knows a boy across the street from her house who would be just perfect."

I roll my eyes in disbelief. Short of setting myself on fire, nothing I do or say will ever deter this woman from fulfilling her life's mission—to see me miserably married. Instead of using my mouth to argue, I use it to consume vast quantities of rice, lamb curry, and potato dumplings. After all, independence needs nourishment. To not eat free food laid before you, well, that is a sin. And we all know how holy I like to be.

CHAPTER 34

"I'M GETTING MARRIED TODAY!" squeals Angie as she throws up the bouquet.

"Whoa there, tiger, that's after the ceremony," I say, catching the bundle of pink roses and lilies before they hit the ground and incur any permanent damage.

"I can't believe this is actually happening. Can you believe it?" Angie turns to me, her eyes shining.

I smile indulgently and reassure her that, yes, it is indeed happening. Her smile starts to freeze and fray a little around the edges. "I'm getting married to Antoine, and we are going to be together... forever?" Her bright complexion starts to wane slightly.

We hear a small tap on the door. Angie's mother walks in, looking quite regal in a pale lilac suit. "They're ready for us, dear."

I stand and start walking out the door when I hear it. A small wheezing sound. I recognize that sound. That is the sound Angie made when Mrs. Drummond used to make us run a mile in gym class; that is the sound Angie made when she came in second place at the Ms. Hostess Cupcake pageant. What usually accompanies this wheeze is a deluge of tears.

"Mrs. Wesley, I have to use the washroom, can you give me a minute?"

Mrs. Wesley arches one brow, "Two minutes, Maya. Don't make my baby girl late for her own wedding."

I smile nervously and say, "I won't," before promptly shutting the door in her face.

Turning around, I catch Angie staring at me, her eyes wide with panic. "Maya, what if this is all a mistake?" Angie starts whispering, "what if this is some kind of cruel joke? What if he turns out to be a serial killer or has a toenail fetish?" I snort in response.

"Angie, he loves you." I take a hold of one of her hands. It is ice cold.

"He loves me now, but what about later? I mean, Langston isn't even his child, and he has been wonderful with him. But what if one day he wakes up and he realizes that he can do better? Maya, marriage is so permanent. What if I'm not ready? What if this is a—"

"Angie, look at me," I force her eyes to meet mine. "This is the best case scenario, this is as good as it gets. There is a man who loves you very much, and he is waiting downstairs for you. He wants to spend the rest of his life making you happy. I know it's been tough, and I know it's scary to trust in your own happiness. We like to cling to the crappy bits; that way we're never disappointed. But he won't disappoint you. I promise."

"How can you be so sure?" Angie whispers, her eyes darting across my face.

"Well, I don't usually like to bring this up, but psychics did originate in India. So given that I'm Indian, I'm obviously part psychic, and I foresee a very happy future ahead," I say solemnly.

That earns me a watery giggle, "Oh Maya, you are a nut!"

I wipe away a small tear before it can hit her cheek and ruin her flawless makeup, "You know… if you are serious about ditching this thing, I do have a scooter tucked away across the street. We can drive off into the sunset and leave this nonsense behind. Granted, we'll only be going 20 miles per hour."

"And ruin my dress and shoes? I think not!" Angie says, scowling and shoving me away. Looking at herself once again in the mirror, she re-arranges her ample bosom and carefully pulls the veil over her face. Exhaling, she turns towards me, "I'm ready."

There is a fierce knock on the door, "Maya, that bladder better be emptied out by now or I'm going to have to come in and help."

I stand up abruptly, "Ready, we're ready in here." By Mrs. Wesley's tone, I had a feeling she would be all too happy to rip my bladder out entirely.

Mrs. Wesley opens the door once again and smiles beatifically at her daughter. "Honey, you look so beautiful. Let's walk down that aisle together, shall we?" As she offers her daughter the crook off her arm, I quickly slip out of their way.

***

"Do you take this…"

"I do…"

"Will you promise…"

"I will…"

"I now pronounce you…"

A few simple words later, my best friend had turned from smart-mouthed Angie Wesley to Mrs. Antoine Wingman: wife, mother, and extraordinary woman. Tears prick at the back of my eyes and I think my heart is going to burst out of my chest due to the sheer pride I feel when I look at them.

***

A microphone turns on, followed by a screech and a tapping sound, "Ladies and Gentleman, I'm not sure if the bride and groom are allowed to make speeches, but we wanted to say a few words. So if you would kindly indulge us, we would be most appreciative." The hum in the banquet hall quiets and we all turned our attention to Antoine as he nervously clears his throat, "There are a lot of people we want to thank for putting this together. My incredible sisters, for being able to book a date at Olivet Baptist Church, I know that wasn't easy. My mother, for being able to throw together a wedding in a matter of weeks, and on New Years Eve of all days. Thank you, Ma, for understanding that I wanted to spend the New Year with my beautiful wife Angie Wingman," he pauses to kiss his new wife, a move that is met by wolf whistles and applause. Antoine's eyes glance out over the crowd, "I'd also like to thank a very special friend, Maya Khan. Thank you for seeing what we were, before we were smart enough to see it ourselves. Thank you for always believing in us. Thank you for fighting for us. We will never forget it." Angie nods and blows me a kiss.

The tears that I held in check all through the ceremony are now running in rivulets down my cheek, and I'm gasping for air. Sniffling and trying to keep my nose from running, I desperately go through my little purse looking for a tissue. The closest thing I can find is a tampon. I am seriously tempted to shove it up my left nostril to stop the oncoming flood.

"Tissue?" a deep voice says to my right.

"Oh, yes, please," I say, my voice quaking as a fresh wave of tears threaten to overtake me. I keep my eyes lowered and grab the proffered tissue. I don't want the entire reception area to see my waterlogged face.

"Sorry, I don't normally cry. It's just that I'm the Maya Khan that they were thanking and it was the love-liest—"

"I know who you are, Maya Khan," I glance over at the hand that has a new batch of fresh tissues. Clean cuticles are attached to long, lean fingers that flow into a masculine wrist smattered with reddish, blond hairs. I glance up the arm and into the face of Eddie. My Eddie—no, not my Eddie, I correct myself vigorously. Eddie Holden belongs to no one, least of all me.

CHAPTER 35

"WHAT ARE YOU DOING here?" I say hoarsely.

"I came to see the hot maid of honor that everyone was talking about," he smiles back easily. The—the—the nerve of the man! The nights I had lain awake wondering about him, worrying about him, and he has the nerve to come over to me and act like we're friends?

But today is not about me. As much as I want to slap him, claw his eyes, and maybe tear out his hair (Indians are a very passionate and sometimes violent group of people), I won't. Because it is Angie's wedding day, and I will not ruin it.

I draw myself up to my full 5 feet 4 inches and attempt to look down my nose at him, except he's a foot taller than me, so the effect is lost. "Thank you for the tissue. If you'll excuse me I have to go um... check on the gift table." With that, I regally sweep past him and remind myself (forcefully) that nothing good ever happens around Eddie Holden.

***

"What are you doing out here?" I hear a voice ask behind me a few minutes later.

"Checking on the gift table," I answer, not bothering to look up.

"Out here? On the sidewalk? Outside of the banquet hall?" Frustrated, I finally turn around and face him.

"What do you want, Eddie? Is this fun for you? You pursue, I run? I give in, you back off? I'm tired and weary of the games and the lies and the engagements. You want to be with Matisha, go be with her. I am not standing in your way."

"Matisha and I are over," he says, taking a step towards me, the snow crunching under his shoes. He looks so good, his hair windswept, his glasses fogging up ever so slightly from the cold. Who gets turned on by foggy eyewear? I do, apparently. I mentally shake off the emotions. I do not like this man, I repeat to myself, I do not like this man.

"You are talking to the wrong person. I gave up caring after the tenth time I called you on Raj's behalf asking you if you were okay." I wrap my arms around myself to ward off the cold. I can't believe he chased me out of my best friend's wedding. The bastard. Enough of this nonsense. I brush past him to go back into the reception.

"I love you, Maya," Eddie says as he grabs my arm, halting me mid-stride.

"You're not allowed to say that," I look up at the sky and try to keep my tears at bay, "when you love someone, you don't hurt them. And you hurt me— badly, Eddie. I don't want to be the second runner-up. The ol' stand by until something better comes along."

"Maya, I know I screwed up. But please hear me out. I want to make this up to you. I want us to be together." He takes hold of my chin and pulls my head up to look into his eyes.

"You have one minute," I say, my voice quavering ever so slightly. "I have a wedding to get back to. I'm the maid of honor, you know. The sole reason those two are even married."

He nods and smiles ever so slightly. "Maya, I love you. But when I first met you, you scared the crap out of me." My eyes widen in surprise. He continues, "I had my life all mapped out. My fiancée, the business, my best friend. And you knocked it all over without even trying. No one has ever distracted and infuriated me the way you have."

"But why?—" I try to interrupt, he silences me by placing a finger in front of my lips.

"Sorry, I only have one minute, I need to use every second to convince you that what we have is rare. Please don't ignore it because I screwed up." I purse my lips, trying my best to look unimpressed. "Let me make it up to you. Give me the chance to show you that I want you and no one but you. Be with me. Please?" the last word ends in a husky whisper.

I open my mouth to say no, except he kisses me, and it feels so good that I can't help but kiss him back. He tastes like peppermint and comfort. In the midst of our kiss, I swear I hear fireworks. "Do you hear fireworks?" I murmur against his lips.

"Yes," he says, kissing me again. "But that's because there are actual fireworks."

Startled, I pull back and am chagrined to realize that the sky is lit up with bright specks of light. Explosions of color reverberate throughout the night around us.

"Happy New Year, Maya," Eddie says, pulling me close and rubbing his nose against mine.

"Happy New Year, Eddie," I let him kiss me again. My insides have turned to mush. "You," I sigh into his neck, "You have a lot of making up to do."

"I can't wait."

"I haven't forgiven you yet, you know."

"I know."

"I really have to pee."

"I figured. You were doing your little pee-pee dance," Eddie entwines his fingers in mine. "Let's get you back inside where it's warm."

That sounds wonderful.

ACKNOWLEDGMENTS

First and foremost I would like to thank my best friend Paula White who told me my kernel of an idea deserved to be made into a book. Thank you for always pushing me to follow my dreams, no matter how zany they are. Thank you mom and dad for your support and blessings. Thank you Mahi for always keeping me humble. Thank you Dien Truong for reading every painful draft of this novel, over and over again until (I'm sure) your eyes bled. A very special thank you to Steven Edward Weaver. There are no words to describe just how much I love and appreciate your strength and support. I could not have done this without my wonderful graphic designer Ahmed Ghazi or my equally gracious editor Julia. It was serendipity meeting you both when I did and I cannot thank you enough. And lastly to my very special nieces Safa and Farzana. You two inspire me and amaze me every day. I am so proud of how beautiful and intelligent you both are. To all of my friends and family, I thank you for your good energy and infinite blessings.

ABOUT THE AUTHOR

TANIMA KAZI LOVES TO READ: her love of reading inspires her to write. Born in Dhaka, Bangladesh, she has had the pleasure of living in many different countries such as Saudi Arabia, Canada and the United States, where she currently resides in Wheeling, Illinois.

She is working on her second novel and avoiding the beckoning call of Netflix binge watching. Traveling, writing and eating are her favorite past times.

Please visit her at www.tanimakaziwriter.com She would love to hear from you!

11952305R00160

Printed in Great Britain
by Amazon.co.uk, Ltd.,
Marston Gate.